IN A COTTAGE
IN A WOOD

ss Green is the pseudonym of Caroline Green, an
ard-winning author of fiction for young people. Her first
vel, *Dark Ride* won the RONA Young Adult Book of the
ar and the Waverton Good Read Award. *Cracks* was
ommended on Radio 4's Open Book programme and
old Your Breath won the Oldham Book Award. She is the
riter in Residence at East Barnet School and teaches
iting for Children at City University. Her debut adult
vel *The Woman Next Door* was a No.1 ebook bestseller.
a Cottage in a Wood is her second adult novel.

@CassGreenWriter

D1368282

Also by Cass Green

The Woman Next Door

IN A COTTAGE IN A WOOD

CASS GREEN

HarperCollins*Publishers*

This novel is entirely a work of fiction.
The names, characters and incidents portrayed in it are
the work of the author's imagination. Any resemblance to
actual persons, living or dead, events or localities is
entirely coincidental.

HarperCollins*Publishers*
1 London Bridge Street
London SE1 9GF

www.harpercollins.co.uk

This paperback edition 2017
4

First published in Great Britain by
HarperCollins*Publishers* 2017

A catalogue record for this book is
available from the British Library

ISBN: 978-0-00-824895-6 (PB b-format)

Typeset in Sabon by Palimpsest Book Production Ltd,
Falkirk, Stirlingshire

Printed and bound by CPI Group (UK) Ltd, Croydon, CR0 4YY

MIX
Paper from
responsible sources
FSC™ C007454

For all the orphans I know,
and the ones I've never met.

1

Neve stares up at the nicotine-yellow ceiling and thinks about the long journey between here and her own bed. Or at least, the sofa bed in her sister's flat.

She has a fierce longing for ice-cold Diet Coke and paracetamol. Her head is already starting to hurt and she hasn't been asleep. She needs to pee, badly.

Squinting at the small travel clock that blinks with neon aggression on the bedside table, she sees it is 03:00. They got here about two. The sex had taken about fifteen minutes, tops. Maybe she had briefly fallen asleep after all.

Whatsisname sighs and gently farts in his sleep.

Christ.

He told her he had his own software company and was in London for a conference. But it didn't ring true. Surely no one held conferences a few days before Christmas? Plus, he said 'pacific' instead of 'specific' and smiled in a glazed, uncomprehending way at a couple of her more acerbic comments. He didn't seem bright enough to have his own company.

Now she slowly begins to extricate herself from the bed, placing her bare feet down onto the rough, worn carpet. It feels greasy and gritty. She curls her toes with a shudder

1

and spots the squished comma of the condom lying next to the bed.

The air smells of hot dust from the ferocious radiator that's within touching distance of the bed, with a base note of damp.

The outside of the hotel – which was grandly named the *Intercontinental, London* – had looked alright with its jaunty blue and white awning, potted plants and fairy-lit windows.

Neve has always been a sucker for fairy lights.

But the room, with its shabby MDF table and undersized kettle, feels like the kind of place travelling salesmen go to commit suicide. There's a white extension cable snaking across the middle of the floor and she makes a mental note that she mustn't trip over it on her way to the bathroom. The wallpaper is the textured sort popular in the 1970s, splashed lumpily with a jaundice-yellow emulsion.

Whatsisname's (Greg? Gary? Something like that) wheelie case is sitting open on a chair next to the table. The arm of a jumper hangs languidly towards the carpet. She pictures him getting ready earlier, selecting a shirt that would mean the best chance of getting laid. Well, it had worked.

Self-disgust puffs through her like hot steam. She has some-how bypassed the numb, unconscious part of this scenario and gone straight to the hangover and guilt. She's suddenly appalled by the idea of him waking and suggesting she come back to bed. Or, worse, wanting conversation.

This whole thing had seemed like a good idea at the time.

Her own office party – dinner in an uninspiring Italian restaurant, followed by drinks in a bar near Waterloo – had ended early because, in her view, her colleagues were a bunch of lightweights, all making excuses about babysitters or night buses or *I've-had-quite-enough-haven't-you?* Well, no, she hadn't, clearly.

Her usual ally and best friend, Miri, was too pregnant to last beyond eight p.m. and Neve'd had to work hard, again, not to make a wistful comment about the fun they'd once had on nights out. She knew that Miri might as well be emigrating to the other side of the world soon. Nothing was ever going to be the same again between them. Watching Miri expand and step tentatively into this new world, she felt jabs of real grief.

So when someone decent looking had come over and bought her another bucket-glass of Merlot, she hadn't said no. Plus, she wasn't wearing her contacts and was drunk enough that everyone looked quite attractive in their own way. And he was Irish and therefore exotic.

She can almost hear Lou saying, 'You're thirty now, Neve,' in that mouth-like-a-cat's-arse way she reserves for her only sister.

A wave of misery washes over her and she carefully gets up and starts to hunt for her knickers among the discarded clothes on the floor. She spots them lying in a forlorn figure of eight where she'd shucked them off earlier.

She'd already been thinking this was a mistake by then. The kissing – hard up against a doorway outside the bar – hadn't been that promising. His tongue had been a muscular slug that poked and jabbed at the inside of her mouth as though on a mission to find something.

Now Neve fumbles for her bra and, once on, reaches for the gold silky top she'd bought especially for the night out. She'd been delighted with it at the time because it was half price, but wearing it she'd discovered that it made her sweat under the arms. She'd spilled red wine down it earlier too. She wrinkles her nose as she rolls the top over her head and down her body.

'You leaving?'

The voice makes her jump. She turns to see Whatsisname

looking up at her from the rumpled bed, propping himself up on pale, muscular arms.

'Yeah,' she says, 'Um . . . I'd better get going.' She smiles as though they'd just had a casual coffee together instead of a joyless, drunken shag. 'I'll just . . .' she hooks a thumb in the direction of the bathroom and then goes in, closing the door behind her as she pees.

She quickly washes her hands and avoids her reflection, aware it will only make her feel worse in the circumstances. Maybe she is faster than he expected, because when she comes back into the room a minute later, he's leaning out of the bed, vigorously checking the pockets of his trousers that are pooled next to it.

He stops and regards her with a sheepish shrug.

Realization burns. 'What the actual fuck?' she says. 'Did you think I was going to take your *wallet*?'

Her head is far too sore to be speaking this loud. But it's better than smashing him in the face with the travel kettle, which she might do otherwise.

'I don't really know you, do I?' he says, defiantly raising his chin.

'No you don't,' she hisses, hunting for her bag and shrugging on her coat. It feels as though these actions take far longer than they should.

Finally, she is able to take the few paces to the hotel door.

'By the way, you're shit in bed,' she says as she wrenches it open. 'Merry Christmas, arsehole!'

She wants to slam the door behind her but it's on one of those safety hinges and, instead, it gently closes with a disappointing sigh.

The word 'Bitch' is lobbed through before it shuts.

Outside on the street, she pulls her fake fur coat together at the throat. Fury pumps through her. She half thinks about going back and giving him a further piece of her mind.

4

But instead, she walks away, her high heels ringing out against a pavement that's glossy with recent rain. She swallows down a surge of self-pity and blinks hard, trying to concentrate on which way to go.

Neve has a terrible sense of direction. Several boyfriends, and Lou, have claimed not to believe quite how poor it is, as if getting lost often is some sort of affectation. As if it is a choice, to experience the freefall sensation of panic when you don't really know where the hell you're going.

At the end of the street she stops and considers which way to turn.

There's some sort of factory on the opposite corner and she's sure now that they passed it. So she heads off that way, praying that she will find herself somewhere near Waterloo. If she can get over the water to the Embankment, she can probably find a night bus.

Her shoes chafe the backs of her heels and her teeth are gently chattering with the bitter cold. Whatsisface had a fashionable beard and it feels now as if a cheese grater has been taken to her chin. She'll have to slather it with E45 when she gets home or she'll look like she's been sunburned. And Lou will be all over that in the morning.

It's like being seventeen again, and not in any good way.

Neve takes another turning and begins to feel the usual thrum of worry that she's going in the entirely wrong direction to where she wants to be. But she keeps moving and soon finds herself on a promisingly major road. Tall brown buildings soar on either side, glass-fronted windows lifeless, and a long row of bikes for hire seem to be resting like a tired herd.

Before long, she can see the distinctive glass sphere of the IMAX building by Waterloo and she lets out a breath of relief that curls in the frigid night air.

She's grateful for the few other people around now, either party-goers draped in tinsel, laughing and shouting to each other, or London's invisible army of workers dressed in cheap, sensible coats; heads down, hurrying from one service job to another.

Neve isn't nervous about walking alone in London at night. It's the sort of thing her parents would have fretted about but now . . . well, there's only Lou and hopefully she's asleep. She has only once been the victim of a crime, when her phone was stolen from her bag in a nightclub. The thief had clearly decided it wasn't new enough to keep anyway, because it had been dropped in the beer and dirt and found by the doorman.

She hurries on, wondering whether Miri will find this a funny story tomorrow or give her friend the new look, the one that is just ever-so-slightly disapproving.

Neve tries to remember exactly where she can get the night bus to Kentish Town. Then, with a cold plop of realization in her stomach, she remembers taking her keys out of her bag that morning because a pen had leaked in the front pocket. She can picture them, still lying on the big kitchen table. Frantically, she begins feeling around inside her bag now, but knows by the lack of heft in the pocket that they're not there. She closes her eyes for a moment and says, 'Shit-shit-shit-shit-shit.'

Lou will have a field day with this. The whole house will get woken up.

She can hear her now, with her martyr face on: 'It's about time you took control of your life.'

Neve has been staying with her sister, brother-in-law and their two children since breaking up with Daniel, six weeks before. It feels so very much longer.

If she could go and sleep under her desk, she would, but

she'd need a key for that too. It's too cold to hang about, and anyway, it will probably take forever to get home. Maybe her sister will be up with the baby by then.

She hurries on towards Waterloo Bridge.

2

It's surprisingly quiet. Apart from the occasional vehicle hissing past on the damp road, she has the bridge to herself. She stomps onward, ignoring the bright blue corona of the London Eye to her left and the comforting glowing face of Big Ben across the water. Normally she gets a thrill from these sights; loves the reassurance that she no longer lives in a tiny village near Leeds. But it's too cold and too late for that.

Here, exposed on the bridge, the knifing wind feels mean and personal so she tries to tuck herself down into her coat, tortoise-like.

When she sees the figure ahead of her, she has the disorientating sensation that it is a hallucination, or even something ghostly. It's partly because of the paleness of the woman's skin and hair, combined with the clingy, bone-coloured dress. Maybe it's the sheer incredulity she feels on registering that the woman wears no coat in the small hours of this December night.

The woman stands on the left, facing towards Blackfriars Bridge and the gold-lit Parliament, staring out over the water. She is very still.

Neve involuntarily shivers at the sight of the woman's thin, bare arms, which hang by her sides. In one hand she carries a small, silver clutch bag.

As Neve approaches, the woman turns to her, with a hopeful look on her face. Neve feels the stab of embarrassment of the Londoner, despite the late hour and the strangeness of the encounter. She dips her head but can tell the woman is watching her. She turns, reluctantly, to face her again.

'Look, are you okay?' she says. Her voice sounds hoarse from the cigarettes she smoked with Whatsisface earlier. 'Haven't you got anything else to put on?'

The woman shakes her head in a quick, sharp movement and then smiles with something like sympathy. It's almost as if Neve is the odd, vulnerable one rather than the other way around.

Make-up-less, apart from a slash of scarlet lipstick, the woman is startlingly beautiful, with wide pale eyes and a full mouth. Unlike Neve's thick, dark blonde hair, the other woman's is so pale it's almost white. It is pinned at the sides and falls in silky waves around her thin, white shoulders. Her waxen skin is almost blue from the cold.

She's clearly not poor, thinks Neve, eyeing her. The dress is made from some kind of ivory silk and clings fluidly to her slim frame. It's almost unnatural, the way it hangs in a sweeping circle around her feet. A princess dress. The words float into Neve's brain from some childish part of herself and she's a little ashamed.

'What are you doing here?' she asks with a sigh. This one brief exchange means she now has a sense of responsibility to this woman. It's why no one usually bothers in London.

She should know better. She delves into her handbag and pulls out her purse.

'Look, I haven't got much,' she says, 'but I can probably stand you a night bus. What happened to your coat?'

A particularly vicious gust of wind sweeps across the bridge, making both women take a step to the side. The bitter cold is ramping up Neve's headache now and the other woman's silence is starting to get on her nerves. Maybe she doesn't speak English?

Neve has had enough and is about to walk away when the other woman finally speaks.

'You're lovely,' she says. Not only is she English, but she has the refined, smooth voice of the girls who always looked down on Neve at school. The swishy-haired ones who dominated the sixth form common room.

'I'm not, not really.' Neve feels strangely annoyed by this compliment. 'I can see how cold you are, that's all.' She pauses. 'Look, I've just had a totally shit evening too. Is this about a bloke? Have you had a row with someone?'

The woman makes a non-committal sound that Neve takes to be assent and takes a step closer.

'He's not worth it,' she says. 'Trust me. And no offence, that's a lovely dress and everything but you really will get hypothermia wandering about like that.'

'What's your name?' the woman says quietly. Neve sighs again. Why did she get sucked into a conversation? Her instinct is to tell the woman to mind her own business but she is too tired now. Her heels hurt. Her head aches. It's freezing here.

'It's Neve.' Neve wraps her arms around herself as a shudder of cold mingles with a yawn.

'Neve . . . what?' says the woman.

Neve stares at her.

'Why?'

'Please?' says the woman, and her eyes sparkle. She makes a small, desolate sound in her throat. Neve takes another step towards her.

'Hey,' she says. 'Don't cry.'

'*Please*,' says the woman emphatically. 'Can you just tell me your name?'

Neve stares at her for a moment before replying. 'Neve . . . Neve Carey. Um, what's yours?'

'Isabelle,' says the woman in barely a whisper, and then, with more force, 'Neve, will you do something for me?'

She pictures herself getting on the night bus with this strange wraithlike creature and both of them rocking up at Lou's. Clearing her throat, she has to work hard not to sound sulky.

'Uh, yes, I guess,' she says. 'But it depends on what it is.'

Isabelle opens the clutch bag and produces a small brown envelope. 'I want you to take this.'

Neve hesitates and eyes it suspiciously. 'What is it?'

'It's a gift. For being kind to me.'

Neve takes a step back and holds up her palms. 'Look, I've done nothing. I just don't want you freezing to death on my conscience. I'm not that kind, trust me. I'm actually a bit of a cow. Ask anyone.'

'You *are* kind,' says Isabelle quietly. 'I can sense it. Will you take this, just to humour me? Say you will. Say it.'

Neve stares back at the woman, discomfited by her intense, strange manner.

A passing car washes them with its headlights. For a moment Isabelle looks cadaverous, her eyes sunk in deep pockets of shadow.

'It's important,' she says fiercely. '*Please*.'

Neve is so unnerved now that all she can do is thrust out her hand and take the envelope.

Isabelle's shoulders droop and she seems to shrink in on herself.

'Thank you,' she says quietly. 'Thank you so much.'

She fumbles inside the bag and, after producing a mobile

11

phone, turns away and whispers something quietly into it. The she returns the phone to the bag and looks at Neve. Her eyes are gleaming now, as if she is close to tears.

'You should go,' she says thickly. 'I'll be fine here.'

It's tempting.

Neve sighs heavily.

'Come on,' she says, 'let's get the fuck off this freezing cold bridge. Where do you need to get to? I can—'

'No.' The sharp retort makes her gasp. 'I'm sorry. But you need to go now. Leave me here. You shouldn't be—'

She seems to bite the end of her sentence off and, for the first time, Neve sees that she is terrified in a way Neve has never witnessed before in real life.

Neve crosses her arms.

'No way,' she says. 'I'm not leaving you here. It's bloody cold and—'

She yelps as Isabelle lunges, kissing her quickly on each cheek with cold, dry lips. Her grip is surprisingly strong. Neve feels a flash of fear as Isabelle's lips brush her ear.

'I'm sorry. Please forgive me. And keep it, if you can bear to.'

Then she turns to face the water and, in one neat movement, climbs over the side of the railing and jumps into the river.

3

Neve sits in the back of the police car now, wrapped in a silver thermal blanket as blue light smears rhythmically across the windows. The hiss and crackle of the radio begins to fade as icy rain pounds onto the roof of the vehicle.

The RNLI had arrived first, confusing her with their jaunty logo because she thought they were people who rescued you at sea. They came with astonishing speed after she made the call. Later she would learn that one of their emergency stations was situated close to Waterloo Bridge.

They arrived before the police. Neve's phone had died before she could finish the conversation with the operator so for ten surreal minutes before the police car had arrived, she'd stood on the bridge alone, looking down at the boat as it turned slow circles in the blackness below, its spotlight swishing back and forth. She half thought about hurrying away and leaving them to it. But it seemed desperately sad that this stranger should have no one apart from the emergency services rooting for her to be found.

So instead she kept up the vigil, staring into the depths

below. Her heart had jolted when she saw something white swell and roll in the water, then she realized it was a large plastic bottle. The sensation of relief, that she wouldn't have to jump in and attempt a rescue, had almost buckled her at the knees.

Later, she would understand that no one would expect her – someone with only average swimming ability – to try and rescue a drowning woman from the Thames in winter. But guilt periodically comes in a bright, sharp jab under her ribs. This at least is a sensation she recognizes.

When the police arrived she'd told them what happened in jerky, shocked sentences. They'd gently encouraged her to start again from the beginning and tell them the whole story.

Now here she is, in the strange aftermath and she can't stop shivering. Every now and then a particularly strong shudder jerks through her, which makes her clench her jaw. It's unnerving. She read somewhere that shock can be dangerous in some physiological way she doesn't really understand and wonders whether she ought to ask for something from the ambulance crew.

She looks out the window and sees through the condensation and raindrops that one of the RNLI men is talking to the policewoman. It's the small, Northern one with tight curly hair and an efficient air about her. The policewoman nods and then glances at the car. Neve draws back, as though caught doing something wrong.

The door of the police car opens, but it is the young black officer who pokes his head in and peers at her.

'You alright, love?' he says gently. He has pretty eyes, thickly lashed, and a cold that clogs his voice and makes him fumble for a tissue. He honks into it and regards her.

Neve nods.

'Look,' he says, 'we have been informed by the rescue crew that the tide is very strong tonight and the weather is taking a turn for the worse. They've made the decision that they aren't going to continue the search.' He pauses. 'Do you understand what I'm saying?'

His formal words are countered by the kindness in his face.

'I think so,' she says in a small voice. 'There's no hope. Will she just . . . stay down there?'

He makes a face.

'Probably not,' he continues, 'but it can take a little while for, uh, people to wash up at this stretch of the Thames.' He pauses. 'Was she a friend of yours, the woman who jumped in?'

Neve swallows, picturing the moment again.

The shocking speed of it all. Cold, dry lips on her cheek and clawed hands gripping her shoulders. The bright flash of the dress as she tipped herself up and over into the black water.

'I was just walking past,' she says. 'I don't know her at all. I was just . . . going home and there she was. I started talking to her. And then she . . .' she swallows. 'She just did it. Right in front of me.'

The policeman makes an indeterminate sound of sympathy, his head to the side.

It's only now Neve remembers the envelope, realizing she must have dropped it on the pavement in the shock of the moment. 'Look, she gave me something,' she says. 'An envelope? There was something really strange about it. I only took it to stop her being weird.' She swallows again, feels a tremble judder through her and then she laughs, loud and inappropriately. 'But it didn't work, did it!'

The policeman nods. 'We've got that, also her phone

and bag. In a bit we'll get a written statement and then get you home. Bit of a rough night. You'll feel better tomorrow.'

Neve nods gratefully, her eyes brimming.

4

It's almost six a.m. when the police car pulls up in front of Lou and Steve's building on a leafy street in Kentish Town. It's still dark outside. Several windows are lit. A handful of people are quietly closing front doors, slinging bags over shoulders and jamming in earbuds, walking, hunched with fatigue, down the road to the tube.

Neve thanks the two police officers, noticing the lingering look from the attractive black one. As she closes the car door she realizes gratefully that she is so late home her sister will almost certainly be up, tending to her eleven-month-old baby, Maisie.

The car pulls away and Neve makes her way carefully down the slippery steps that lead to the kitchen.

Lou and Steve live on the bottom two floors of the tall Victorian building and she is hoping she can alert Lou's attention through the window rather than ringing the bell and waking the entire household.

But she realizes with a sinking heart that all the lights are off in the kitchen. It would be typical if Maisie had chosen to sleep through for the first time ever, on this of all nights.

Then she sees her sister, swaddled in the long baggy cardigan she wears as a dressing gown at the sink, Maisie on her shoulder, as upright and alert as a meerkat. The baby sees her aunt and waves sweetly, opening and closing her fingers over her fist.

Neve returns the wave with a weak smile. Lou turns and Neve sees rather than hears her shocked yelp. Lou disappears back through the kitchen door and a few moments later the front door a level up is noisily unbolted and opened.

Lou stands in the entrance and peers out at her sister as she climbs the steps. Her face is puffy and Neve can see right away that she has had a bad night. Lou's eyes look small and pink, like a rabbit's. She has patches of dry skin on her cheeks, which are flushed, as though she is the one teething and not Maisie.

'God, look at *you*,' she says. 'Is this you just coming home? I thought you were in bed. Oh . . . Neve? What on earth is it?'

Neve doesn't have any more tears but is suddenly overcome with the need for human comfort. She stumbles towards her sister, longing to hide her face in the woollen softness of her ample shoulder. To be held like a child and told everything will be okay.

'I can't really . . .' says Lou with a sharp laugh, 'Maisie, stop wriggling!' The little girl pushes against her aunty with hands and feet and revs like a car in protest. All three of them awkwardly clash against each other.

Cheeks flushed, Neve walks off into the kitchen.

She should know better, she thinks. They've never exactly been huggers, her and Louise.

She goes to the kettle and can feel it has only recently boiled. She opens the neatly labelled jar of coffee and taps some roughly into a mug that says, 'WORLD'S NICEST

MUMMY', knowing it will annoy Lou that she is using this cup and that she isn't bothering with a spoon.

'What's wrong with you?' says Lou from the doorway. 'Has something happened?'

Sloshing water from the kettle into the cup, Neve then fumbles in the drawer for a spoon and adds two spoons of sugar before lifting it to her lips and chugging the bitter, lukewarm coffee down. Lou and Steve don't believe in proper coffee.

'Honestly, Neve,' Lou continues in a low, tolerant voice, 'Lottie is getting to an age when she's going to start asking questions about why her aunty has stayed out all night. You can't just come in looking like something the cat dragged in when you are in a family home. Don't you think that it's time you—'

'I watched a woman commit suicide tonight. Right in front of me.'

Lou's eyes widen and she slaps her free hand across her mouth.

'Oh God, no. Where? On the tube?'

Maisie grizzles. She buries her face into her mother's shoulder, squidging her legs up and rounding her back.

Lou swings from side to side. She is always moving to some maternal metronome inside her, even when she isn't holding a child. She shushes and pats the baby's back, her eyes pinned to Neve's face.

'Where? What happened?'

Neve goes to fill the kettle again and Lou bustles over.

'Here, let me get that. You sit down and tell me everything. You look awful. Are you warm enough?' Lou is finally in her comfort zone. Looking after people's physical needs is what she does best.

Neve does as she's told, sitting, and shakes her head to indicate that no, she isn't warm enough. She can't envisage ever being warm again, in fact. Lou leaves the room and comes back with a travel blanket from the sofa. Neve wraps it around her neck and shoulders, trying to ignore the vaguely sickly smell emanating from it, thanks to various small, dirty hands.

As Lou makes her another coffee she begins to tell her about what happened, starting with walking across the bridge.

'Wait,' Lou interrupts her straight away, a deep frown on her face. 'Was this after your work thing? Have you been at a police station *all night*?'

Neve sighs. She's tempted to lie then she thinks, why should I?

'I'd been back to someone's house,' she says, as a compromise. The hotel really does sound so sleazy. Despite their decidedly agnostic upbringing, Lou has turned a bit Christian since meeting church-goer Steve.

She looks her sister directly in the eye as she says this and Lou looks down at the baby's head and pats her back gently.

'Okay,' she says patiently. 'Go on . . .'

Neve tells her the rest of the story in a series of terse sentences.

'What a thing,' says Lou in wonder. 'What a terrible thing.'

They sit in silence.

It is only as Neve is slipping gratefully into her chilly bed and fighting off the returning shivers that she remembers she didn't tell her sister about the strange exchange with the envelope.

I wonder what was in it, she thinks as scrambled images race across her mind. Finally, as she begins to warm up for the first time since she left Whatsisname's hotel room, she tips into sleep.

5

Neve doesn't have any difficulty in recalling what happened when she wakes. There's no moment of mental filing from night to day. It's right there at the forefront of her mind.

A woman talked to me and then she jumped off the bridge.
Isabelle. Her name was Isabelle.

She cracks her sore eyes open and gazes up at the white meringue swirl of the ceiling rose above her.

From downstairs she hears the squawks and shrieks of CBeebies, Maisie's low-level grizzling and the rumble of Steve's voice.

The thought of being with them all makes her groan and turn her face into the pillow.

Steve has never actually said he doesn't want her there. Neither has Lou.

But she sees the looks that slide between them when she's forgotten to wash up, or left a glass and plate on the patio. Her toiletries had been a growing skyline on the bathroom shelf and every morning she sees that they have been tidied and grouped together. Steve practically follows her around with a dustpan and brush.

It's not like she's deliberately taking the piss. She really *is* grateful that they're putting her up like this. It's just that mess seems to follow her. She can enter a room and within minutes has laid her keys in one place, her handbag somewhere else and where did she put her phone again?

Steve doesn't drink much, doesn't smoke and doesn't even swear. He runs, he cycles, he plays five-a-side football with people from the large insurance company where he works. He has two comfortably off parents and likes to think of himself as a hands-on dad to his daughters.

He is almost completely lacking in a sense of humour.

Unfortunately, people like Steve bring out the worst in Neve. The little pursed crease at the corner of his mouth as she sloshes more red wine into a glass, or says, 'Fuck me, it's cold,' only eggs her on.

She'd passed him on the way back from the shower early the other morning, dressed in only a towel. He'd kept his eyes so averted it had given her a wicked urge to drop the towel just to see what would happen. He'd probably have spontaneously combusted, like that picture of the sad stockinged leg in a pile of ash she'd seen in her dad's old *Unexplained* part-work magazine as a little girl.

Steve's prudishness has got worse since an evening a couple of weeks before. They'd all got unexpectedly drunk together. Steve only had a couple of beers but had loosened up enough that Neve found herself quite liking him.

But she'd made a smutty joke while helping him load the dishwasher after Lou had stumbled off to bed and he'd reacted as though he'd been bitten by a snake. Neve can't even really remember what she'd said now. Somehow, his brain had interpreted this as her coming on to him in some way and ever since he'd avoided eye contact.

He clearly thought she was some sort of mad sex fiend

now who would jump on him, were it not for the restraints of him being married to her older sister.

It was all so tedious.

Neve gets out of bed feeling like an old woman and wraps herself in her dressing gown before heading to the bathroom. Thank God it's Saturday, although these days, the pleasures of the weekend are tempered by being a) more or less homeless and b) miserably single.

When she goes into the kitchen she sees Steve at the sink, carefully cutting sandwiches into fingers. He has already been for a run; she can tell by the ruddy glow of his cheeks. He will no doubt have a long cycle later, just at the time the girls are needing their tea. Neve has noticed this, that he manages to live exactly like he had before kids, yet gets praised for the little he does with them.

'Morning,' she says and goes to fill the kettle.

'Lou told me what happened,' says Steve, without preamble. 'That sounds a bit grim.'

She's about to reply when a high fluting voice floats through from the adjoining sitting room.

'What's grim, Daddy?'

Lottie appears below them. She peers up, scrutinizing them. Neve loves her four-year-old niece but somehow always feels as though she has been assessed and found to be wanting in some way. Maybe it's a genetic thing.

She has black hair like her mother, but it bounces and jiggles around her head in spirals. Her eyes are very pale blue, like Steve's, and her small snub nose is dusted with dark freckles.

Steve reaches over and chucks her under the chin.

'Never you mind, Miss Lotts. Are you ready to go to the Heath?'

But Lottie is not to be deterred so easily.

'Did something happen to Aunty Neve?' she says. Neve and Steve exchange glances.

'Why would you say that?' says Steve.

The little girl hoicks her cuddly lamb higher under her armpit and regards them both seriously.

'Because Mummy said you must be nice to her today and you said *God, I'll try but I'm not promising anything.* And then Mummy hit you on the arm.'

Steve barks a sharp embarrassed laugh. 'Well . . .'

Neve smiles weakly.

'I'm fine, Lot,' she says. 'Nothing wrong with me, look.' She holds her arms up and does a strange little turn. She's not sure why she has done it.

Lottie runs back into the living room, mind already elsewhere. Steve ferociously begins organizing snacks, head bent as he chops carrots and decants houmous into a Tupperware pot.

Neve makes herself coffee and toast.

'Anyway,' says Steve now in a low voice. 'Sorry about the . . . thing . . . that happened. Must have been rough to see.'

'Thanks,' murmurs Neve. 'It was.'

Half an hour later the family are ready to go. Maisie arches her back and complains as she is strapped into the buggy, while Lou says encouraging things with a bright, cheerful voice that feels like nails on glass to Neve's ear.

They call goodbye to Neve, who collapses with relief onto the sofa and takes out her phone, grateful that she remembered to charge it when she got home.

Her thumb moves across the screen and before she can stop herself she has stroked up Daniel's number. She hovers over it, filled with a dragging desire to speak to him.

Before she can change her mind she taps out a message.

Can I come round 2 pick up few things?

24

She hesitates and then adds an *N* and an *X*. Just the one.

Neve is suddenly desperate to tell him what happened last night and once again begins to shuffle through the pack of images in her head.

She thinks about the first sight of her, Isabelle, looking across the water. It seems strange now that Neve's first thought wasn't that she was a potential suicide. Ridiculous, in fact. But she'd been cold and tired. Still a bit drunk, not to mention a little humiliated by what had happened with Whatsisname. She wasn't really thinking straight.

With a shiver she remembers those last seconds; the cold lips on her cheek and the whispered words in her ear.

What had she said? She should remember a soon-to-be-dead woman's last words. Isn't that the very least she can do?

Neve holds her head tightly in her hands and stares at the wooden floorboards splashed with pale winter sun, trying to dredge up the exact memory.

But it has gone.

So instead she taps on Safari and searches for local news about a woman jumping off a bridge. Of course there is nothing. She realizes as she is doing it that this is not even news for London. She wonders how many people have thrown themselves into the Thames in the last year. Probably loads.

Her phone pings with a text and she snatches it up.

Not around much this week and away for Xmas. Can we make it in the NY.

There's no question mark. No *D*. And no *X*.

And before she gets any warning that it is coming, she is crying. Hard, hot tears course down her face and she clamps her arms around herself, rocking with grief.

6

Neve's office is set to close for Christmas a couple of days later.

Portland Cavendish Crafts is a publisher of specialist magazines on Gray's Inn Road. Across from the reception desk at which Neve sits for eight mind-numbingly boring hours every day is a stand filled with various magazines with cheerful titles in colourful fonts, titles such as *Cross Stitch Crazy* and *Creative Craft Weekly*.

When she had first started here, she'd vaguely thought she might become a journalist. Wasn't this the kind of career thing successful people said? They were all, 'Oh, I started out making tea and now I am the Controller of the BBC,' and the like. She imagined herself laughing fondly about the funny old magazines she used to write for, before she was taken on in some blurrily defined way for a more glamorous position elsewhere.

She doesn't particularly want to be a journalist anyway, which is a good thing because five years on she's still answering the telephone and saying, 'PCC, can I help you?'

More often than not she says, 'No, I'm sorry, this isn't

the Police *or* the Press Complaints Commission,' and, 'No, that's *IPC*. It's a different magazine company.'

The rest of the time she photocopies things and tries to do as little work as humanly possible while still getting paid a salary. A terrible salary, but it had been just enough to live on when she was with Daniel.

Now that she is staying with Lou and Steve, it's almost but not quite enough to live on. But it certainly isn't enough to live on judging by the flat shares she sees circled pointedly in Biro by Steve on the dining room table.

This is one of the things that causes icy licks of fear in Neve's stomach late at night.

Now she attends to the few admin jobs required before the office closes and ponders miserably the thought of a whole week under Lou and Steve's feet.

His prim parents are coming for Christmas Day and she can already feel the claustrophobia of sitting around the table and wishing someone else would have a second glass of wine.

She hears a loud out-breath now and looks up to see Miri, bent over the photocopier. Her friend is tiny – barely five feet – and with her swollen body is now almost as wide as she is tall. She kneads a fist into her back and groans quietly.

Neve told Miri all about the woman on the bridge as soon as she was back at work. Once, Miri would have been agog at a story like this but late pregnancy has made her formerly feisty friend oddly fearful about the world. Miri looked away from her as she described the moment Isabelle jumped off the bridge; Neve had sensed she didn't really want to hear it, even though she had made the right noises and hugged her friend awkwardly, the hard bullet of her belly nudging Neve's side.

A few moments later she had scurried away, eyes gleaming. It made Neve feel as though she was the one who had done something shocking and violent.

She's gazing balefully at her friend now when someone comes through the double doors and stops by the desk. It's Fraser, the editor of *Modeller Monthly*, a magazine filled with stories about model trains that is, bafflingly to Neve, one of CPP's best sellers.

He's only in his thirties but favours tweedy academic-looking jackets and, with his unfashionable glasses and thin pale hair, looks much older. He behaves as though he's the editor of a major broadsheet and heaven help anyone who cracks jokes about the readership, as Neve has done many times.

It's why, she thinks, he likes to throw his weight around with her, and gets her to do silly little admin jobs he's perfectly capable of doing himself.

She pretends not to notice him, so he has to clear his throat. It's childish, but she takes her pleasures where she can in this job. Looking up, she rewards him with a beaming smile, all teeth and sparkly eyes, which makes the tips of his ears flush almost purple.

'Uh, yes, Neve,' he says, quickly, 'I wonder if I can trouble you to do something for me.'

Neve leans over, conspiratorial, and says, 'Fraser, you know that serving your needs is what I live for.'

She's hoping Miri will hear and that they can snigger about it later, but she glances over to see that Miri has finished her copying job and gone.

'I did actually email you about this earlier,' Fraser says pointedly and Neve, chastised, lets her grin slide away.

'Phones have been crazy,' she lies.

'Yes, well, anyway, there was a problem with some of the subs for *Creative Stamp Monthly* and *Weave It*,' he says. 'I need you to send out a standard apology letter to the readers affected.' He pauses and his eyes gleam as he adds, 'There are quite a few. Should keep you busy for a while.' He hands her a sheet of paper, dense with names and addresses.

Neve takes it from him and murmurs that she will get on to it. As he moves away with his quick, pigeon-toed walk, she watches him go and thinks there's no sport in this job any more. She is suddenly filled with an overwhelming weariness.

She turns the switchboard to the answering machine and goes to the Ladies to hide for a while. Inside the cubicle she blows her nose furiously until the desire to cry passes.

When she is washing her hands she hears a flushing toilet. She'd thought she was the only one in there and is relieved when it's Miri who emerges from the cubicle.

'Christ on a bike,' says her friend. 'I swear it would be easier to wear a nappy and be done with it. That's the sixth time I've had to pee since nine.' She pauses and sees Neve's blotchy face. 'Oh, what's the matter, honey? Thinking about Mum and Dad?'

One of the many reasons Neve loves Miri is that her friend is capable of mentioning Neve's orphan state.

Neve shrugs and washes her hands. When she speaks, her voice is thick and snotty.

'Not really. Just . . . this place, you know? Can't believe I'm still here sometimes.'

Miri washes her hands and regards her in the mirror, her brow creased and her eyes soft.

'Well you're not alone there,' she says kindly. 'Anyway, not long now until the holidays.'

Neve snorts, impatiently.

'Yeah, I'm really excited about Christmas,' she says, deadpan, then makes a doomy face in the mirror.

'Spending it with Mr and Mrs Tight Arse?' says Miri doing a pert, rabbitty gesture with hands bent like paws.

'Yep,' says Neve. 'Yay.'

Miri sighs. 'You know I'd have you to mine in a shot,' she says, 'but I have several million aunties and uncles coming over in order to create my own festive hell.' She slips into a broad Indian accent and waggles her head, 'You need to eat a bit more, Amira-Ji, or that baby is going to come out a lanky bean like his father.'

Neve laughs as she throws the tissue into the bin.

'Arjan is dreading it,' continues Miri with a sigh. 'It's his first one where he hasn't been on call and he'd rather be there. Can you imagine preferring to help sick people than have a family gathering? That's my lot for you.' Miri holds her hand up with a flourish, as though revealing words on a banner. 'The Sharma family: Not quite as much fun as a winter vomiting virus.'

Neve laughs and feels cheered up, a little.

Miri pauses before speaking. 'Hey, I've been meaning to ask you. Did you find out anything else about that woman? The one who killed herself?'

Neve shakes her head, mood instantly sinking again. 'I tried Googling it,' she says. 'But I think too many people in London top themselves for it to be news.'

Miri makes a disapproving sound in her throat. 'That's depressing. Still,' she says, perking up, 'for all you know, they may have rescued her. Why don't you ring the police and ask someone? You have the right to know. You were there, after all.'

Neve takes her mobile out into the stairwell for privacy.

It takes ages for her to be put through to anyone who can help. She starts off with 999, then is directed to another department. Finally, after being on hold for almost five minutes, she's connected with a bored-sounding woman who tells her someone will look on the system for further information and then puts her on hold again.

Neve sighs and entertains the possibility of hanging up. But no, she needs to see this through.

Eventually a different woman comes to the phone. She sounds a little warmer.

'Hello, you were asking about the suicide from Waterloo Bridge on December twenty-first?' she says.

'Yes, that's right.' Neve's heart speeds up and she finds herself clutching the receiver, her hand damp. There's a pause.

'I'm afraid a body was found the following morning.'

'Oh . . .' Neve puffs out the word in a sigh. She didn't know what else she had been expecting, but the news still feels electric and cold in her stomach.

'Did you know the individual?' the woman continues brightly.

'Well, no, I was just there. You see . . .'

She finds herself recounting the whole thing again, while the woman on the other end of the phone clucks, 'Oh dear' and 'What a shame,' at key points.

When she has finished, the woman lowers her voice a fraction before speaking again. 'Look,' she says. 'It's very common in these situations to feel guilty and think you could have done something. But put it this way, this was someone who was serious.'

'What do you mean?' says Neve, sitting forward in her chair.

'Well,' there's a pause, 'she made certain provisions to make sure she sank quickly.'

Neve quickly scans her memories of what the woman, *Isabelle*, had looked like. There was no coat that could be filled with stones, à la Virginia Woolf. She wasn't carrying anything. So how on earth did she weigh herself down enough to drown? She pictures that silky dress, clinging to Isabelle's thin frame. The swishiness of it and the jarring sense that it was from another, more glamorous time.

'I just don't get it,' she says miserably. 'She was only wearing an evening dress.'

There's a brief silence and then the woman speaks all in a rush. 'Look, I'm not sure whether I ought to release this information without the family's permission but you were the one who had to see it all so, well . . .'

She clears her throat and lowers her voice further. 'It was the hem of her dress, you see,' she says. 'She'd sewed lead curtain tape all around the bottom of it. This was enough extra weight for someone of that size to sink.'

Neve's stomach lurches. 'Oh God,' she says. 'That's awful.'

'Yes, it's terrible,' says the woman. 'She had obviously done her homework. In that stretch of the Thames, most people are rescued before there's any prospect of drowning, you see. Such a shame. She really meant business, the poor thing.'

7

'No more for me, thanks Stephen.' Steve's mother Celia puts a small, neat hand, tipped with shell-pink polish, on top of her glass of wine. She has been nursing the same glass for the last two hours.

Her husband Bill is engaging their son in a lengthy discussion about the shortcomings of the M4 and the A406. This is a follow-on from the same conversation earlier.

Steve nods and is trying to look interested, while simultaneously shooting looks at his small daughter, who is sitting with a mutinous expression on her face. Lottie has been recently reprimanded by her grandmother for whining and looks ready to blow at any moment.

They are sitting at the table with the wreckage of Christmas dinner in front of them. The gold tablecloth is a battleground of spilled peas, which Lottie had refused to eat, rings from glasses and small lumpy mounds of red wax from the festive candle that is melting like a squashed volcano in the middle of the table.

Neve stifles a yawn.

Today seems to have been going on for an eternity. At five a.m. she was woken from a dream about Daniel by the study door opening and the sound of feet padding across the floorboards.

She'd kept her eyes firmly closed, then felt laboured breathing hot on her cheek. After a moment Lottie had announced in a stage whisper that, 'Mummy and Daddy say it is too early to see if Santa has been.'

'That's because it *is* too early,' Neve had groggily replied. Then, when Lottie showed no sign of going back to bed, 'Why don't you go and have a look on your own?'

She hadn't even been aware, really, of what she was saying; she'd only wanted Lottie to go away. And she certainly didn't remember saying, 'Yes, you definitely are allowed to get started on the presents,' as was later claimed by the little curly-haired Judas.

But it turned out she had committed a crime of major proportions an hour later when she heard raised voices from the sitting room.

Lottie had gaily skipped away and unwrapped everything under the tree, including everyone else's gifts. She had eaten a whole selection box and was starting on the handmade Belgian chocolates meant for her grandma before anyone else got up.

Lou had been tearful because a special moment – when the family all discovered the presents together – had been ruined. She had been planning to film the whole thing. Lou was, in Neve's opinion, an obsessive chronicler of her family life. She would have unfollowed her sister on Facebook because of this, had she been able to get away with it.

Steve, surveying his guilty-faced daughter, and the colourful piles of ripped paper, wore an expression that wasn't at all Christian. Neve was in the doghouse.

He spent the rest of the morning cooking and refused all offers of help, while retaining a beleaguered air.

Lou has been brittle with tension all day. She doesn't like

Celia and Bill, Neve knows this. But she seems to think that if she refrains from criticizing them, even to Neve, then she will somehow find a deeper reservoir of tolerance.

Neve has resolved to be the model guest for the rest of the day. When Bill resorts to one of his favourite topics of conversation – namely, the fact that the 'UK is an island with limited resources and it's time something was done about our border controls' – Neve smiles sweetly and suggests she clear the table and wash up.

Celia regards her as she hands over her smeared plate.

'So how is the flat hunting going, Neve?' she says. Neve hears Lou quietly sigh.

'Bit slowly,' she says with a small laugh. 'Everywhere is so expensive. But I am looking!' She sets her jaw as she picks up more plates, hoping for a quick exit from this conversation. But Celia isn't finished.

'Have you ever thought about moving back to your home town?' she says. 'Do you have any people there? Remind me. I mean,' she adds, hurriedly, 'I know you don't have your mum and dad any more, but is there anyone else? Wider family?'

Lou shoots her a panicked look. Celia knows full well that Lou and Neve are the only ones left. Steve has two siblings with five children between them, several aunts and uncles, and his grandparents only died in the last couple of years. He's positively rotten with family, thinks Neve. He has no idea what it is like to be an island that only contains two, yet is still somehow crowded.

She feels a sharp tug of love for her sister now and the urge to say something shocking and untrue, like, 'No one that isn't inside,' but knows her sister will be even more upset with her.

Neve decides to ignore the question.

'Shall I make you some tea, when I'm done washing up?'

Wrong-footed, Celia blinks at her without replying.

Neve's phone buzzes in her pocket then and, despite herself, she can't resist sliding it out and glancing at the screen.

It's from Miri and says simply **SHOOT ME NOW**. Neve smiles weakly.

Lou is watching her with a similar expression to the one she keeps flicking towards her eldest daughter. Neve knows that her sister is wondering, constantly, about whether she is in communication with Daniel. Neve decides to put her out of her misery.

'Miri says hi,' she says.

Bill seems to wake up at this. 'Miri. Now that's an unusual name. English girl, is she?'

'Yes,' says Neve as she heads towards the kitchen. 'Her full name is Amira Sharma-Kapoor.' She looks back over her shoulder and adds, 'She was born in Croydon.'

At the sink she can't stop the grin at the silence in her wake. She can picture Bill and Celia exchanging glances. She attacks the washing up with fast efficiency, hoping that no one will offer to help her.

Bill and Celia retire to the sofa now and Celia is tasked with trying to put batteries into one of the few plastic toys Lottie has been allowed to have. Everything else has a wooden, utilitarian air about it and screams 'educational'. Neve had played it safe and stuck to the present she was instructed to buy; a stacking game with colourful wooden balls which Lottie hasn't looked at since opening.

Maisie starts to grizzle and Lou takes her off into another room. She still occasionally breastfeeds her and knows she will get a frosty reception from Celia, who once declared that there was 'no need for letting everything hang out'. Neve, having seen what having two children has done to Lou's breasts, guiltily half agrees with this sentiment.

*   *   *

As she washes up, Neve thinks back to the Christmas before. She and Daniel, who didn't speak to his parents any more and was without familial ties, had holed up with wine, beer and a range of deli food from Marks and Spencer. They watched *Breaking Bad* in one long marathon, stopping only for sex and food breaks. There was no tree and they sent no cards.

It had been her best adult Christmas.

Her heart feels sand-bag heavy inside her chest as she remembers them emerging, blinking into the daylight for a walk on Boxing Day. They'd walked hand in hand on Hampstead Heath and stopped for hot chocolates in the funny old café that never seemed to change.

It's hard to think about what they talked of now.

So much of their time together – almost four years – had revolved around going out, getting stoned, getting drunk. Laughter. Music. Sex.

Fun.

During his 'up' times anyway. There were other periods when Daniel turned his face to the wall for whole mornings or afternoons and was monosyllabic. She used to tell herself it was all part of his arty personality and that his up and down moods were somehow fuelled by creativity.

Daniel was a musician, who played in a couple of bands and also did the occasional bit of session work, mainly classical guitar. He was a few years older than Neve – thirty-six on his last birthday. When, shortly after, he had quit both the bands on the same weekend, she'd told him he was having an early mid-life crisis. Then he took off, to Ireland, to visit a friend, so he said.

And while he was away, she was so angry with him that she got drunk and slept with his friend and band mate Ash. When he came back it turned out he had been 'trying to get his head together' and had decided it was time they got married. Neve didn't want to get married. But she didn't want him to know about Ash either and she had ended up blurting *that* out within two hours of him getting home.

She'd moved out a few days later. There's no prospect of being forgiven. Daniel was 'betrayed', as he put it, by his first love and had sunk into a deep depression after this. Now, he says Neve has opened up old wounds, and inflicted new ones.

She still doesn't want to marry him. But she wishes they could slip back into their old life and just carry on as they were. Why did things have to change?

Taking a tray of teas and coffees into the living room, Neve sees that Lottie has built a teetering tower out of her building blocks and is concentrating with a scrunched brow and chewed lower lip on getting the final piece on top. Steve is helping and Celia is sitting close by and handing over marbles.

But as the final one is put into place, the whole thing collapses and scatters coloured glass in a surprisingly wide arc.

Lottie gives a frustrated squeal and says in a clear, bright voice, 'Buggering cunty bollocks,' just as Lou walks back into the room.

Celia sucks in her breath. Steve glares at Neve. Lou looks as though she is going to burst into tears.

'Where on earth has she learned language like that?' says Celia.

'That's what Aunty Neve said when she stubbed her toe on Daddy's bike,' says Lottie, eyes bright, picking up on the charged atmosphere. Neve forces a laugh and reaches for a cup of coffee. She takes a sip and scalds her mouth.

'Oops!' she says and glances around the room at the looks of disapproval and disappointment. 'Sorry. I promise to rein it in.'

'Yes, why don't you?' says Steve, furiously snatching up bricks. 'Why don't you just do that?'

Neve suddenly feels an overwhelming exhaustion wash over her. She would happily lay her head down on the carpet and sleep right now.

'I said I'm sorry,' she says in a small voice.

'But are you?' Steve's face is rigid and Neve experiences a jolt at how much dislike she sees there.

'Er. Yes, I am?'

'Because,' says Steve, 'I don't know.' He gets to his feet. It is actually possible to see his internal temperature rising. 'It seems to me as though you get a bit of a kick out of disrupting things.'

Injustice flashes bright inside her chest. 'That's not fair.'

Lou says, 'Steve,' warningly.

But Steve is only just starting. Lottie creeps towards her grandmother's legs and leans against her, thumb in mouth and eyes wide.

'No, Lou, you know that you feel the same way. You said it would be for a week or so and how long have you been here now, Neve?'

'I'm not sure, maybe a month, but I'm trying—'

'Six weeks,' he cuts across her. 'And not only do you leave a trail of destruction everywhere you go, you come in at all hours after doing God knows what. It's like you think you live in a student squat, rather than a family house.'

'Steve, please!' snaps Lou. 'It's Christmas Day! This isn't the time for that conversation.'

'It never is the time!' Steve's roar shocks everyone, including, it seems, himself. He snaps his jaw shut and blinks furiously.

Neve gets up from the seat. She can feel it building inside her, and she knows she should just leave now. Say nothing else.

She also knows she won't do that.

'But you're not so perfect, are you?' she says, with a half-smile.

Steve laughs. 'What's that supposed to mean?'

'Well,' says Neve, 'I've noticed that it's always Lou who does the donkey work with the girls. You somehow manage to go out with your mates and do all your wanky sports, don't you? While my sister looks like one of the walking dead most of the time.'

'Neve!'

'Sorry, but it's true.'

'If you care so much about your sister, you could help out a bit, couldn't you?' barks Steve.

'Really,' says Celia now, her face pink with outrage. 'I must say that you are being very ungrateful after everything my son . . . and daughter-in-law have done for you.'

Neve can't help it. It literally slips out of her mouth, as involuntary as a cough or a belch. 'Oh you can fuck off, Celia.'

Celia's mouth drops open and it occurs to Neve she has never seen this happen quite so cartoonishly before.

'How dare you speak to my wife that way!' bellows Bill.

'STOP IT!' Lou bursts into tears and the sound sets off Maisie from her bedroom. Lou is almost panting, her fists clenched at the sides of her head. She looks just like Lottie for a moment.

Neve feels her anger dull and makes a move to touch her sister's arm, alarmed. But Lou shakes her hand away as if it burns.

'Just stop it, all of you.' She looks at Neve, her eyes gleaming. Her expression is one of genuine puzzlement when she says, 'Why do you have to spoil *everything*?'

8

Dearest Granny,

Can I just say that everyone is really overreacting?

Look, I've always been funny about blood - you
know that. Remember when Rich broke his nose
playing rugby? And I fainted and gave myself
concussion? Then there was the time Mummy cut
her finger when I was little and I got all hysterical.

It's what I do. Funny old Izzy, etc! Big drama
queen. As Dad always says.

And this time there were what you call them -
extenerating (???) circumstances. I hadn't eaten
my lunch and was about to come on, so I was a
bit wobbly.

The stupid thing about it is that the paint didn't
even look that realistic, not really.

We were in art and because it was almost
Halloween, people were telling silly stories and trying
to scare each other. And Sasha Picket, who always
has to be at the centre of EVERYTHING, thought it

would be really funny to cover her hands and arms in red paint.

She let out this horrible shriek and when we looked at her, her eyes were all wide and mad.

Everyone says that almost straight away she went, 'Out, out damned Spot!' and then cracked up. But I don't really remember any of that.

All I know is that everything went tight and hot and there was no air. I wanted to make myself really small. I don't remember screaming like they all said I did. I think they're exaggerating about that part.

But anyway of course there was a big hoohah about it and all the teachers went nuts.

I am FINE.

F.I.N.E.

Okay? Promise!

So you can stop worrying about me. I hate school, but there's nothing new there.

Can't wait to see you and to give you and Bruce the biggest cuddles. Tell him I'm taking him for walkies SOON! Hope he's being a good boy.

All my love,

Izzy xxxxx

I miss Mummy so much. She never went off the deep end like Dad does. I know you miss her too xxxx

9

January crawls along with skies the colour of cement and unseasonable temperatures. Sad little patches of bright daffodils break out in the parks and are largely ignored, like early party-goers. No one feels they have earned these signs of spring yet.

It all adds to a sense in Neve that everything is off kilter. She has been thinking about the woman, Isabelle, a lot. One night she even found herself contemplating calling the Samaritans. Not because she is depressed – she knows that a general feeling of my-life-is-shit-right-now is on a different continent to real mental illness – but because she thought maybe someone could explain to her what kind of thoughts were going through Isabelle's head that night.

She keeps trying to step inside that moment again, when Isabelle spoke into her ear with that harsh whisper. Could she, Neve, have grabbed hold of her and stopped her doing what she did?

Could she have been kinder when she saw her there?

Every time she thinks about how irritated she had been at the hold-up to her journey home, she feels a nauseous lurch of guilt in her stomach. If only she had a bit more information. She forgot the woman's surname as soon as the police had revealed it. Why didn't she make a note of it somewhere? And how *could* she have forgotten? This feels like a terrible thing.

They have reached an uneasy truce at the flat. She has apologized, and so has Steve, but they both know their only regret is having upset Lou.

Lottie and Lou and the baby have all been felled by a vicious cold. Neve has the constitution of an ox but can feel a general sniffly misery pulling at her senses and knows it's only a matter of time before she gets sick too.

At least she might get a day off work.

Miri is on maternity leave now and Neve is keenly aware of the space she has left behind. Two of her closest friends have moved away from London in the last year, both because they have married and started reproducing. There are invitations to go to Wales and to Sussex, or wherever it was, to visit, but she feels curiously dispirited by the prospect of admiring their wood burners and their big gardens and hearing all about how they 'should have done this years ago'.

This particular morning has crept by with soupy slowness. There is an uneasy feeling at PCC because of a rumour that a German magazine company based in Beckenham are interested in buying the company and merging it with one that specializes in magazine part-works.

Neve has finished up all the jobs she has been asked to do this morning and now sits staring down at Facebook on her phone and giving desultory swipes at various posts.

She remembers that she had stuffed some letters into her bag this morning before leaving for work. A small pile was building up on the table and she knew Steve was going to start getting all twitchy about it soon, so she had resolved to take it to work to read and dump, depending on what it was.

Flicking through now she finds a couple of bills, an interesting-looking letter in a white envelope, which turns out to be from an estate agent of all things, and finally she opens an A3 brown envelope, knowing it is bound to be something to do with tax, or National Insurance, or some other unpleasantness.

But inside, she is surprised to see first a compliment slip with 'Met Police' printed at the top and a couple of sentences scrawled in blue Biro beneath.

Ms Carey, we were asked to pass on this information. Kind regards.

There is no signature.

Neve flicks the switchboard over to automatic and feels her heartbeat kick faster as she unclips the compliment slip and looks at the letter beneath.

The paper is thick and creamy; official-looking. The letterhead says 'Beswick, Robinson, Carter, Meade, Solicitors and Commissioners of Oaths'.

The address is in Salisbury.

Neve quickly unfolds the letter, ignoring the lights that have started to flash insistently on the switchboard.

Dear Ms Carey

We have been instructed to act on behalf of trustees of the will of Miss Isabelle Shawcross, who died on 21st December 2016.

We would be very grateful if you could ring the office and arrange a time to come in at your convenience to discuss a matter that relates to these instructions.

We look forward to hearing from you.

Yours sincerely,

L. Meade (Solicitor)

At first, all she feels is relief. Seeing the police logo, and then the solicitor's header, she'd had a terrible feeling of having been found guilty of some crime she doesn't remember committing. She stole a traffic cone, drunkenly, a couple of years ago and for a strange moment had been sure they were finally coming for her.

The switchboard is lit up like the flight deck of a 747 now so she forces herself to pick up the phone and start routing calls where they need to go. She isn't concentrating and one caller comes back to switchboard, annoyed at being sent to the IT office, rather than the post room as they had requested.

All the while her mind buzzes with questions.

How did the solicitor's firm get her name? The police, presumably. That was easy enough to answer. But why on earth did this solicitor want to see her?

It couldn't be that she has been left something in her will, because they only met just before she died. Neve doesn't know much about it, but she knows wills have to be signed and witnessed well in advance of someone's death.

So what else can it be?

Realization dawns and she actually says, 'Oh,' out loud.

Of course. The family want to speak to her, as the last person to be with Isabelle. To thank her? Or to have a go at her? Why didn't she stop her from jumping and so on. As if she hasn't tortured herself with that thought enough.

Neve shudders and scrunches the letter up before throwing it neatly into her recycling bin.

She doesn't tell anyone about it over the next week. Miri never seems to be around and she knows exactly what Lou would say. She'd go on about 'the right thing to do' and guilt trip Neve like she always does. So she leaves it, not expecting to hear anything further.

But a week later, another letter arrives in the post.

Dear Ms Carey

Further to my letter of 15th January regarding the estate of the late Miss Isabelle Shawcross, we would be extremely grateful if you could call the office. We urgently need to discuss a matter that relates to these instructions.

We look forward to hearing from you.
Yours sincerely,
L. Meade (Solicitor)

This time the person who has signed the police slip has written, We would be grateful if you could attend to this. We cannot pass on personal information under The Freedom of Information Act 2000 but this is no longer a police matter and we have limited resources in terms of fielding enquiries. Thank you for your consideration.

Neve is in the hallway, having arrived home from work as she opens this one.

Sighing, she takes her phone into the study to make the call.

Two days later, she is on a train to Salisbury.

The solicitor wouldn't explain over the phone. But she insisted it was in Neve's interests to come to the office to discuss this in person. 'In your interests'. Those were the exact words. It's all very mysterious.

Neve drains the last of the coffee she bought at Waterloo and looks out of the window as the tightly packed buildings of south London change to Surrey commuter towns and then green fields.

She has a book, something Lou has foisted upon her, which looks a bit worthy, and a copy of *Grazia*, which she can't be bothered to read either. Squeezing her earbuds into her ears, she plays Tom Odell on her phone and tries to settle into the journey.

Neve would have liked to have done this the above-board way.

But there was simply no chance that she would have been allowed a day off so soon after the Christmas holidays. So at seven a.m. she had sent her direct boss, office manager Kate, a short text saying, So sorry. Food poisoning from a curry! Bleurgh! Been up all night. Better stay close to a toilet today!

Which, thinking about it, might have sounded a bit desperate. Daniel, who was a maestro at telling lies like this, always said she needed to keep it simple. But being naturally honest, she always felt the need to embellish.

The bad night's sleep part was true anyway. She'd been lying in bed worrying about money the night before. Neve managed not to think about money too much, as a rule. It was a necessary evil, and that was all. She had no real desire to be rich, but she wasn't someone prepared to rough it either. She and Daniel had spent a few nights in a squat when they were first together and she vividly remembered how miserable it had been, lying in a smelly room and feeling colder than she had ever been in her life.

But yesterday she'd had another automated text from the bank, reminding her she had reached her overdraft limit and now being charged £1 a day for further withdrawals. The ticket to Salisbury was paid for on her credit card, but that was coming close to being maxed out.

And the worst thing was, she couldn't tell Lou how broke she really was.

When their father had died, eighteen months ago, the sisters had inherited a small amount of money each – £15,000. It would have been more, but for him having been persuaded into taking out a bad mortgage arrangement on his property.

Lou had put her share into a university account for the children. Neve had had every intention of saving at least some of it, but she had two big credit card bills to pay off at the time.

And then she and Daniel had really needed a holiday. They'd gone off to Spain for the Benicàssim music festival and had a brilliant time. Well, what she could remember of it, anyway. Parts of it were still a bit of a blur.

But somehow, within five months, her bank statement was showing her the impossible information that she had just £500 left in her savings account. Neve feels so ashamed at how she has ripped through her inheritance that she has been clinging onto this £500, determined not to spend it unless it is something that her dad would have thought appropriate, which most definitely ruled out credit card bills. When she and Daniel were together, they somehow muddled through. Now it looks as though she is going to have to dip into this small pot of money after all.

Neve had gone from her A levels to a job as a live-in au pair in London, working for a rich American couple with a pre-teen daughter. She had only to ferry the girl, Tabitha, to various activities and clubs and do a minimal amount of housework. Everyone told her she'd lucked out and she knew it was true. Then she met Daniel and when the Schwarzes located back to Colorado, she moved in with him.

She's never really had to look after herself before, or live alone.

And she is on borrowed time with Lou and Steve.

When they were children, Lou used to harbour small resentments about the division of the parental affection. Neve was always the one having accidents or requiring medical attention when they were little: contracting a serious stomach virus that required hospitalization at two, falling out of a tree and breaking an arm at five, smashing a tooth after tripping over a paving slab at eight. Their parents used to joke that they would settle down for a family picnic somewhere and within moments Neve would have been stung by a bee, or fallen in the stream. Somehow this used to be seen as endearing when she was younger.

She wasn't confident this was how Lou saw it even then.

These thoughts are still swirling corrosively in her mind as the famous spire of Salisbury cathedral finally comes into view. It is a crisp blue day and as she steps out of the station and begins to follow the directions from Google maps on her phone, she starts to feel more positive.

Soon she finds herself in the big market square, packed with stalls selling fruit and vegetables, children's clothes or mobile phone accessories. A jumble of pointed roofed buildings line the top of the square. Neve checks the address once again on the letter. Heading across the square, she finds herself outside a modern-looking shopfront with tinted glass and a sign bearing the name 'Beswick, Robinson, Carter, Meade'. A man in overalls is currently washing the large windows and he moves to one side with a grin as she heads towards the door.

Pushing it open, she looks around a small reception area. A middle-aged receptionist with blonde coiffed hair and bright pink lipstick sits at a curved reception desk.

Neve says, 'Hi, I have an appointment with . . .' but the receptionist holds up a finger imperiously and lifts the receiver to her ear. She smiles brightly at Neve as she speaks to the caller.

'Beswick-Robinson-Carter-Meade-solicitors-how-may-I-direct-your-call-today?' she says all in one breath, still beaming at Neve, who shifts on the spot.

Finally, she has the woman's attention and a few moments later is directed to wait in one of the chairs for visitors.

The square leather chairs are very low to the ground and Neve settles her five-feet-nine-and-a-half frame into it awkwardly, knees to the side. The glass coffee table is covered with copies of *The Lady* and *Country Life*. She pretends to study her phone while she waits.

After a few moments she hears her name and looks up to see a woman about her own age smiling coolly down at her.

Her glossy red hair is twisted in a neat knot on top of her head and she wears a white silk top and a tight black skirt with high heels. Neve feels a stab of something uncomfortable. She always feels wrong-footed by uber-professional people like this. Really, she'd been hoping the solicitor was some middle-aged twinset and pearls type. She wouldn't feel any need for comparison then, she thinks, placing her hand over a mark on the knee of her trousers she's just spotted.

'Miss Carey?'

'Yes.' Neve gets up with difficulty from the low chair and shakes her proffered hand. She always finds this ritual odd when between women. The other hand is small and cold and perfectly dry. Her own feels sweaty and ham-like in comparison.

'I'm Laura Meade, would you like to—'

Before she can finish her sentence they are all distracted by the door to the street opening with almost violent force.

A tall bear of a man with curly dark hair bursts in and looks as if he has forgotten why he's here. Bright blue eyes peer out of a chubby, unshaven face. He's wearing some sort of brown corduroy jacket, baggy trousers of an indeterminate colour and wellies that are thickly rimed with claggy brown mud.

A black Labrador bounds in after him, heading for Neve and burying its face in her crotch.

'Oh!' she laughs and fusses with its ears in an attempt to distract it.

'Jarvis!' the man barks. The dog, ignoring him, leans its considerable weight against Neve's legs, almost pushing her over. She grins but when she glances up, sees that Laura Meade is bright red. She keeps looking between Neve and the man, and the receptionist, one after the other. Then she seems to gather herself.

'Richard,' she says coolly to the man. 'Didn't we cover everything earlier?'

'Don't suppose I left my bloody phone in here?' Richard's voice is rich and fruity, like an old Shakespearean actor's.

Laura looks at the receptionist, who is taking all this in with bright-eyed avidity. She shakes her head.

'I'm afraid not,' says Laura.

'*Bugger*. Better try the bank then,' he says with feeling. And then he's gone.

Neve sees a look pass between Laura and the woman on reception, whose eyebrows are almost at her hairline, and wonders what she isn't getting about this whole scenario.

'Apologies for that,' says Laura now, gesturing towards some double doors behind the reception desk. 'Do come through.'

Neve follows the solicitor into her office, and the door is shut.

10

'You've got to be fucking kidding me,' says Neve five minutes later. 'Sorry. I didn't mean to swear. Sorry.'

She picks up the glass of water she was offered on arrival into the office and puts it down again, sloshing a little onto her trousers as she does so.

Laura Meade regards her with an expression she can't quite read.

'I assure you, I'm not,' she says. 'Look, I appreciate this is a shock. It is why I wanted you to be here in person. I thought this had to be a face-to-face conversation, rather than being discussed by letter or over the phone.'

'But how?' Neve blurts out, her voice too loud. 'I mean, how can she have given me a fucking *cottage*? Sorry. But how? She didn't even know me.'

Laura nods patiently.

'It's a special type of bequest,' she says, 'that can be made separately from a will. It applies when someone dies intestate, like Isabelle did, and is known as *donatio mortis causa*.' She pauses. 'Basically, it's a deathbed gift.'

Their eyes meet and both look away at this uncomfortable term then Laura continues crisply. 'There are a few basic requirements for this to be legally binding,' she says, 'and they have all been met, however unusual the circumstances may be.'

'But why me?' says Neve after a moment.

Laura sighs. 'We can only guess that she wanted to make this bequest to the last person she saw before she took her life.'

Neve thought of the envelope, clutched in Isabelle's thin, white hand.

She never even saw it fall to the ground when she'd dropped it a couple of minutes later. The shock of the other woman climbing up and throwing herself into the cold, dark water had thrown it violently from her mind. 'What exactly was in the envelope?' she says.

Laura lifts a coffee cup to her lips and takes a sip before placing it carefully back on its coaster.

'It contained the deeds to the cottage, plus a written note. You may remember she also recorded a message into her phone, confirming your name, just before . . .' she clears her throat '. . . just before she did it.'

'God,' says Neve quietly. 'I don't know what to say.' After a moment, she adds, 'Did *you* know her?'

Laura seems to lose her professional veneer for a moment and makes an anguished face.

'We were at school together, years ago, but we weren't really good friends. She was . . .' she pauses. 'She ran with a bit of a different crowd. I hadn't heard from her in years. Then . . . well, then we received this.'

Neve chews her lip.

'I can't take it, anyway,' she says.

'Why not?' Laura slightly tips her head to the side.

'Because!' Neve lets out a humourless, stressed laugh. 'Because it's not right. And what do her family say? Don't they mind?'

Laura looks down at her skirt and brushes something off before looking up at Neve again. The shutters are back down now.

'She only has a brother,' she says. 'And . . .' she pauses. 'I have no idea whether he wanted it or not.'

Neve shakes her head in wonder.

'I just can't understand why someone would do this though, with a complete stranger. I mean, why not leave it to, I don't know, Barnardo's, or Battersea Dogs Home or something? Why a random person on a bridge?'

Laura sits back in her seat with a sigh.

'We can't possibly know what was going through her head now,' she says, wearily. 'But she clearly had a desire not to be alone when she killed herself. Maybe she just wanted to say thank you, retrospectively.'

'Well, it's the saddest bloody thing I've ever heard.' Neve's eyes fill with hot tears and she swipes them away, furiously. 'I wasn't even that nice to her,' she says. 'I was impatient to get home. All I did was say I'd stand her a night bus and ask where her coat was.'

'Well,' says Laura, her gaze fixed on Neve's face. 'All we can assume is that this is more kindness than she would have had otherwise. Maybe it was enough.'

There's a pause. Neve swallows and finds a tissue in her handbag, which she uses to blow her nose, more loudly than she intended.

Laura pushes an A4 padded envelope across the table towards her.

'This really is happening quite legally, Neve,' she says in a gentle voice. 'You own Petty Whin Cottage and everything in it. It's all yours now.'

11

Neve walks robotically back to the station afterwards, all thoughts of having a wander around Salisbury and finding somewhere cheap for lunch forgotten. She has a strong desire to get straight on a train and try and make sense of what has just happened.

She's lucky with trains and is able to run for the Waterloo-bound one that is just leaving.

Finding a table to herself, she begins to investigate the contents of the envelope. There's a bundle of papers, including the details of a lease. At the bottom of the envelope there is a small keyring in the shape of a dog, with a grubby suede covering that is worn away in patches, revealing carved wood underneath. It looks ancient, thinks Neve, spreading out the lease document and studying the address.

Petty Whin Cottage
Briarfield
Stubbington Lane
Cador
Near St Piron
Cornwall

Neve reaches for her phone and taps the Google app, before typing the name of the cottage into the search box. There are no entries for the property, but she learns that the odd name comes from a yellow flowering plant native to the area.

Cornwall.

She's never been there. She'd wanted to ask Laura Meade if the cottage was by the sea, but it didn't seem right. It might have sounded as though she actually wanted it. But the very word makes her picture blue skies, roses climbing up the front of a whitewashed cottage. Healthy sea air. Her heart rises a little, despite herself.

There isn't anything much online for Cador, except, worryingly, a headline from the *Cornish Times* about a drugs bust. Neve assumes it is too tiny for mention, but St Piron seems to be a small town that's a few miles from Truro.

Next she Googles the name 'Isabelle Shawcross' and after a couple of unhelpful entries about an American law professor she sees a news story from a site called *West Cornish Life*.

Christmas Suicide of Local Woman

A woman has died after apparently jumping into the Thames on 21st December. Isabelle Shawcross, who grew up in the St Piron area of the county, was 34 years old and left no husband or children. It is believed she had been living in Australia for some time before returning to the UK. The police say they are not treating the death as suspicious, but the coroner has yet to fix a date for the inquest. Her brother, local landowner Richard Shawcross, was unavailable for comment.

Searching further, she finds only a black American woman called Isabel Shawcross on Facebook and nothing else.

Bizarre. Isabelle seems to have been someone with almost no internet presence.

Neve finds herself tapping the words 'cottages for sale, Cornwall' into Google.

On the Rightmove site a list appears and she begins to scroll through it, quickly finding an astonishing difference in the range of house prices here, from a run-down two-bedroom cottage at £75,000 right up to places going for several million.

But right now, £75,000 sounds like a miraculous, almost magical amount of money. All of a sudden, Isabelle's last words appear in her head . . . 'And keep it, if you can bear to,' and the back of her neck prickles.

When the train pulls into Waterloo station, Neve drains the last of the warm gin and tonic, her second on the train, and begins to gather her things.

Over the course of the journey, she has made a series of plans:

1. Sell the cottage immediately. Pay off debts. Get own flat.
2. Say NO to cottage. How can I possibly accept???Find a way of contacting Isabelle's surviving relative. Hand over cottage.
3. Sell it. Sell. SELL.

Walking across the concourse at Waterloo towards the tube station, at first Neve ignores the man pointedly staring at her, taking him to be a creep. But when she hears her name she looks at him properly and feels her stomach plummet.

It's Fraser from work, gazing at her with a triumphant expression.

'Well,' he says, as commuters stream past them in both directions. 'Looks like you have made a full recovery.'

'Does, doesn't it?' says Neve. She has to stifle a yawn that rises from nowhere. She's suddenly very, very tired.

'I think we'd better have a word tomorrow, don't you? A little chat about responsibility?'

He's so pleased with himself that his face has turned the colour of ham. Neve sighs.

'Bugger off, Fraser,' she says, just as another man comes to stand right next to him, his expression one of injured puzzlement.

Without waiting to hear a reply, Neve turns away and hurries to the tube.

She can't face going home.

Everything is buzzing inside her now. The tiredness has turned into a wired energy. She needs to go out, to do *something*. To find a way to make sense of the mad day she has had.

On the Northern Line, she makes the snap decision to get off at Camden station. She'll go to the pub where she and Daniel used to hang out. There's bound to be someone there who wants to have some fun. There might be a live band. Maybe Daniel will even come along. She can pretend it's just like old times.

It turns out that most of her old crowd are there. By ten o'clock she's standing outside, smoking a joint with her back against the wall and laughing so hard she almost starts to pee.

She's with a drummer called Bick, a friend of a couple of years. No one knows where Bick comes from, exactly. He has a strange accent that is part American and part Scandinavian. He is six foot five and his shaved head gleams like polished ebony. Tribal scars nubble his cheekbones and rows of earrings stud his upper lobes. His sexuality is what he refers to as 'fluid'. He's the most beautiful man Neve knows.

She has told everyone about the cottage over the course of the evening.

Most agree that she must sell up straight away. A tiny, birdlike girl called Darcy, an ardent clubber, is of the opinion that Neve should go and live there. There was some talk of jam-making and a mass visit from them all at a date in the summer. Also possibly a music festival in the 'grounds'. Everyone, including Neve, is hazy on the specifics but it sounds like the best idea for a while.

Bick is talking now and Neve smiles soppily up at him.

'I think I love you, Bick,' she slurs and puts her hands on his chest, raising her mouth to kiss him. But Bick steps back, laughing.

'Neve, honey, I absolutely would, don't get me wrong. But you've had a very weird day and I think you need to go home.'

Deflated, Neve stands back and almost falls off the kerb.

'*I'vegotafuckingcottage,*' she says as one word.

'I know you have, darling. I know you have.'

A few minutes later he folds her into a taxi with assurances to the sceptical driver that she isn't going to be sick. Neve manages to pass on Lou and Steve's address. But when they reach the junction of Camden Road and Kentish Town Road, Neve leans over and gives new instructions, filled with a sudden second wind.

The driver eyes her warily, then changes direction.

A few minutes later, the car pulls up outside Daniel's flat. The flat that was once hers and Daniel's.

She pays the driver with the money Bick had insisted she

take and stands on the pavement, staring woozily up at the top floor. A fox appears from the alleyway next to the house and regards her brazenly before slinking away. There's a car alarm going off on the next road along.

Swaying slightly on her feet, she wishes fervently now that she hadn't thrown the keys back at him during a fight. All she wants is to creep in and go to bed. She wouldn't even bother him; she'd only sleep on the sofa. It seems so reasonable that she could do this. Who could possibly object to her sleeping on their sofa?

But there is no option other than to wake him up, now she's here.

She wobbles up the steps and peers at the row of buzzers. Funny how unfamiliar it looks in such a short time. Focusing hard on not missing the target, she presses her finger squarely onto the buzzer and keeps it there. Then she removes it and does it again.

'Hello?' Daniel's sleepy voice crackles from the intercom. She feels a happy rush that he is so near and she will see him within mere moments.

'S'me!' she says.

'Who?'

Neve pauses, frowning.

'S'Neve,' she says a bit less cheerfully.

There's a silence.

'What do you want?'

Neve sways and tries to concentrate on what's happening. This isn't working out as she had expected.

'To go to sleep,' she says honestly and pushes the door, confident that it will have been released.

Nothing happens so she buzzes again and, a few seconds later, it opens and reveals a stony-faced Daniel.

He's wearing an old T-shirt she has always loved, which says *Revolution is Just a T-Shirt Away* in white letters on black, faded to soft grey now, and pyjama bottoms. His hair is tousled and hangs over his eyes and he's grown a small beard since she saw him last. He's never looked more attractive and desire floods her entire body, hot and quick.

'Neve? What the fuck?' he says as she moves quickly and snakes her arms around his back. She breathes in the familiar smell of him and feels her groin squeeze in anticipation.

'I've missed you,' she says and starts to nibble and kiss his neck. 'Let's just forget about all of it. I have a cottage now.'

'What?' Daniel tries to step back. 'What the hell are you talking about? And get off me, Neve, you're completely wrecked.'

Neve slides her hands around his waist and over his firm buttocks, looking at him impishly through her lashes. She can feel the beginnings of a hard-on against her stomach as she pulls him closer and he makes a small sound in his throat. She's not sure whether it's a sound of being turned on, or a disgusted 'tut'.

'Not too wrecked,' she says in a low voice. 'We were always good together like this, weren't we? Remember, I know what you like.' She tries to peel his pyjama bottoms down and is suddenly thrust backwards so hard she almost falls down the steps.

'Stop it!' yells Daniel. 'Just fucking stop this!'

'Danny? What's happening?'

A sleepy high-pitched voice seeps from the staircase and Neve stares over his shoulder to see a girl she recognizes from the pub, standing behind Daniel. She's wearing one of his T-shirts and coils of blonde hair spill over her shoulders. Yawning like a cat, she then blinks hard at Neve.

'What's going on?' she says, awake now. 'What's going on, Danny?'

'Danny! No one calls him Danny! Who the fuck are you

to be standing there like that and calling him fucking Danny?'

And with that she bursts into violent sobs.

Danny regards her with a look that makes her actually clench her toes inside her shoes.

'Just go home, Neve,' he says. 'You're only embarrassing yourself. You need to accept things and move on, alright?'

12

Neve remembers several things as her alarm clock, which by some miracle she managed to set last night, goes off with the intensity of a road drill next to her.

1. She was given a cottage yesterday.
2. She went to Daniel's and humiliated herself.
3. When she got back to Lou's she threw up in the bathroom.
4. Then she cleaned it up.

She definitely cleaned it up. Didn't she?

Scrambling out of bed, she smashes her knee into the frame in her haste, and swears. She pulls on a hoodie with shaking hands and, thrusting open the study door, heads down the landing to the bathroom.

Lou is just emerging through the door. She is wearing rubber gloves and holds a bucket filled with cleaning products.

'Lou, I'm so sorry, I swear I meant to sort that out.'

Lou regards her younger sister. She doesn't look angry. She looks exhausted. Her nostrils are inflamed and red, her skin porridge-coloured.

'You didn't do a very good job,' she says in a flat monotone. 'Luckily I went in there first. Steve's having a lie-in.'

'Lou, I really am—'

Maisie begins to wail.

'Forget it,' says Lou and her voice is sharp now. 'Just forget it, Neve.' A surge of shamed affection for her sister washes over her and she goes to touch her arm but Lou pushes past and goes down the stairs.

It takes two paracetamols, a double strength ibuprofen and a triple espresso to give Neve the physical means to be able to walk into the office just before nine. The pounding in her head is more muted now, but her stomach occasionally shivers with nausea and her hands are shaky.

She vows to belatedly sign up to whatever the Dry January thing is on Facebook later. Dry half-of-January has to be better than not doing it at all.

The morning creaks by a second at a time and she tries to bury herself in admin jobs that have built up since the start of the week.

Mid-morning, Fraser and a couple of the other editors sweep into the office, and the sleepy energy instantly changes. This is partly because they are all wearing suits; even Fraser looks quite dapper in a dark blue pinstripe, despite the cut being a good fifteen years out of fashion.

Neve weakly turns on her smile of greeting, which slips when she sees the mean shine in Fraser's eyes and notices the man he is showing into reception. Small and bespectacled with close-cropped grey hair, it's his companion from Waterloo yesterday.

'Miss Carey,' says Fraser brightly. He has never called her this before. He somehow manages to make it less respectful than if he had used her Christian name. 'Can you please organize for some coffee in the conference room?'

'Yes, sure,' she says, even though she isn't supposed to leave reception. The party of five men sweep past her and she notices the stranger frown at her, in obvious recognition from the day before. Her heart gives an anxious jolt and she feels clammy sweat beading her hairline. She grabs the bottle of Diet Coke on her desk and takes a long swig.

One of the picture editors, a shy young woman called Edie who wears 1940s-style clothes, comes into reception then. She stares at the retreating backs of the men, chewing her red-lipsticked bottom lip; brow creased.

'Edie,' hisses Neve. 'What's going on?'

Edie comes over in her neat little dress covered in sprigs of cherries, thick tights and 1940s sandals. Her blonde hair is twisted into victory rolls at the side of her head. She fixes large pale eyes on Neve and makes a face of dismay.

'That's Holger Meier,' she says in a low voice. 'He's one of the directors from Brahmen Klein.'

'Shit . . .'

Brahmen Klein is a huge European media company. She's been too preoccupied to think much about the rumours in the office. Now all she can do is remember the shocked expression on the face of this man, who has power over her future, as she told Fraser to 'bugger off'.

'Oh God,' she says. Edie sighs.

'Yeah. I'd better get back to updating my CV,' she says. 'I suggest you do the same.'

Neve doesn't make the coffee.

Instead, she thinks about the moment Isabelle Shawcross whispered hot breath into her ear; breath that was on a countdown to being her last. She thinks about the fact that she is going to lose her job; if not today, then soon.

She thinks about last night, and Christmas, and the

reception she is going to get from Lou and Steve when she gets back.

She understands that Daniel is now part of her past and will never be in her future again.

The switchboard begins to light up in front of her and she watches it as though from behind a sheet of glass. Then she picks up her coat and handbag, and leaves the building for ever.

Lou is out with the girls at one of their classes when she gets home. She is struggling under the awkward weight of a bunch of flowers that cost more than £40, bought after transferring the last of her dad's money into her current account. They're a mix of gerbera in bright purples and yellows. She knows that Lou loves gerbera.

She carefully arranges them in a vase on the kitchen table, making sure she wipes up the spills of water she leaves in the process, then hunts for paper and a pen. All she can find is a drawing pad of Lottie's, covered in stick people and attempts at cats in crayon, and a felt tip pen. Finding a sheet that leaks colour through from the drawings on the other side, she rips it out and begins to write a note.

> Lou and Steve. I'm so grateful for everything you've done for me. I'm really sorry I've been such a nightmare. I do love you, whatever you might think. xxN

Then she takes the duvet cover, sheets and pillowcases she'd taken from the sofa bed that morning and tips them into the linen basket. Getting the vacuum cleaner out of the hall cupboard, she gives the room a thorough clean.

She can't take everything but she'll think about that later.

This is only for a few days, to get her head together. She manages to stuff a surprising amount into a small wheelie case and a rucksack, which she hoists onto her back, wobbling under the awkward weight.

A few minutes later, she leaves the flat, closing the door with a quiet click behind her.

13

Neve sleeps for most of the nine-hour journey to Penzance from Victoria, head resting on her bunched-up fake fur coat, her hoodie a makeshift blanket. It's not comfortable, but in her exhausted, hungover state, it's enough.

She barely notices the movement of the coach or the stops at pick-up points along the way. It is only the insistent *wah-wah* wail of a baby that finally tugs her back to consciousness and at first she's convinced it's Maisie crying. She opens her eyes and is about to call for Lou when she realizes she's looking at a grubby purple-grey patterned seat back. There is an elderly man next to her, who nods at her with a big smile.

He has cottony white hair over a pink scalp. A pair of bright blue eyes peer merrily out of his craggy face.

'Gosh, you've been out for the count,' he says and offers her a Polo mint from the packet held in his shaky hand. 'I half wondered if I should give you a nudge to make sure you were alive.'

Neve hasn't quite regained the power of speech and simply smiles weakly. Her mouth feels foul and lined with wool, so she takes the Polo with a nod of thanks.

'Where are we?' she says, and suddenly remembers her and Lou saying, 'Are-we-there-yet,' over and over again to annoy their parents when they were little and going on family holidays. The memory gives her a dull ache under her ribcage when she remembers how she had left her sister this morning.

'We're about five miles from Truro, I think,' says the man. 'Better give my daughter a call and let her know we're almost there!'

Neve smiles vaguely and then fumbles in her bag for her phone; it is on five per cent battery. The phone has taken to hiding calls and messages from the home screen and she is grateful for this now. Pushing the uncomfortable thought that Lou and others might be trying to contact her, she looks out of the window.

They're on a motorway. She has no idea which one. Neve doesn't drive – something both Daniel and Lou have nagged her about at different times – and she has only the dimmest notion of major roads.

Looking at her watch she sees it is now half past eight, but it feels much later. The darkness outside increases her feeling of being far away from anything.

The old man is still looking at her and she shoots him a nervous glance. He immediately smiles again and Neve hopes she won't be forced into uncomfortable conversation for the rest of the journey.

Instead she roots inside her handbag for her earbuds. Her phone is almost dead, but he doesn't know this. Jamming them into her ears she sees the old man is jabbing a large finger at his mobile phone. It is the sort that looks like a toy, with large buttons designed for the elderly.

He begins to speak in a loud voice. Her own dad never seemed to understand that phones had sensitive microphones either.

'Hello, flower,' he says. 'It's Dad. I'm just calling to let you know that we won't be all that long into Truro now.' There's a pause and he says, 'Uh-huh, right,' then abruptly, 'Well goodbye then. See you soon.'

Neve turns herself around to face the window, jamming her earbuds further into her ears. Her hands tremble. Something is starting to fracture inside.

Dad used to call *her* Flower. The old man's conversation has had the effect of an uppercut punch to her diaphragm. She gasps a breath and her eyes prickle. The man makes a gentle 'tsk' sound and thrusts a man-sized tissue at her. She takes it gratefully and blows her nose.

'Are you alright, dear? Is there something I can do?'

'I'm fine. Thank you.' Her voice is a tiny, lame thing. Neve manages a weak, watery smile.

'I don't want to be nosy,' he says. 'But are you visiting friends or family in Truro?' He looks genuinely concerned. 'Is someone going to meet you off the bus?'

Neve wants to tell him the truth. But it's too bizarre.

'Yes,' she says. 'I'm all sorted. And really, I'm fine now. Thank you again for being so kind.'

He gives her a small nod.

Turning back to gaze out of the window she sees they have turned onto a dual carriageway. Before long signs are announcing they are in Truro.

These sudden swerves of grief take her by surprise, eighteen months after her dad died.

At first the loss had been a constant, gnawing ache. Her heart, which hadn't yet recovered from losing her mum, felt like a lump of beef that had been whacked all over with a meat tenderizer.

But as time moved on, the nature of the grief changed. In some ways it was almost crueller in the way it took her. She'd find she hadn't thought about it for a day or so and then it would suddenly bloom painfully in her chest, as violent as a physical assault. And the same thoughts would slam into her: an orphan.

Really? It was such a desolate little word.

She and Lou had lost their mother to cancer a year before their father died. Their dad, who had met his wife when they were both eighteen, had seemed to shrink as the space in the small semi in a Yorkshire village had swelled. Their mother had been a loud presence, prone to outbursts of emotion and jollity, while Dad was a quiet, reserved man.

They were older parents, only having Lou at forty, then Neve at forty-two. Neve had been a bit embarrassed about their age, especially as one of the girls in her class had a mother who was only seventeen years older than her.

They'd been foster carers for a time before Lou came along and would receive the odd Christmas card from people who had briefly lived with them. Neve used to feel a bit jealous of these mysterious troubled children with dramatic lives. As though they remained in the home as shadows, still jostling for her parents' attention.

Neve occasionally fretted that they would start fostering again as she got older, picturing brooding teenage girls with violent tendencies moving in and taking over her bedroom. But her parents said they'd 'done their bit' and that this part of their lives was now behind them.

The brain aneurism that killed her father hadn't given any warning and the doctor told her and Lou that he had most likely been carrying it around for a long time, like a tiny ticking bomb.

Neve had been away with Daniel, visiting musician friends in Brighton. It was one of their lost weekends, passing by in a blur of drinking, dancing and weed and it wasn't until late on Sunday afternoon that Neve had realized she had lost her phone. It was only when she and Daniel wearily arrived back in the flat that she noticed the flashing lights on the barely used landline recorder and discovered the messages from Lou saying she had to get to the Whittington Hospital immediately.

He died half an hour later after she erupted onto the hospital ward. Everyone said that he had waited for her.

Lou had never voiced what she thought about being the one holding vigil at the bedside for two long days. But the look on her face when Neve finally roused the courage to meet her eye had felt like being sandblasted. They have still never spoken of that final day.

Neve is keenly aware now of how little she visited her father in the period after Mum died. She kept meaning to go and spend more weekends with just the two of them.

They had a particular routine. He would cook her proper Welsh rarebit and they would eat it on trays, each with a Guinness, watching reality television he had recorded on his Freeview box. Her dignified dad had a weakness for anything like that, and despite reading hefty non-fiction about history and politics, he could converse with the best of them about what was happening on *The Voice* or even *America's Next Top Model*.

When she thinks about the fact that she will never, ever get to do this with him again she experiences a vertiginous swoop in her stomach, as though someone has just pressed a button and taken the floor out from under her feet. It's a sensation of falling through space. She is no longer tethered to anyone other than Lou, who has her own family now.

Neve sighs and roots in her handbag for her make-up bag. It's the hangover and the uncertainty of what she is doing that is making her feel like this; she just needs to get a grip.

Stretching out the stiffness from her neck, she waits in

the aisle to get off the coach. People groan and gather bags from above their heads, gazing blearily out of the window.

Neve thanks her seating companion, who lets her go first and begins to move towards the doors. There's a pinch of worry in her stomach about arriving somewhere in darkness. She hasn't really thought this through. The words 'as usual' rise up in her mind as though someone has whispered them in her ear.

Standing at the side of a road with a car park on one side and residential houses on the other, she watches people purposefully walk to cars or stamp their feet in the cold and look around for lifts. The old man gives her a final wave and she watches as he laboriously climbs into a small white car. A woman with glasses and a dark ponytail is in the driver seat and he leans over for a kiss, talking all the while. Neve has a sudden urge to call him back and tell him everything; about Isabelle Shawcross and the cottage, about work, about Lou. About her mum and dad . . .

But it's too late now. She begins to shiver as the shocking temperature – always so much colder outside of London, she thinks, despite her Northern heritage – begins to bite, making her eyes sting and her nose stream.

She takes an experimental sniff and realizes with disappointment that she can't smell the sea. It can't be that far away, can it? Neve thinks again that she knows nothing about Cornwall and experiences a queasy lurch of anxiety about this whole plan.

Pulling her coat around her and yanking on a lilac beanie with flowers on the side that she had found in Camden market, she goes to a central area and attempts to work out which bus she should get to this Cador place.

It's no good though, she can't see any bus that will

help. When she'd looked this up hurriedly on her phone in London, it had seemed relatively straightforward. But now . . .

A bus driver is about to close his doors when she reaches out her hand and quickly steps on board.

'Mind yourself,' says the driver, a bald man in his forties with a tattoo curling up his neck to his fleshy, pink ear.

'Sorry,' she says with an apologetic smile, 'but can you tell me where I'd get a bus to a place called Cador? It's near St Piron?'

The driver sighs and then picks up an iPad. He swipes at it and then looks up.

'No buses from here go there. Best bet is to get to St Piron on the 198 and then you'll have to walk.'

'Oh,' says Neve, doubtfully. 'Er, thank you.'

It is only twenty past ten but feels like the middle of the night. Neve's back and bottom ache after nine hours on a coach, then another hour being rattled on a hard seat. The bus seems to hare with dangerous speed through small villages lit by a few streetlights, but most of the journey is spent tearing around dark, twisty country roads.

When she is finally disgorged at the side of a road and told by the disinterested driver that to get to Cador she needs to walk 'a couple of miles . . . maybe a bit more', it starts to become apparent that this is definitely one of her more ill-thought-through plans.

Knowing her battery won't hold out for much longer, she uses her phone as a torch only in short bursts. Luckily, there seems to be a main road lit by street lamps that leads in the direction she has been told to follow. Her headache has returned and she is desperate for something to eat and drink. All she has left is a mouthful of water in a bottle and a couple of pieces of gum. Her wheelie case squeaks in complaint as she drags it along behind her, shoulder beginning to cramp.

A couple of men pass her at different times. The second of the two, a weasely guy with an ugly moustache, stares at her just long enough for fear to surge up her throat. She hastens her step.

Eventually she comes to a row of shops, all closed. Then she spies something that feels like a beacon above the doorway of a fish and chip shop; a glowing sign that says simply, 'Taxi'.

Neve hesitates, gnawing on her bottom lip as she thinks this through. She has no job. No prospects. She's only intending to come for a few days but her remaining £400 is going to have to last. She'd had vague images of cooking giant batches of chickpea stew and holing up in the cottage with a pile of books until she worked out what to do with her life, back in London. The £400 seemed like a fortune, put like that.

But now she wants a taxi so badly she is incapable of doing anything but walking across the road towards the light. She tells herself she must do this for her own safety.

A few minutes later she is climbing into a saloon car. The thin-faced, middle-aged driver puffs vigorously on a Vape and regards her in the mirror.

'Where you wanting, then?' he says.

'Can you tell me how much will it cost to get to Cador?' The driver regards her.

'That'll be thirty.' His voice has a slow, West Country drawl.

This seems like an outrageous sum and Neve feels a flash of anger that she is being ripped off. She is of the view that everywhere outside London is cheap. The cost of this will clean out her purse. But she doesn't really have any choice.

'Okay,' she says grudgingly, mentally thinking she wouldn't have given the miserable git a tip anyway.

She tells him the rest of the address. The driver punches it into the satnav then pulls away.

Before long Neve realizes that Cador is considerably further than the two miles the bus driver specified. For once it feels that, in taking this taxi, she is doing the sensible thing.

The driver doesn't say a single word as they drive. While she would ordinarily welcome this, part of her feels the need for some reassuring conversation.

There is pure darkness on either side. Neve tries to suppress the queasy sensation that they could be going anywhere. This is like pitching into nothingness. Their journey is mirrored in miniature as a blue line on black on the satnav mounted on the dashboard.

'How far away are we?' she asks. Her voice sounds loud in the humming peace of the car interior.

The driver shoots a look at her in the mirror.

'Almost there. You here on holiday?' he says, and grins to himself, as if this concept is funny.

Neve frowns. What's he getting at? Is it really such a strange idea to holiday here?

'Sort of,' she says cautiously. 'But just for the weekend.'

Belatedly, she thinks of all the stories she has read about rapist taxi drivers. She would never get into any old mini cab in London. What was she thinking? Why should different rules apply here?

She pictures the scene through a camera, complete with eerie soundtrack. He's going to pull up to a dark house that's obviously unoccupied and watch her fumble her way inside.

Alone. With no one around for miles to hear her scream.

The car heater seems to be pumping out a nauseating fog of heat and sweat prickles in her armpits.

Shit . . .

They turn off the main road. The surrounding darkness seems to be solidifying into a tunnel now, swallowing them as they move forwards.

'Right oh,' says the driver after a moment. 'I can see Stubbington Lane up ahead but it looks a bit narrow. More of a track.'

Neve peers at the window but can only see her own pale face reflected back at her.

'Is this Cador then?' she says doubtfully. 'Isn't it a village?'

The driver taps the satnav. 'Nah, just a collection of houses,' he says.

'Oh,' says Neve. She was prepared for this being rural, but had pictured the cottage being in a small village at the least. She'd foreseen a village pub, a shop with a blue bike parked outside, and an attractive display of local produce in the window.

The car turns and slowly begins to make its way down a narrow track, pitted with potholes. The driver grumbles quietly about his suspension as the car jolts and bumps its way forwards. Neve holds onto the seat with clenched, sweaty hands. The car comes to a stop.

'Well, this is as far as I can take you,' says the driver. His tone is softer now. 'You going to be alright?'

Neve swallows what feels like a solid bolus of fear in her throat.

'I'll be fine,' she says, trying to quell the shaking of her voice.

'You sure?' he says. 'Your friends definitely going to be in?'

The taxi driver being a rapist suddenly seems like a small concern. She has to bite her lip to stop herself from asking him to come with her to the door, and possibly to stay over.

Neve reaches into her bag for her phone and switches

on the torch app, praying she will get at least a few minutes before the battery dies completely.

'It's alright,' she says, straightening her back. 'What do I owe you?' Then, hurriedly, 'Think we agreed thirty pounds?'

After she has paid and left the car it reverses into a small lay-by, and turns awkwardly. She watches the white head-lights illuminate the bushes, then the two red tail-lights seem to blink off as the car exits the lane, leaving her alone.

14

Taking a deep, wobbly breath, Neve holds up the phone and attempts to splash the narrow beam around, to get her bearings. Tall trees line one side of the track, thin and silvery trunked. She can't see how far back they stretch, but there are no other houses to be seen.

Luckily, the icy beam reveals enough of the muddy, potholed way ahead for her to be able to walk forwards in small, nervous steps. She pictures herself twisting an ankle, or worse, and having to lie in the mud until someone – *who?* – comes to help.

The night seems to be filled with scritches and scratches and scurryings. A bright moon peeps out from behind lacy skeins of cloud and reveals a gap in the bushes, filled by a rickety wooden gate. The beam of light picks out the words *Petty Whin Cottage.*

This is it, she thinks, before tentatively opening the gate and walking through.

She realizes now she had been carrying a vague mental picture of the cottage: white stucco paint, maybe a plant growing up the front. Possibly a thatched roof.

It's too dark to see the cottage properly but first impressions are of a squat, low property that feels distinctly unwelcoming. Its overall shape reminds her of the ugly old cricket pavilion they used to smoke in after school.

Louder rustling in the bushes nearby now makes her heart thud harder. Neve tries to breathe slowly, forcing herself not to run towards the cottage, knowing this will set off full-blown panic. Her foot goes into a pothole and she feels her ankle give, painfully, just as she had pictured.

'Shit, shit, shit,' she breathes, hobbling the last steps to the front door. She has been carrying the large set of keys in her other hand as a weapon since she left the relative safety of the car. Something about this had been reassuring but now she is picturing complicated locks that must be opened in some magical sequence she doesn't know.

Neve points the iPhone's beam – thankfully still holding out – at the doorway and attempts to find the key that is most likely to fit the main lock.

There appear to be three locks: a deadbolt style at the top and bottom of the door and a Chubb. Why so many? It seems excessive.

The Chubb is straightforward, but she uses the others in the wrong order and the door doesn't yield. Her fingers are trembling with fear and cold and the bunch of keys slips from them and lands by her feet. Neve cannot help the squawk of misery that bursts from her, part-wail, part-curse. She bends over to grab at them, expecting at any moment to feel a meaty hand circling her neck, or the cold blade of a knife against her throat. Her shoulders are tortoised up to her neck – as if *this* would protect her – and she is lightly panting now.

She has forgotten the order she tried the keys before and anyway, they look identical.

'*Shit, shit,*' she says through gritted teeth as another attempt fails.

She tries again and this time – hallelujah! – feels the beautiful click of the mechanism releasing. Two more to go. She quickly unlocks the bottom one.

There is another loud rustle in the bushes now, like something large is forcing its way through towards her. Neve cries out, stabbing the last key into the lock.

The door opens and she almost falls through the front door into the chill, dusty air inside.

The iPhone's light blinks out.

It is an even deeper darkness here, inside. So absolute it almost has a texture.

Breathing heavily, Neve dabs trembling fingers along the wall until she finds the nub of a light switch.

A sickly glow emanates from an old-fashioned glass shade above her head.

She is in a narrow hallway, standing on a worn runner of carpet in faded pinks and greens.

A wooden coat stand just to the right of the doorway has a single jacket on it – a Barbour – and a pair of wellies stand neatly underneath, every bit as if someone has pulled socked feet from them mere moments before.

She's aware now that a strange smell is coating the inside of her nostrils. She can almost taste it.

Neve's heart thuds against her ribs as she timidly opens the nearest door and peeks inside. The smell of old potpourri with a hint of damp wafts out. Fumbling with the light switch on the inside of the door, she finds it doesn't work and gently closes the door again. She has the sensation of trying not to wake someone, or something, up. Maybe the house itself, whose atmosphere feels like a held breath.

This thought gives her stomach such a fearful twist that she strides to the end of the corridor, forcing herself to thrust the door open confidently. Her feet crunch on something gritty on the carpet.

Moonlight pools on a lino-covered floor. She slaps at the light switch and two long strip lights stutter and buzz into life.

Neve looks around and lets out a small moan of dismay.

She doesn't really know what she had been expecting. Maybe a large, friendly room with worn flagstones and dried herbs hanging neatly above an Aga. Not that she would have had the faintest idea what to do with an Aga. But she'd hoped for something warm and homey.

It certainly wasn't this. Clumps of mud and dirt cover the floor and the bin is overflowing with rubbish that smells so bad she has to cover her face with her hand. There's a draught coming from somewhere.

The 1970s lino flooring and mud-brown cupboards are bad enough. But she never expected it to be so *filthy*.

There are white bits of some material she can't identify scattered around the sink area. Approaching cautiously, she sees what they are.

Feathers. White ones, and some grey and black too. Grimacing, Neve dips a quick look into the sink and then rears back with a squawk, crashing against the big kitchen table behind her. She has to steel herself to edge forwards slowly to take another look.

'Oh God.' She covers her mouth as a wave of nausea brings sweat prickling to her temples.

It's a magpie.

Dead.

Neck bent, sightless eyes like small dull holes. The feathers still have an oily sheen, black with a blueish tinge, and the white chest has a rust-coloured bib of blood. One wing is twisted and the bird's claws curl inward, grotesquely. Neve's nose twitches in protest at the odour of old fish and sweetish rot.

Her mother had been terrified of birds. She can still recall the prickly horror of Mum's pallor and tight too-bright voice when a sparrow had been trapped in their bathroom. Now, illogically, Neve's as afraid of this dead thing as if it were capable of attacking her.

Swallowing another surge of nausea, she reaches for a tea towel that's hanging by the sink and, whimpering, begins to wrap it around the bird's body, trying not to touch it. This strategy proves to be useless. When she tries to lift the package, the bird falls with a dull plop back into the sink. Breathing heavily through her mouth she tries again. This time she is forced to touch the cool damp feathers as she bundles the bird up into the cloth and she shudders all the way to her toes.

There's no obvious key for the back door so she awkwardly opens the broken window, which is small and deeply recessed into the wall. Neve slings the whole package outside. She'll deal with it in the morning when she has more resources.

Then she stands for a moment, breathing heavily, in the silent kitchen.

What a welcome.

Daniel would have called that dead magpie 'serious bad voodoo'.

She imagines Lou saying, in her usual weary tone, 'Best get rid of it, then.'

Neve begins to look in the cupboards and finds bin bags and a dustpan and brush under the sink. She clears up the broken glass. Then, she finds bleach spray in the cupboard, and squirts the whole area around and in the sink until her nose begins to sting, drying it using kitchen towel from a roll attached to the wall.

There's a broom resting to the side of the sink and Neve uses it to get the worst of the dirt swept from the lino. Emptying the filthy contents of the bin, which seem to contain lots of takeaway cartons, cans of beer and a stinking, fetid nappy, she ties the bag inside three more until she can no longer smell it. She can deal with it in the morning, when she finds the back door key.

When she has finished she allows herself to finally take stock of the room.

There is a pine table, on which sits a small pile of junk mail and newspapers, and a decent cooker that must have been about forty years younger than the rest of the kitchen.

Neve starts to shiver and, opening up her rucksack, begins pulling out clothes. It's so cold in here that the only possible course of action is to layer as many items on top of each other as she can. The over-imaginative voice at the back of her brain says this will also make it harder to stab her, when the knife-wielding maniac currently lurking upstairs decides to make his move. Then she remembers there *is* no upstairs and can't decide if this is reassuring or even scarier.

Fewer nooks and crannies for an axe-wielding rapist to hide in.

But an even smaller space in which to be trapped with him.

'*Stop it*,' she says out loud, even though the sound of her voice ringing out in the silent house frightens her even more.

Neve roughly swipes her eyes and her fear begins to shift into something else.

She is sick of herself, sick of still being scared of the dark at thirty years old. What would Lou do if she was here right now? Neve pictures warmth and light and the reassuring sound of a kettle boiling for a hot, comforting drink. Lou wouldn't be afraid.

That's when she notices a plastic A4 file has slipped onto the floor under the table. Reaching for it she sees the words

'PETTY WHIN COTTAGE. ESSENTIAL INFORMATION'
printed on the first page.

How strange to imagine Isabelle Shawcross writing this. Had she written it in anticipation of her own death? If so, Neve thinks, why leave the place in such a horrible state?

A hard shiver, of cold this time, ripples down her arms and back. Neve flicks through the pages, quickly looking for information about heating.

It is all there, under 'ESSENTIALS'.

The heating system is a bit ancient, she reads, *but it works perfectly well once you get the hang of it. Look in the cupboard in the hallway and you will see a boiler. There is a torch on the shelf to your left. You need to light the pilot light first by holding down the red button for at least 25 seconds. You might have to do this a couple of times!*

Reading these words from beyond the grave, written in such a clear and friendly voice, feels almost indecent now and Neve once again registers the odd contrast between this helpfulness and the disgusting state of the place.

With a sense of purpose, she goes to the stair cupboard. It's much larger than she first realized and recessed back into the wall. There seems to be a pile of blankets in there, presumably spare bedding. There is no cupboard light, but there is a small Maglite torch, which, thankfully, works. She painstakingly follows the instructions to light the boiler, which looks like a relic from a different era.

It takes her three attempts before a tiny blue light starts to lick at the small glass window on the front.

Triumphantly, Neve places the torch back on the shelf and closes the door to the cupboard. Rattling, clanking radiators begin to come to life around the property and a smell of hot dust begins to fill the air.

This small achievement attained, she takes a deep breath and begins to investigate the rooms.

The floor is filthy and gritty but Neve decides she will find a Hoover and do a thorough cleaning job first thing in the morning. She'll just have to keep her shoes on tonight. There is no prospect that she would be removing any clothes anyway.

A bedroom, a bathroom and small study lead off the narrow hallway. The bedroom appears quite neat and tidy, to her relief, but when she opens the bathroom door, she grimaces at the sight of the toilet. 'Oh *yuck*,' she says out loud, reaching over and flushing away the dark mass that had been lurking there. There's a worrying clunking sound as she flushes. She washes her hands.

Neve now looks properly around the bathroom. It's quite big, with an avocado-coloured bath and toilet. But there's a surprisingly modern addition in the form of a cubicle with a decent-looking shower. Neve can't imagine the cottage ever being warm enough for this, but takes it to be an encouraging sign for the morning.

Inside the bedroom she realizes two things simultaneously: it's a perfectly nice room, and yet there is no way she is going to be able to sleep in here tonight.

The thought of climbing into that bed, which might still retain the shape of Isabelle's body – might hold the smell of her – is too downright creepy. Again, she wishes fervently that she was a practical sort of woman who didn't knock on wood for luck, or sometimes avoid cracks in the pavement.

No, the only thing for it, she thinks, is to grab some blankets and try to sleep somewhere else.

The small study is filled with a desk, some bookcases and a large metal filing cabinet. She had at least hoped for a futon.

Feeling a little calmer now, Neve goes back to the kitchen and resolves to investigate whether there is anything to eat or drink.

The fridge, which she notices is also relatively new, is empty and pristine, smelling of lemony detergent. This seems strange, considering the mess elsewhere. But at least there are no mouldering yoghurts or liquefied vegetables of the sort frequently found in her student fridge.

What was going through Isabelle Shawcross's mind, the last time she looked around this kitchen? Neve wonders. Did she know she was never coming back?

A thought strikes her then and she goes to the table, reaching for the newspaper on top of the pile. It's a local paper, *The Truro Advertiser*, and the date reads 13th December 2016.

That was the week before she killed herself.

A woozy feeling passes over her.

Food. She needs something to eat, having only had a sandwich and a chocolate bar since she left London. Her hangover is gone but a bone-deep weariness drags at her limbs as she begins to investigate the contents of cupboards.

There isn't much here; just a small tin of tomatoes, and handful of dried pasta, the bag folded over and resealed. Some peanut butter. On the counter top there is a container of decent coffee to Neve's surprise, and while she doesn't normally drink it black, she makes herself a cup and loads it with sugar from a small, chipped bowl.

A short while later she sits at the table and starts on her small meal of pasta with tinned tomatoes. It's bland and unpleasant but she is hungry so she eats every mouthful and then has a few spoonfuls of peanut butter straight out of the jar.

Once she has finished eating she goes to plug in her phone, leaving it on the counter and knowing it will take some time to show signs of life again. Her battered old iPad, with its cracked screen, is also dead but she only has one charger. The phone is the priority right now.

Investigating the living room, she discovers that there is no television and her stomach gives a little flop of disquiet. Surely everyone has a telly? Sighing, she studies the bookshelves and finds a copy of *Jane Eyre* which she has read several times before.

There are a few photos on the mantelpiece and Neve studies them now.

One shows a small blonde girl, smiling toothily with her arm slung around the neck of a large, golden Labrador, who seems to be grinning up at something to the left. It's hard to tell whether this is Isabelle. Neve wishes she had concentrated more on that oh-so-brief exchange on the bridge. It doesn't seem right that she is in the other woman's house when she can barely even remember what she looked like.

Another picture is in black and white. A couple in full evening dress smile into the camera. The woman is tall and blonde and the man dark; slightly shorter than her. The woman has a merry look about her, but he appears more severe.

Neve feels sure these are Isabelle's parents. She wonders when they died. And then she looks more closely at the picture and her heart seems to tumble over in her chest.

The woman is wearing a dress that looks very like the one Isabelle wore when she jumped to her death. Could it be the same dress? It's a little more fitting on this woman, who has a more voluptuous figure, but the colour is the same, perhaps a little brighter. Age will have faded it somewhat, she is certain. But there's something about the way it flows around the woman's hips and thighs that feels so familiar. Neve takes a step back and blows air out through her cheeks.

She imagines this woman – Isabelle's mum – getting dressed all those years ago; dabbing perfume on her wrists, maybe asking her husband to help put on the pearl necklace that lies on her collarbone. Perhaps excited about the glamorous evening ahead of her.

And then she pictures Isabelle Shawcross painstakingly sewing lead lining into the hem. Then, on that freezing night, gazing down at the viciously cold water rolling beneath the bridge before taking her own life. Maybe wearing the dress gave her comfort in some way. As though her mother were there with her, embracing her as she fell, as she would have once rocked her small body in her arms.

Neve closes her eyes for a moment and finds she has made a small sound of distress. This feels like the saddest thing in the world. She suddenly thinks of her own mum's clothing; shapeless jumpers and Marks and Spencer slacks that smelled of Comfort fabric conditioner and whatever it was that made her mother indescribably herself. She sways with the pain for a few moments until she has ridden it out. Here, at last, is something she has in common with her benefactor.

Then she forces herself to look at the next picture. It is of a woman in her sixties, with short grey hair and glasses. She is sitting on a bench with her hands in her lap and a wall covered in roses behind her. She has a basket of flowers and some gardening gloves next to her on the bench.

Neve turns her full attention to the final photograph now.

It shows a tiny girl with cherubic blonde curls, who is sitting on a flagstone floor, surrounded by Lego. She has a neat little pinafore on, with a daisy on the chest and a look of concentration on her face as she attempts to click two pieces together.

Neve smiles at the picture and suddenly remembers sitting like this as a toddler herself. They had similar tiles when she and Lou were little, in their first house. Her earliest memory is of running her tricycle into the kitchen table and cutting her head. She remembers sitting on those tiles and howling with outrage and pain at the blood.

Lou, no doubt, was off doing something benign and helpful, she thinks.

Moving away from the mantelpiece, she finds a radio, a modern DAB one that is already tuned to Radio 6. It has been left on; the button turned almost but not quite to the off position.

Neve turns it on and tries to settle in the chair as an old Pulp song begins to play.

Despite the coffee and the adrenaline still fizzing around her body, she begins to feel sleepy, and, gathering the blankets she'd found earlier around her, attempts to snuggle down and read on the sofa. There are two lamps that throw soft light across the room and it is almost cosy.

It's really quite comfortable and she is almost getting warm. She opens the copy of *Jane Eyre* and begins to read.

She is aware of a heaviness dragging at her eyes after a couple of chapters and resolves to close them for just a minute or two.

After all, everything is far too weird for her to sleep.

She comes to with a violent start, certain something is on her face. With a squeal she dashes it away, realizing it is her own hair.

But then her brain registers something else that's wrong.

She is in total, thick darkness.

Shock pings her upright on the sofa.

With a drench of pure, cold terror, Neve realizes there is someone else in the room.

15

There is another noise then, a quick, soft thump. Neve's on her feet and reaching for the nearest object, which happens to be the empty coffee mug. An involuntary sob rips from her throat.

'Who's there?' she forces out. 'What do you want?'

Something warm and bony brushes past her leg. Shrieking, she stumbles towards the door, painfully slamming her knee against the coffee table on the way. Her body braces with the expectation of being yanked backwards by the arm, or hair, as she crashes into the hallway.

She stops, still braced, but her head is full of the whoosh of her own blood, furiously pumping around her body.

Then she hears it. A deep throbbing. It's something motorized and living all at the same time.

It takes a moment for understanding to seep in and then she starts to laugh.

'What the *hell*?' she says. 'How did you get in, you stupid bloody cat?'

Reaching down, she lifts up the heavy, warm animal and holds it to her chest.

'Were you here all along? Eh?' she says and rubs her

face on its soft head. The relief is only temporary though because the darkness crowds in all around her. The sound of her breathing and the cat's purring is loud in the hallway.

Neve holds the cat like a living shield to her chest, and forces herself to walk to the hall cupboard. Inside it, her fingers close gratefully around the rubbery handle of the torch and she switches it on, eyes greedy for light.

The cat struggles and jumps from her arms, landing squarely and silently, before scurrying back towards the sitting room.

She tries to breathe slowly and think encouraging thoughts as she heads into the kitchen to find the folder.

There is a perfectly reasonable explanation for the lights going off.

This is the countryside. Things are different here. More . . . unreliable.

If only she had done the sensible thing and read the folder from cover to cover on arrival, instead of glazing over at all the practical information, this wouldn't have happened.

No one has cut the lights.

No one is waiting in the house to slash her with a knife, rape, or strangle her.

All shall be well, and all shall be well and all manner of thing shall be well, she repeats an old saying of her father's inside her head as she walks on trembling legs down the terrifying hallway and into the kitchen.

Flicking through the folder she quickly finds what she needs to know.

The electricity is on a Pay as you Go scheme. There's a key on the shelf under the stairs and you can get it charged at most Post Offices. There is currently enough on there to last a week or so.

Neve thinks about the radio, which Isabelle must have left on. That was probably draining the meter.

Wearily, she looks under the kitchen sink and is relieved to find a number of small tea lights and a box of Cook's matches. Glancing at her phone on the side she presses the home button and sees it managed to reach thirty-seven per cent battery life before the electricity died.

She carries her small mercies – candles, matches, phone – back into the sitting room, then lights the five tea lights and places them on the mantelpiece.

The room is all shadows and flickering flame but Neve is surprised to realize she is no longer spooked. The grim arrival, then being plunged into darkness and the surprise feline visitor, have exhausted her adrenaline stocks for the night. She's too tired to be afraid now. She pulls the blanket around herself.

The cat comes purring into the room again and jumps up onto her lap, where it proceeds to knead her leg with curved needle claws. Neve rubs its head, grateful for the companionship. She's always been a dog person but this animal is a comfort.

Her phone must have found a signal in this spot because she now sees there are several missed calls from Lou, plus a series of texts saying things like **Where R U?** and **Pls call me**. Resolving to ring first thing in the morning, she pulls the blanket, which smells faintly of washing powder, around her body and waits for daylight to come.

She doesn't know how long she has slept for, but when she wakes, pearly grey light is seeping through the curtains. Her neck is stiff and her mouth feels foul. Her knee throbs and at first she can't think why, then she remembers the drama in the middle of the night. Looking around she sees the cat has gone. It almost feels like a dream now, like there never was a real, breathing cat purring like a furry engine in her arms at all.

Blinking gritty eyes, she looks around the room, seeing it in daylight for the first time.

The surfaces have a few old-fashioned trinkets on them; brasses and a couple of small, ceramic dogs. It feels like a room belonging to a very old person.

Depressing.

But then she notices something odd.

Frowning, she gets creakily to her feet and walks over to the window that must face out onto the front of the cottage. It is small and bubbly with age and there are sprigged white curtains at the sides.

But this isn't like any cottage window she's seen before.

The glass is covered in metal bars.

The incongruity of bars on a window in the middle of nowhere feels like a problem too strange for her tired brain to compute. She stands there for a moment, trying to shake off the last clinging moments of uneasy sleep.

It is bitterly cold again and she wonders if the heating has gone off. But when she gets to the cupboard in the hallway and checks, the pilot light is still flickering away like a blue tongue.

She opens the door to the bedroom and the first thing she notices now is that this room also has bars on the windows. Hurrying to the study, she finds the same thing.

Neve stands in the doorway, chewing her lips uneasily.

Surely this isn't normal for the countryside?

She and Daniel once lived opposite drug dealers, whose front door had an extra layer of bars. But even there, in a dodgy bit of central London, they hadn't felt the need to bar their own windows.

This is the middle of nowhere. What possible reason could there be for such high security?

Something unpleasant occurs to her as she remembers all the locks on the front door.

Isabelle must have been frightened to go to these lengths. Of what though? Or who?

This is nothing like the country idyll Neve had been hoping for.

It's more like a fortress.

She's too exhausted, achy and in need of coffee to feel as frightened as she had the night before. But she can't stay, that's quite clear. This was a mistake. As usual she has run headlong into a situation without thinking through the consequences.

This thought ferments like sour milk as she gets her soap bag and goes into the bathroom. She will have a shower, phone Lou, then think about what to do next.

The bathroom is cleaner than she thought, she now realises. Once she has flushed the disgusting toilet and swirled some of the pungent yellow cleaning fluid lurking at the back, it's quite acceptable in here. There is even a stack of clean, fluffy towels in an airing cupboard and she peels off her musty, sleep-worn clothes with a feeling of gratitude for this gesture.

The bathroom is empty of toiletries, apart from a brand new plastic dispenser of soap, and a bottle of bleach and a cloth that sit to the back of the toilet. Checking for a cord and a switch, she is relieved that it isn't an electric shower. Standing under the powerful jet of water she closes her eyes, allowing her clenched, tense muscles to unknot. Frothing shampoo into her hair, she then begins to shave her legs and armpits. It's pure habit, but the sensation of sloughing off the old so she can emerge, brand new, is pleasing too. She begins to feel her spirits rise a little.

Padding back to the sitting room and her case in a towel, she shivers and quickly dresses in clean underwear and socks, but with all the layers she wore the evening before. The radiators don't seem to be up to much, despite the clanking sounds they make at regular intervals.

Her eyes are drawn to her phone and a guilty feeling tugs at her. She really ought to have called Lou last night. But it was late when her phone finally came to life again.

Her stomach rumbles and she almost cheers when she discovers the scrunched remains of a half-eaten chocolate bar in the depths of her handbag. She devours it in two bites while she frets about the problem of topping up the meter and getting some provisions in for later. Sipping cold water from a delicate china mug she found hanging on a hook above the sink, she wonders where she will find some manner of corner shop.

There must be something, surely? She simply needs to investigate the area and it will be fine, she is sure. She can do this. She is a grown woman. With a *cottage.*

But first there's something she must do. Taking her water back to the sitting room, she sits in the same spot and pulls the blanket over her knees to get comfortable. As her thumb moves to find Lou's number, the phone comes to life as if by magic.

The screen tells her it's Lou.

'Oh hey,' she says, 'I was just—'

'Where the *hell* are you?' Her sister's voice is nasal and thick, her tone clipped.

'You won't believe what has happened,' she says, 'I only got here last night and then my phone was dead and—'

'—so your phone was dead for an *entire day and an evening,*' says Lou. It isn't a question. 'It's *so dead* that you couldn't even send me *one* little text, just *one line* so that I know you're alive?'

'Lou, c'mon,' she says with a laugh that sounds hollow

to her own ears. 'Of course I'm alive, I mean, what did you think I'd—'

But Lou isn't going to allow her to finish any sentence. She is off again, shouting now. Neve has to hold the phone away from her ear in what might have been a comedic way, in other circumstances.

'What did I *think*?' she yells. 'I thought *all sorts* of terrible things! I thought you might have even gone and done the same thing that bloody woman did! Thrown yourself off a bridge!'

Neve lets out an irritated breath. 'Don't you think that's a bit melodramatic? I did leave you a note!'

'Saying what?' Lou's voice has a hysterical edge now. Neve winces. 'Saying nothing at all! I had no idea whether you were leaving for good, or something bad had happened to you, or anything at all!'

'Look, if you'll let me speak for a moment, I'll tell you what's happened, alright?'

Sulky silence thickens on the other end of the phone. Lou blows her nose, loudly.

'Okay, so that woman? Isabelle Shawcross?' Saying her name out loud in the quiet house feels strange and uncomfortable. Neve swallows and continues. 'Well . . . you won't believe it but she has only gone and left me her cottage.'

'What?' snaps Lou, her tone disbelieving. 'You only met her for five minutes. How can that be true?'

Neve suppresses a sigh. Who would make up a story so outlandish?

'It's a special sort of bequest,' she says patiently, parroting Laura Meade. 'A donati morto . . . can't remember the name. But it's all legal. And anyway, it's in Cornwall and everything was shit at work yesterday because of the Germans – I think I'm losing my job – so I walked out and decided to come here and check it out. And like I said, my phone died and then I had all sorts of trouble finding my way in here in the dark and it was only this morning that I was able to call.'

Silence.

'So let me get this straight,' says Lou thickly after a moment or two. 'You walk out of a job maybe, oh, days before getting a redundancy package, but let's put that to one side, and you head off to a dead woman's house on your own without telling anyone?'

'Yes! But what the hell, Lou? It's no skin off your nose.' Neve is sharp now. It's too early for all this judgy stuff. Lou can be so superior. 'What's your problem?'

There is a pause.

'My problem,' says Lou, quietly, 'is that I haven't slept for six months. I'm surrounded by snot and nappies and I feel so *ill and bloody pissed off* that I could just walk out on the lot of them, and then I have to worry about you, *as usual*, because having two needy children of my own isn't enough.'

Stunned, Neve manages to stutter, 'That's not fair!'

'Isn't it?' Lou's tone is so bitter that Neve actually recoils. She has never heard her sister like this before.

'I'm sorry,' Lou continues, 'I forgot that we always have to make allowances for *Neve*. We always have to laugh it off when she is selfish and self-centred, and, and . . .' Lou bursts into tears '. . . and everyone always runs around making things better but they never do that for me, do they! It's typical that you should get given a bloody cottage for doing precisely nothing!'

'Look, Lou . . .'

'Oh forget it,' says Lou nasally. 'It's always been like this. Mum and Dad let you get away with murder and now it doesn't even occur to you to behave any other way.' She blows her nose again. 'Enjoy your cottage. If you make any

99

other major life decisions maybe you can do me the common courtesy of at least dropping me a text.'

She hangs up.

Neve's hand trembles as she puts her mobile on her lap.

It was like there were a thousand grievances that had been lining up inside her. How long had she been carrying all *that* around?

Neve's mind shifts unpleasantly to the night their father died.

The sisters had hugged in the horrible little hospital room they had been led to by the nurse, who said they should wait there while their father was 'sorted out'.

Neve remembers now that Lou murmured, 'You weren't *there*. I couldn't find you,' in a voice thick with tears. She kept saying it, but never mentioned this again afterwards.

Was that it? She couldn't help not getting the messages. And this is completely different.

Guilt mixes with indignation now. She is a grown woman, as Lou is always telling her.

She no longer has Daniel. If she wants to take off somewhere alone at no notice, then surely that is her right? Surely that's the whole point of not being weighed down by babies and mortgages like Lou. She'd chosen those things; Steve with his boring hobbies, and the two babies. It wasn't Neve's fault that Lou was struggling now. It wasn't *her* fault that she had been given a cottage by a complete stranger. She doesn't even want it, not really.

The carriage clock ticks in the thick silence that surrounds her.

Neve stares up at the barred window and suddenly feels that the room is very small, the walls squeezing in. She needs to make a plan; to get an idea of where she is and how she can get around.

She picks up her phone and taps Google, but there's still

no 4G. She didn't notice anything about wi-fi in the folder. She goes to the kitchen and flicks through it again, ignoring the stuff about bin timetables and septic tanks, trying to find the properly useful part about getting online.

But there's nothing. Neve lets out a breath. No television and no wi-fi? This is surely more than anyone could put up with.

She puts on her coat and goes to the front door to check the temperature outside. The sky is grey with thickening clouds above the trees.

She wishes she had something waterproof to wear as she pulls on her hat. Then she remembers seeing the wax jacket on the coat rack.

But when she goes to the hall and looks at it hanging there, missing the shape of the dead woman who once wore it, she can't bring herself to put it on. So instead she shrugs on her fake fur and pulls on her boots.

There's bound to be a bus stop, she thinks and, picking up the large bunch of keys to the house, she opens the front door and steps out into the chill air. She can't spend another night here without food for a start.

She'll work something out. She'll have to. It's not like she has anywhere else to go. She can't go back to Lou with her tail between her legs. She just can't.

16

Outside, Neve forces herself to walk a few steps before turning to get her first, unadulterated view of the cottage.

She lets out a long, slow breath. Comparing it to the old cricket pavilion at school had been optimistic, she now sees.

The building is a blunt, grey rectangle, painted in a drab, scabby covering that is flaking off like dry skin. The two front windows, obviously covered in bars from here, seem to stare back at her from under a glowering, low-slung roof. It looks as though it may have been built in the 1950s, rather than the nineteenth century, as she'd imagined when she first heard of the place. In fact, it couldn't *be* further from the rose-clad, whitewashed property of Neve's imagination.

Petty Whin Cottage is, quite simply, hideous.

Disappointment tumbles coldly inside her.

As she casts her gaze to the right of where she stands, she sees there was once a reasonable garden here, even to her untutored eye. There are two flower beds, edged by rockery. But everything is overgrown and tangled, as if nature is gradually creeping closer to the house, ready to swallow it up in green, subterranean light.

Thanks for sodding nothing, Isabelle, she thinks and heads quickly towards the gate through to the lane.

Better to get moving.

At least it is daylight now.

Neve looks across at the trees lining the other side of the lane. No way of telling how far the woods go. The words of the old nursery rhyme drift into her mind.

> In a cottage in a wood
> A little old man at the window stood.
> Saw a rabbit hopping by
> knocking at the door.
> 'Help me, help me, help me,' he said.
> 'Before the hunter shoots me dead.'

'Oh for God's sake, get a grip,' she says aloud and hurries down the lane to the main road, shivering inside her coat.

She's tempted to drown out her thoughts with music while she walks and her fingers toy with the earbuds in her bag. But this is such an unfamiliar place and she has no idea, really, where she is going. She walks on, quietly congratulating herself for doing the sensible thing for once.

When she reaches the main road, she stops and looks around uncertainly.

She thinks the taxi driver turned right into Stubbington Lane last night, so Cador is . . . back that way? But there was nothing there as far as she could tell.

Neve begins to walk in the opposite direction, down the steep hill.

A low mist clings to the horizon, giving the view an almost unearthly feel. She pulls her collar higher around her neck against the chill, damp air. Every breath feels like it is being sucked through a cold sponge and her cheeks are soon wet from the tiny droplets in the air.

It is bitterly cold and her toes inside her boots are starting to tingle with pins and needles. She quickens her pace a little.

At least there is a pavement. She is grateful for it when the occasional car thunders past and misses it sorely when it disappears and she has to walk at the side of the road.

Fields on both sides melt into the smudgy horizon.

It is ten minutes of walking before she comes to a couple of houses, set back from the road by driveways. They are the first signs of life in this vista of fields and grey, grey sky.

It really is the middle of bloody nowhere.

A few minutes on she sees a sign showing somewhere called Polmeath is one mile to the right. A village, surely? Trying to ignore the nagging worry that she may get completely lost, Neve sets off at a steady clip down the road. It is a bit narrower than the one she has been walking on, potholed and muddy. She walks close to the hedge and shoots nervous glances over her shoulder, looking out for any cars that may come barrelling this way.

The road begins to rise and she is sweating now under all her layers, puffing with the effort of the climb.

When, finally, she reaches the brow of the hill, she sucks in her breath.

The sea.

The colours are bleakly beautiful. The water is gunmetal grey with tumbling white-tipped waves. It almost merges with the ominous clouds gathering at the horizon. The sky has a lilac tinge like something unearthly is boiling there. Neve pictures a giant hand pointing through the clouds; a Michelangelo finger offering its judgement on her. This image makes her chuckle to herself, and feeling energized by the sight before her, she pulls a deep, clean breath of salty air into her lungs.

A slice of sunlight pierces the cloud just then, bathing the sea in a spray of gold light that feels like a gift just for her.

She says, 'Oh,' out loud and pushes her hands deep into her pockets, rocking on her heels a little as she takes it all in.

Mournful cries of seagulls fill the air and Neve looks up to see them wheeling and twirling above. She feels a powerful urge to walk on the sand now and begins to hurry down the hill towards the sea.

There's a sign pointing to a coastal path and Neve picks her way down a steep zigzag that's treacherous with mud and stones. Her boots keep sliding beneath her and nettles and sharp jaggy plants catch at her fake fur coat, and, once, her hair. This, she realizes, is not the way most people get to the beach.

But finally she is stepping down onto the damp sand and looking around with a half-smile.

The wind is much stronger down here. Neve watches the suck and pull of the waves as they claw at the shoreline.

There's an old rowing boat back near the cliffs. It is tipped on its side, encrusted with barnacles, streaked with brown rusty stains and frilly with colonies of seaweed. Narrowing her eyes against the chill wind, she sees that there are recesses all along the cliff. Caves?

She loved rock pools and caves as a little girl. It was something she did with Lou for hours and hours. She pictures bringing Lou and the girls here in the summer and realizes, for the first time, that she has imagined staying at the cottage for any length of time.

This is good for me, she thinks. All this sea air will blow away the crap in my head. I can be a new person.

But it's as if someone has pressed some cosmic switch now because the sky begins to close in like an immense bowl of smoky glass. Deciding she can come back to the beach for a proper walk another time, she begins to hurry back up the path and towards the road just as the first fat drops of rain start to plop onto her head.

This detour now feels like a mistake, and grimly Neve heads back to the main road, thighs aching with the climb. As she reaches the top, she pauses, rain running down her face. The thought of being in that place with no lighting, no television and no decent food is more than she can bear. Neve resolutely quickens her pace. Surely she'll come to the village at some point soon?

The road is narrower here and Neve carefully walks along the muddy grass bordering it. As she reaches a curve in the road, a lorry comes careening around a corner so fast she cries out and almost throws herself into the bushes.

Shaking with shock and the effect of the cold mizzling rain soaking through her coat, she trudges on for what feels like an impossible amount of time. She passes fields where cows crowd the gate and regard her sorrowfully, as though even they're wondering why she is so stupid as to be walking along this road.

When she sees the sign for somewhere called Marak, her heart leaps. It's not where she intended to go when she started this walk, but any village will do now. She pictures a roaring fire and a ploughman's lunch. Maybe some chips on the side. She'll have a hot chocolate too, or, no, maybe a hot toddy. She's earned it.

Walking past a farm and several semi-detached bungalows with a 1950s look set back from the road, Neve stops, heart speeding up as she contemplates the terrible possibility that she has just experienced Marak in its entirety.

She's mourning bitterly for the cosy pub that never was as she turns and walks back the way she came. At least she will end up back at the cottage this way but it has been an entirely wasted journey.

The rain whips her face and plasters her hair against her head.

Cars pass, hissing on the wet road.

Neve hates Isabelle Shawcross now; hates her for killing herself and leaving Neve her stupid, ugly cottage with its weird window bars and lack of wi-fi. For fooling her into thinking coming here was a good plan.

But what other option does she have? Daniel doesn't want her; Lou hates her right now and Miri isn't the only close friend she has lost to motherhood in the last couple of years. She has no skills, no job. And Lou was right; what was she thinking, walking out of PCC without even bothering to wait for the redundancy package she must surely have rights to?

Neve has painted a vivid mental image of herself ending her days surrounded by cats, alone and unloved forever, when the volume of rain seems to double and everything suddenly feels so much worse. Her knee and ankle both ache from the various misadventures of the evening before and her coat is now sucking in so much water it feels like she is carrying the weight of another person on her back.

She is forced to walk on the road again and when she comes to a bend, she presses herself against the wall and hopes she'll live to see the other side.

This isn't just miserable but dangerous now too.

Neve somehow senses the vehicle behind her before she can see the lights so she turns, but it feels like less than a second later that a massive, black four-by-four looms out of the mist. It's going too fast. She cries out and throws herself back against the wall as it passes less than six inches away from her.

The tail lights are small bright suns in the hazy rain-soaked air as it comes to a stop.

Neve approaches, breathing heavily.

The window lowers smoothly and a middle-aged woman with short grey hair and small dark eyes peers out at her.

'God, I almost hit you!' she says. 'Are you alright? I never expected to see someone actually *walking* on this road.'

'I'm okay,' says Neve shakily. 'It's probably my fault.'

The woman's face softens. 'You do look cold. Can I give you a lift?'

Neve doesn't hesitate. Clambering into the car and offering profuse thanks, she is suddenly self-conscious about her bedraggled state. She finds a tissue and blows her nose loudly, trying to smile gratefully as she does so.

'So where shall I take you?' says the woman.

There's a question, she thinks but attempts a bright smile. 'Anywhere down here will be great, thank you,' says Neve. 'I'm off to the right in a cottage down a track in the middle of bloody nowhere, so anywhere, really . . .' She pauses. 'I was trying to find a shop and I walked miles but there was nothing.'

She trails off, aware that she is doing her usual thing of babbling from nerves. The woman pulls off into the road, frowning ahead.

'Well, there is a garage about four miles this way,' she says, 'and a Spar in the village at Polmeath. But really you'd need the big Sainsbury's that's on the other side of Cador.'

'Oh God, really?' Neve pictures herself trudging miles along the side of the road, bags of shopping whitening her fingertips and yanking painfully on her shoulders.

The woman nods sympathetically then abruptly slows down as a tractor appears ahead as if from nowhere.

They crawl behind it for a moment until it turns off the main road into a narrow lane.

Neve gazes out at the narrow ribbon of road ahead, flanked on each side by low walls. It feels as though they are driving inside a tunnel, there's so little light and the headlight beams seem to cut into the grey drizzle ahead.

'I'm Sally,' says the woman. 'Sally Gardner.'

'Neve,' says Neve. 'Carey.'

Sally pauses. 'I'm guessing you're visiting someone around here?'

Neve's tired attempt at a bright laugh seems too loud in the interior of the car. 'I'm not sure you'll believe me if I tell you why I'm here!' she says.

'Why don't you try me?' says Sally. '*Where* is it you said you were staying?'

Warmth blasting from the heater is beginning to bring Neve's numb fingers back to life. She flexes her toes in her boots. The fake fur coat smells like wet dog. But the loneliness of the last twenty-four hours is beginning to melt away. She feels that she never wants to leave this car, which is so high and neat and smelling of leather seats and air freshener.

'It's called Petty Whin Cottage,' says Neve. Sally looks at her so sharply she says, 'Do you . . . know it?'

Sally stares ahead and Neve can see that she is choosing her words before speaking again.

'Yes,' she says finally, and then, 'I take it you are a friend or relative of Isabelle's then.'

'Oh,' says Neve, prickling with the awkwardness of this encounter. 'No,' she adds hurriedly. 'I'm so sorry. You obviously knew her. But I'm not a relative. Or even a friend. I'm just . . . staying there.'

The oddness of this seems to hang in the air. The other woman doesn't speak and Neve is unable to leave the silence unfilled.

'Look,' she blurts out. 'It's all so weird and horrible but I didn't know her at all. I just happened to be there, you see, when she . . . when she did it.'

She hears a sharp intake of breath as Sally lifts one hand

off the wheel and covers her mouth with it. They meet eyes for a second and Sally's shine in the bleak light of the car.

Neve is surprised to find her own voice thickened by emotion as she continues.

'I talked to her a little because she had no coat and seemed so lost but it never even occurred to me that she was about to do what she did.'

The silence drags on uncomfortably long before Sally speaks again.

'You poor, poor girl,' says Sally. She clears her throat, and then, 'So, if you don't mind me asking you, why are you here *now*?'

Neve hesitates, thinking about how to frame the words. Saying them in the pub the other night, when it all felt unreal and still a bit of a laugh, was one thing. The next time had been to her sister and that hadn't gone well. This woman obviously knew Isabelle Shawcross. Was she going to judge Neve harshly for receiving this strange, unwanted gift too?

Taking a steadying breath first she speaks again, choosing her words with care.

'That's the strange thing,' she says, 'I got a letter out of the blue from a solicitor in Salisbury, you see, and it turns out . . .' she pauses, 'well, it turns out she has left me the cottage under some strange type of will arrangement.'

Sally glances at her, her expression too blank to read, and Neve ploughs on, 'I don't even really want it, to be honest. I never asked for it.'

Sally is quiet again and the hum of the engine, combined with the tick-tock of the wipers, drags at Neve's exhausted brain. She blinks heavy, sandy eyes and wonders if she should have made something up, instead of telling Sally the truth.

It sounds mad. The other woman probably thinks she has picked up a lunatic.

Eventually, Sally breaks the silence.

'We'd heard on the grapevine that she hadn't left it to her brother . . . but, well we did wonder who . . . um,' Sally falters. 'Well, I'm not surprised you're a little in shock,' she goes on. 'I think anyone would feel that way.' Neve glances at her and the other woman flashes her a quick, warm smile.

'And I'm guessing by that dance with death just now,' says Sally, 'that you have no car?'

Neve shakes her head. 'Never needed one in London,' she pauses. 'I don't even drive,' she says with a laugh. It strikes her then that there has been no sign of a car parked at the cottage. Surely Isabelle had some means of getting around, living out here?

'Did Isabelle own a car?' she asks and Sally darts a quick, sharp look her way.

'Yes, she did,' she says after a moment. 'She very generously gave that to my son, Matty, a few weeks before she died. But we had no idea about what she was planning.'

'Oh, right. Good,' says Neve, awkwardly. She hopes fervently that it didn't sound as though she felt she had the right to the car, as *well* as the cottage.

She's distracted by them slowing down and she realizes with disappointment that they have reached Stubbington Lane. The thought of going back into that depressing bungalow squeezes her throat. She hasn't even managed to get the electricity sorted out.

But instead of driving down the lane to Petty Whin Cottage, Sally stops in the road and turns to look at Neve.

'How about I drive you to Sainsbury's now, and you can get some provisions? And then maybe later you can come over to mine for some supper. We only live a few minutes from you.'

Tears well in Neve's eyes and she blinks them away furiously.

'Are you sure I'm not keeping you from anything?' she says, trying and, she knows, failing, to keep the neediness from her voice. Sally smiles kindly and pats her hand.

'I was thinking about tackling some paperwork, which is terribly boring and you are saving me from that, so no, it's really no trouble at all.'

'Thank you *so* much,' says Neve with feeling. Sally nods briskly and starts the engine.

Sainsbury's sounds like a wonderful place right now. Neve can get in some groceries and maybe even sort out the electricity problem.

Things are looking up.

17

Sally goes off to do some shopping of her own while Neve walks into Sainsbury's and almost sighs with relief at the bustle and life around her. There's a Costa Coffee near the entrance and Neve buys a large triple shot latte and a muffin. She eats the muffin where she stands, grateful for the instant blood sugar lift, then carries the coffee awkwardly in one hand as she steers a small trolley down the aisles with the other.

She enjoys selecting items, choosing basics such as toilet roll, soap, milk, tea and more coffee, along with cheese, olives, crisps, some good bread, wine, plus a couple of French sticks to be heated in the oven. It reminds her of when she and Daniel first shared his flat and decisions about dinner felt like they were playing house. This makes her sad, so she takes a large sip of coffee and begins to browse another aisle.

She picks up crackers and some pasta sauces in jars, too, along with some fruit and salad vegetables. Before heading to the tills she makes a last minute decision to buy an elegant pink orchid that stands tall in a small white pot as a thank you present for Sally.

Outside, Neve sees that Sally is in deep conversation on her mobile, looking annoyed and speaking rapidly. She waits, not wanting to intrude.

Sally hangs up and stands immobile for a moment, looking out across the car park, a cloth shopping bag hanging from the crook of her arm.

Neve coughs deliberately as she approaches and Sally turns and smiles.

'I got this for you,' says Neve, holding the orchid plant towards her by the ribbon loop handle. Sally pauses and then smiles as she takes it from her hand.

'Oh, how very pretty!' she says, 'but there was really no need to do that.'

'I wanted to say thank you, for rescuing me,' says Neve firmly. 'I honestly didn't know what I was going to do. I think I'd have ended up hitchhiking back to Truro this afternoon and probably being murdered.'

Sally gives her a slightly puzzled look at this and Neve reminds herself that not everyone gets her humour. Feeling slightly chastened, she tentatively asks about topping up the electricity key.

'I'll show you,' says Sally and they walk across the car park to a row of shops.

'Do you . . . have any idea how long you'll be staying?' asks Sally then.

'Not really,' says Neve, puffing out her cheeks. 'Things are a bit complicated at the moment. I need to get away for a little while.'

'But you will be selling Petty Whin Cottage?'

'Oh yes,' says Neve. 'I should think so. What else am I going to do with it really?' This reminds her of something and, as they are about to enter the Post Office, Neve stops. Sally stops too and regards her curiously. 'Do you have any idea why there are all those bars on the windows?' says Neve.

114

Sally makes a rueful face. 'Well,' she says with a sad sigh, 'Isabelle, God love her, was a very unhappy woman. She was . . . up and down, you know? When she was in one of her up phases she could be great fun.' She pauses. 'Or it could go the other way and she would get these . . . delusions about things.'

'What sort of delusions?' says Neve curiously.

Sally flashes a quick look her way. 'Nothing for you to worry about I'm sure,' she says. 'But, well . . . she never felt very safe in the cottage. She said, well . . .'

'Please, go on,' says Neve.

Sally sighs. 'She sort of became convinced that someone was after her.'

The back of Neve's neck prickles with unease. 'Really?' she says. 'Who?'

Sally places a hand on her arm and leans in conspiratorially. 'She wasn't a well girl, in all honesty. I think she was heading for some sort of psychotic breakdown.' Her face clouds for a moment. 'The dear sweet girl was one of those people who wasn't really strong enough for this world. Do you know what I mean?'

Neve nods vaguely, remembering the way Isabelle had looked on the bridge, with her thin white arms and her wide, desperate eyes.

'It's so sad,' she says. 'What a waste.'

Sally squeezes her arm. 'Yes, it's dreadfully sad. We did what we could but I half think she was always going to do something like this,' she says. Then, in a brighter tone, 'Come on, let's get you back to the cottage.'

Forty minutes later Neve waves as Sally's four-by-four bumps its way backwards down the drive. The rain has stopped and there's a promising swatch of blue in the sky. Neve's spirits feel lighter as she opens the many bolts on the door and hauls her two bulging bags of food into the house and down to the kitchen.

She's grateful that there was no food in the fridge to spoil as she follows the instructions on the electricity meter. She has topped it up for far more than she can really afford, but the thought of being plunged into darkness like last night is so terrible that she can't allow it to happen again. Next she finds a wheezing old Hoover in a cupboard in the hall, which she drags around the carpets and over the lino in the kitchen, until all the floors are free of grit and dirt.

She makes more coffee, heating up milk in a little jug and frothing it with a fork. Sipping it gratefully, she chops salad ingredients and cheese, then constructs a doorstep sandwich, which she eats standing at the table.

Sleepiness washes over her now after her odd night, despite the coffee, and she yawns as she heads into the sitting room. Switching on all the lamps in an attempt to counteract the gloom, despite her niggling worries about the electricity, she settles on the sofa.

The argument with Lou still nags and Neve considers whether she ought to send a conciliatory text. Or at least give her the address, so someone apart from a virtual stranger knows where she is. This is an uncomfortable thought, once again triggering her over-active imagination about being alone here.

Sally's words about Isabelle's delusions bring the memory of the night before sharply back. Maybe it's something about the loneliness of this place, she thinks. But the bars on the windows only make it feel more sinister, not less. Neve makes a mental note to ask Sally later if she has the number of a handyman service, or a builder. The first thing she wants to do with this property, whatever her ultimate plan, is to get rid of those bars.

Neve goes to the mantelpiece and snaps a picture of the

photograph of Isabelle as a baby with her phone. She'll
send it to Lou in a desperate attempt to bond.

No putting it off any longer.

She begins tapping out a message.

Lou,

Look, I really didn't mean to worry you like that but
things have been a bit strange for me for a while and
when this thing happened with the cottage I thought I
should at least come and check it out. It's not really
what I expected to be honest. It's a bit creepy and dark,
plus this Isabelle woman seems to have had some
'issues' and has put bars on all the windows!!!!!

Still, at least the bogeyman can't get in, hey? Maybe
you can bring the girls for a visit soon when everyone
has got over their lurgies. I really am grateful to you
and to Steve for letting me abuse your hospitality for
so long. Who knows, maybe it will be the making of
me, moving to the countryside. I'll be all rosy cheeked
in a floral apron when you see me next. I might even
start making jam.

Love Neve.

PS On second thoughts . . . maybe not the jam part.

PPS Check out this photo of the woman who owned
the house. Sad, isn't it? But reminds me of kitchen in
Gloucester Crescent. Remember when I cycled into the
kitchen table and split my head open? Always the bloody
drama queen, eh?

Neve normally dashes out texts full of abbreviation. But
she nothing else to do. Anyway, it feels right, somehow, that
she write out these missives to the outside world with care.

Maybe she will at least raise a small smile from her sister.
In the past she could always make Lou giggle – when they

were younger they would often roll around in hysterics, clutching their stomachs.

But now she can't even remember the last time Lou really laughed at anything.

Next, she sends Miri a message. She can't quite bring herself to call.

Have you popped yet?

Sorry if I go quiet but I'm in the middle of nowhere and the signal is shit. It's a long story and a bit weird!!!!! Upshot is that the woman who killed herself in front of me has basically left me her cottage in her will.

I know, right?!!!!!

I still can't quite believe it and don't know what I'm going to do. It's a bit of a shithole to be honest and very isolated.

CUE BANJO MUSIC

But I've met some locals and they don't seem to be all pitchforks . . . yet. I am going to dinner tonight so I'll get back to you on that.

I might hang out here for a little while anyway until I work out what to do next. Oh I didn't mention that I told PCC to shove their crappy job up their arses, did I? So, yeah, I'm fucked in terms of job prospects at the moment. But don't worry, I'm sure something will turn up! And if not, maybe I can sell my body to the locals for a few quid a go.

SEE HOW ENTERPRISING I AM . . .

Anyway, hope you're alright and make sure someone tells me when the alien bursts out in all its gory glory.

Love, love, love.

xxxN

There is a tentative band of sunshine on the carpet now and the rain has stopped. She ought to investigate the property a bit more.

Her coat is still sodden though and, hesitating for a moment, she goes to the hall and looks at the waxed jacket she noticed earlier.

She hesitates. It feels creepy to wear something of Isabelle's. But isn't she living, albeit temporarily, in her house? And she has no choice, with her own coat being wet. She reaches for it, decisively. The jacket is a little big on her, but she rolls the sleeves back and appreciates its heavy warmth around her shoulders. It smells of nothing much, which makes it easier to forget she is wearing a dead woman's coat.

Outside she walks around the side of the cottage and into the back garden. There's what looks like a large vegetable patch at the back, rows of bamboo sticks lying forlornly on earth now choked with greedy weeds. A rusty swing seat sits to the side of the vegetable patch and there's a bench that Neve recognizes from the photograph inside.

A wood pile towers at the very back of the cottage, with an axe resting on the top.

Her lurid, violent fears of the night before flash into her mind, stirring up the same queasy feeling of uneasiness. For a moment she has the feeling of being watched from the bushes; of eyes roving over her.

Waiting.

She swallows and rubs the back of her prickling neck as she looks around the garden. The only sounds are birds singing and wind whispering in the branches of the trees that stand tall on the other side of the lane.

There's no one there.

Neve forces herself to continue her circuit of the garden.

Towards the top corner there's evidence of a bonfire. Neve prods at soft, black ashes. Some of it was clearly paper.

Looking closer, she sees the remains of a small book, maybe leather bound. Neve picks it up but it crumbles away in her hands. It looks like there were cardboard files burned here too. She can see the metal spines that have survived the fire. And over there is the distinctive stripy edge of an air mail envelope, the rest destroyed.

Maybe Isabelle did this when she was planning her suicide. Neve imagines her striking a match and watching a life's paperwork curl and blacken before her eyes.

A cold breeze curls around the building then and Neve shivers and pushes her hands into the deep pockets of the jacket. Feeling something there, she pulls out a scrap of paper. It's from a ring-bound reporter's notebook and seems to be a list of chores.

Ring plumber, is the first point, followed by a scrawled list of food items like eggs and flour. Turning the paper over, Neve sees some other words, written in capitals in a strong hand that has almost torn holes in the paper.

HMP LL 14107116. PBH date TBC

She searches her memory for a meaning but can find none.

But suddenly her senses are on high alert. She isn't imagining it. Someone is there, in the lane. A shaft of afternoon sun flashes on something bright through the bushes.

Peering closer she sees a silver vehicle is parked in the lane. Neve hurries to the gate and as she steps through it she sees a man is standing right there, still as a statue.

'What do you want?' she says sharply. The man, in his early sixties, has owlish glasses and closely cropped grey-white hair. He stares back at her with rounded eyes.

He blinks several times and then clears his throat.

'I thought for a moment . . . You look . . .'

Neve glances down at the coat, understanding the confusion. 'But what do you want?' she says. 'Were you *spying* on me?'

The man runs a hand over his hair and then quickly turns and almost runs to the car.

'Hey, wait!' Neve calls as he hurriedly gets in and starts the engine. Then he is driving at speed away over the bumps and ridges of the lane.

Neve stares after him as the car turns into the road and is gone.

What a creep. Why was he skulking around like that? It was obvious he mistook her for Isabelle because she was wearing her coat. But why hurry away so rudely? And had he been watching her through the bushes?

She wishes she'd had the presence of mind to make a note of the number plate.

Just in case.

Neve shivers, despite the warm jacket. She doesn't need any further reasons to be creeped out by this place. *Bloody hell*. Dead magpies. Lights blacking out. And now this weird Peeping Tom lurking in the bushes. None of it is exactly helping with her integration into rural ways.

Grumpily, she glances down at her watch. She'll be picked up by Sally before long and had better get ready. Thank God she doesn't have to spend another evening alone in this dump.

In an attempt to lift her mood, Neve plays some music from her phone via its own small, tinny speaker as she hunts through the items of clothing she has brought on the trip. She doesn't have much, but she is glad to see that she included a black sleeveless dress with a silvery thread running through it. Slipping a light blue linen cardigan over the top, she pulls on a pair of thick purple tights and contemplates footwear.

Apart from her boots, which are currently drying out by the door, she only has a pair of foldable ballet slippers.

But she isn't going to be walking anywhere, she is sure. Sally never exactly said where she lived but Neve hasn't seen any other properties so guesses it must be driving distance away. She twists her hair up into a bun and slicks on some mascara and lipstick.

Feeling more like herself, she heads down to the sitting room to wait. Picking up her phone she sees the temperamental signal has disappeared again. She sighs in frustration. This place . . .

The doorbell brings her out of her reverie and she hurries to the front door.

'I'm Will Gardner, Sally's husband,' he says. His voice is pleasant and well spoken. 'I've been instructed to pick you up for dinner.'

'Oh, hi!' says Neve, flustered. Will is quite attractive, in a silver fox kind of way. He is very smiley and large in the doorway. 'I'll just get my things. Come in!'

Still beaming, Will steps into the hallway behind her.

'Can I just pop through to your loo to wash my hands?' he says.

Neve wants to say, 'It's not really mine,' but instead, she says, 'Of course, do you know where to go?' and then, as a shadow passes over his face, 'I'm sorry. What a silly thing to say. Sally told me you both knew Isabelle.'

'It's quite alright,' he says kindly, adding, 'I'll just be a moment. I got some diesel before coming over this way and the bloody pump handle was covered in it.'

Neve tuts in sympathy and goes to pick up her coat, which is thankfully almost dry, and the bottle of wine from her small stash she plans to offer her host.

Will walks back into the hallway, grimacing. 'Having trouble with the plumbing?' he says.

'Um, not that I've noticed,' says Neve, 'but I only got here last night. Why?'

'Isabelle used to say all the time that it was a nightmarishly unreliable system in this house. I noticed a bit of ominous rattling just now when I went to the loo and flushed. I'd keep an eye on it if I were you.'

'Oh dear,' says Neve. 'I guess I'd better add that to the list of things that will need doing.'

Will gives her a sympathetic smile then looks down at her feet.

'I don't mean to be rude,' he says, 'but are you going to spoil your shoes? Is *is* rather muddy out there.'

Neve stares down at her own feet in confusion.

'Oh,' she says. 'Are we walking?'

Will barks a hearty laugh. 'Oh goodness me, Sally didn't tell you where we are then? It's only a few minutes on foot.'

'Oh!' she says. 'I didn't realize. Let me just . . .'

She goes to get her still-damp boots and grimaces as she slips her feet into the chill insides. Rolling her ballet shoes up, she puts them in her handbag. The whole thing feels intimate and uncomfortable in this small space so she forces herself to give Will a quick grin, which he returns.

'All set?' he says.

'All set.'

Will has a powerful torch and Neve clings to the bobbing white circle of its beam as they walk. It really is only a few minutes' away, accessed by walking a little further down the main road and then turning into another lane, this one in better condition than the one to Petty Whin Cottage.

If the trees surrounding the houses hadn't been there, the two properties would be visible to each other from an upstairs window in each case. Neve feels something in her chest lightening. Maybe she isn't as alone here as she first thought.

Will tells Neve there is a much larger property a little further over that belongs to Richard Shawcross, Isabelle's brother.

'Right,' she says. 'I think I should go and introduce myself to him at some point. I feel a bit funny about the whole house thing.'

Will murmurs an indistinct reply. Then, 'Here we are,' he says.

A sign on the gate says 'The Spinney', then, 'Well, I wouldn't worry too much. Bit of a strange family all round, if you ask me.'

18

10th January 2003

Dear Granny,

I wanted to write and say sorry, both for what I have done and for not letting you visit me here. I know I have caused you a great deal of worry and pain and I wish I could take it back. But I am still not ready to see anyone from the family and I am told you have been ringing up and asking to visit. I'm still trying to process things and maybe being here will help with that but I need to do it on my own.

It was a terrible shock when I found out the truth about my birth mother. I would never have known if I hadn't made my own enquiries and that is what I am struggling with. Didn't I have a right to know?

I know Mummy and Dad thought they were doing the right thing by not telling me the circumstances of my adoption (not the Shawcross way, eh? Stiff upper lips all round) but I now think this was a huge mistake. When I was little and had those dreadful nightmares I was told that's all they were. Bad dreams. Always so much blood in them. It was as if they were brushed away as unimportant. But they were so very vivid that I think some of them were memories. I know I was only tiny when it happened but small children understand so much more than people give them credit for.

Anyway, the most important thing is that my 'cry for help' as they call it isn't something for you to worry about. I am going to get better here and then I am going to travel. I might become a nurse, like she was. I owe it to my birth mother to live the life she was denied.

Don't worry about me. I'll be in touch when I can.

Best love. (And give old Bruce a cuddle for me) Izzy xx

19

Sally and Will's home is, to Neve's mind, what a cottage *should* look like: all whitewashed stone and a thatched roof. The bones of a wisteria – one of the few plants Neve can identify – clambers up around the front door, reaching to fresh white windows above. The front garden is neat and bordered with flower beds and on the front doorstep there is a painted white bench and several colourful pots quietly waiting for spring.

'Come in, come in,' says Sally, smiling. She wears a fisherman's style jumper and slim trousers, her only adornment a pair of small, diamond earrings that wink in her lobes. Neve immediately feels over-dressed and self-conscious, and wishes she had worn her jeans and a jumper.

Will has to duck his head to come through the low front door behind Neve. 'Come through and have a drink,' says Sally. Neve gets a glimpse of a sitting room furnished with squashy flowered chairs around a huge inglenook fireplace. Bookshelves line the walls. The comfort of it all hits her brain like a chemical rush.

She quickly takes off her boots and slips on her ballet

slippers before following Sally into what looks like a kitchen extension with glass doors all around.

The air is filled with the smell of garlic and chicken. Neve realizes too late that she didn't mention that she barely ever eats meat.

'This is gorgeous,' she says, retrieving the bottle of wine from her handbag.

'Oh there was no need!' says Sally warmly, 'especially after the beautiful orchid.' She gestures with her hand towards the window sill and Neve sees the plant sitting there. It is still wrapped in cellophane, with an oddly abandoned look about it. She experiences a small jab of shame. Maybe orchids-in-a-pot from Sainsbury's are not classy enough for these people. Perhaps she should have got something else . . .

'Now then, what's it to be?' says Will, rubbing his hands. 'G and T? Wine?'

'A gin and tonic would be lovely,' says Neve with a smile, and feels herself beginning to relax for the first time in ages. A thin MacBook Air is open on the countertop and she can see iTunes on the screen. Speakers in corners of the room play Billie Holiday at exactly the right volume. Neve lets the husky sweetness of the voice wash over her, remembering how much her mum had loved the singer.

'Just excuse us while we get sorted and then we can have a proper chat,' says Sally, opening the oven. Smells of sizzling meat, lemon and garlic fill the kitchen and Neve's stomach growls in response.

'It's only roast chicken,' says Sally apologetically. 'It seemed like a safe bet – I hope you like it.'

'It smells delicious,' says Neve and it is the truth, despite her semi-vegetarian habits.

Will is preparing drinks with as much care as if he worked in a top hotel bar. Neve watches as he measures out Hendrick's gin and then splashes in Fever-Tree tonic. Piling lime wedges and ice into the tall glasses, he grins as he hands one to Neve.

'Wow,' she says, 'that looks great!' She is aware that all she has said so far is lame, gushing things and resolves to sound a bit more intelligent for the rest of the evening.

'Cheers.' Will clinks his glass against hers. Sally doesn't seem to be having one and is involved now in checking vegetables, wafts of steam curling into the air.

The gin and tonic is strong and delicious. A sense of well-being floods through her and she settles back in her chair, watching the couple bustle about the kitchen in comfortable synchrony.

It's then that Neve notices the cat sleeping in a round basket to the side of the Aga.

'Oh!' she exclaims. 'Hello again, you.' She twiddles her fingers and the cat comes over to rub against her legs, purring luxuriously. She laughs and strokes its long bony back.

'Have you met old Horace then?' says Will.

'He kind of came visiting last night,' says Neve.

Will laughs.

'I'm sorry about that,' he says. 'He's been doing it for years. He was almost more Isabelle's cat really. I hope he didn't give you a fright, the bossy old thing?'

'Well,' Neve grimaces, 'he did a bit. The electricity had gone out and for a minute I thought I was alone in the dark with a serial killer.' She laughs airily as if this is a joke and not the exact thing she *had* believed.

Will and Sally both make shocked, sympathetic noises.

'How awful that you had no electricity,' says Sally, shaking her head. 'You would expect that as a bare minimum, wouldn't you?'

Neve hesitates. She doesn't want to badmouth the woman

who left her an actual house. But the urge to share is overwhelming.

'That's not the only thing,' she says, and takes another sip of her drink. 'The place was in such a state. There was rubbish everywhere and it was really dirty. It looked like some old tramp had been living there.'

'No! That's awful,' says Sally, face creased with concern. 'You poor thing. I have heard about some break-ins around here. Maybe someone had been squatting there?'

Neve takes a large slug of the drink. This is not a good thought.

She tries to lighten the atmosphere a little. 'I could put up with all of that, if I only had wi-fi!'

'Oh,' says Will. 'Well we can help with that, can't we, Sal? She can piggyback off ours until she's sorted? I bet it will reach the cottage.'

'That would be brilliant! If you don't mind?' says Neve, her voice a little too loud.

Sally frowns as she stirs. 'Hmm?' she says distractedly. 'Of course.' Neve wonders for an awkward moment if she is being cheeky by falling so gratefully on this.

'Let's not forget though,' adds Will. 'That Isabelle had some real mental health problems. I think the poor girl just couldn't cope with life, at the end of the day.'

Neve thinks of the folder with its neatly printed instructions about the cottage. Such a contrast to the neglect she'd witnessed.

'I'm sorry our daft old moggie gave you a fright,' says Will. 'I know that place is a bit . . . gloomy.' He pauses and seems to almost shudder.

'Well, how's that drink, Neve?' He comes to join Neve at the table.

Neve glances at her own glass, thrown by his change of subject. The drink *is* going down a bit too easily and she resolves to slow down. The last thing she wants to do is get pissed in front of these nice, well-behaved people.

'I'm good just now, thanks,' she says.

Sally begins to speak again. 'Isabelle was what you might call a bit of a wild child in her teens,' she says. She is stirring gravy with a wooden spoon and looking distant. 'Always getting expelled and whatnot. There was always something a little . . . unstable about her, I think it's fair to say. We didn't see her for years, really, until she came back.'

'Where did she live before?' Neve toys with her glass.

'She travelled all over and then ended up in Australia,' says Will. 'She came back a year ago when Margaret – her grandmother – died. They were very close in some ways.'

'Petty Whin Cottage used to belong to Margaret,' says Sally now. 'She owned the cottage separately to the rest of the estate and then she left it to Isabelle. She was a dear old soul. Very well-liked in the community, you know?'

'Isabelle took it very hard,' says Will.

Neve murmurs an agreement and then the atmosphere changes anyway because a hulking teenager slinks into the room, with the air of a sulky cat.

'Matty,' says Sally. 'It's almost dinner time, darling. This is Neve, our new neighbour.'

Matty is chubby and tall like his father but his brown buttony eyes are his mother's. He regards Neve, who smiles at him, as if he has been stung by a wasp.

'Hi,' she says, uncertainly.

'I've seen you before,' he says and Neve shoots quick, confused glances at his parents. They look as baffled as she feels.

'Oh, I don't think so,' she says with a nervous laugh.

Matty grunts in response and, sitting down at the table, immediately starts tapping away at a mobile phone.

'Now then Matty,' says Will in a warning voice. 'No phones at the table, you know the rule.'

Without complaint, Matty puts down the phone and looks into the distance. Neve is aware that something about him is not quite right, but isn't able to work out what it is.

The awkwardness of the situation forces a bright attempt at conversation from Neve. It's not a question she really wants to ask because it will only be reciprocated but she can't think of anything else.

'So do you guys work around here?' she says, taking a small sip of her gin and tonic. Will has finished his and is already scooping up her glass and asking if she would like some white wine.

He pours her a generous glass of cold Chablis as he replies.

'Well, Sally works for an architectural firm in Truro,' he says in an easy tone. 'And I was headmaster of a school in Redruth for many years.'

She waits for further information that isn't forthcoming. But it is time to eat anyway.

Matty hasn't said a word as they start. Neve tucks into the chicken with relish, quickly forgetting her recent attempts to give up meat. For a moment there is only the sound of clinking cutlery and appreciative murmurs about the food.

'And what about you, Neve?' Sally asks the inevitable question. Neve takes a sip from her glass of wine to buy time, noticing that Will has already drunk half of his. Sally has a tumbler of orange juice, Neve notices now, as does Matty.

'Well,' she says carefully, 'I worked for a magazine publisher for the last few years but the company has gone under and so I'm going to have to find something pretty quickly.' It's near enough to the truth, she thinks.

Sally has laid down her knife and fork and now regards Neve with a frown.

'Oh you poor thing,' she says. 'I don't know what your plans are but I have to tell you that the chances of finding work around here are very slim indeed. You're much better off looking in London.'

Neve makes a face. 'I've fallen out with London a bit,' she says with a laugh. 'I'm hoping a few days here will help me to work out what to do with the rest of my life!'

Neve blushes when she realizes that Will and Sally are both now looking at her with concern and she concentrates on spearing the last of the perfect golden roast potatoes, fragrant with rosemary, on her plate.

'You don't even care that she's dead. Listen to yourselves.' The unexpectedness of Matty's words land in the centre of the table like a football that has been kicked over a fence.

Sally leans across and covers his hand with her own. When she speaks, her voice is low and firm.

'Matty, you know that isn't true. I understand that you're upset, but there is no reason to be rude to our guest.'

Neve blushes and Will flashes her a pained look.

Matty looks at her directly then and the raw emotion in his face almost makes her flinch. Will and Sally have talked fondly about Isabelle tonight, but this is something different. She is looking at real grief. It's familiar enough for her to be able to recognize it in someone else and she suddenly feels ashamed at living in Isabelle's house like this; as though she has any right.

'Come on,' says Sally matter-of-factly, taking Matty by the hand. 'Why don't you catch up on *Sherlock* with pudding in the den.'

The young man gets up as obediently as a well-behaved child. Sally mouths 'Sorry' at Neve and they leave the room.

Will tops up Neve's glass even though it is still half full, then his own, empty one.

'Sorry about that,' says Will now. 'He was fond of Isabelle – well, we all were. That was rude of him, just now, and I can only apologize. Matty is . . .' he pauses. 'He's had some difficulties of his own. He's taking some time out from education at the moment. His first term at uni proved to be a bit . . . stressful. He had a bit of a breakdown. I think that's why he and Isabelle got on well. She understood him. God knows we don't.'

'Okay,' says Neve awkwardly. 'Please don't worry. It's fine. Poor him.'

She pauses. 'Can you tell me any more about her? About Isabelle?'

Will takes another large sip of wine. His eyes are starting to get an unfocused look and his cheeks are flushed.

'We didn't know her all that well in some ways,' he says with a sigh. 'Look, I don't think there is any reason not to tell you this in the circumstances, but she had tried to commit suicide before.' He pauses. 'More than once, in fact.'

Neve sucks in her breath. 'Oh God, really?'

Will nods sadly. 'Yes, I believe she took an overdose when she was living in Australia and there was talk of something even in her teens. And then she decided to come back here to live and, well, it wasn't a good decision for her.'

'Why not?'

Will makes a moue. 'For a while she threw herself into living there,' he says. 'Became very committed to continuing work on her grandmother's garden, that sort of thing. She seemed to glow with energy when she was like that, you know? Almost a bit manic.' He pauses before speaking again. 'Then something happened,' he says. 'I don't know what. But she became very nervous and started thinking someone was watching the cottage.' He makes a face. 'Well, you've seen the bars on the windows, of course.'

Neve nods, with a grimace. A cold finger seems to stroke her spine. She toys with her napkin. 'Did she say who she thought was watching?' she asks after a moment.

Will sits back in his chair, his eyes distant. 'Not really, but she got a bit obsessed about being safe. Kept calling the local police and asked them about installing a panic button, or so I heard. They got a bit fed up with her after a while.'

The words 'safe' and 'panic button' seems to pulse and loom inside Neve's head.

'There was a man lurking about in the lane today,' she says in a rush. 'It felt like he was watching me.'

Will regards her for what seems like a long time before speaking. 'What did he look like?' he says at last.

Neve describes him and he frowns. 'Not Richard then,' he says. 'No idea who that was. Hopefully just someone who got a bit lost.' He takes another swig of his drink. 'Have you met him yet? Her brother?'

'No,' says Neve, trying to pull her thoughts away from dark corners. 'What's he like?'

Will stares down at his glass but is unable to hide the sneery twist of his lips.

'What?' says Neve.

Will flashes a smile at her. 'Oh, nothing,' he says. 'He's just not overly blessed with social skills. He lives in the main house. Have you seen that yet?'

Neve shakes her head.

'Basically,' he says, 'Briarfields is your typical crumbling country pile. But it's not big enough or attractive enough to make any income, nor is it small enough to be easy to manage. Been in the Shawcross family for about a hundred years. Completely falling apart and Richard has neither the money nor the wherewithal to do anything about it. This house and Petty Whin Cottage are all technically part of the estate. They form a triangle.'

Neve absorbs this information. A question that has been bothering her rises to the surface now, buoyed by Will's easy confidences.

'Do you think he's angry that she left the cottage to a complete stranger?' she asks. Will meets her gaze and doesn't respond immediately.

He takes another swig of his wine and then grimaces.

'I don't know,' he says. 'But I can't imagine he is delighted. I mean, would you be, in the circumstances?'

Neve dips her gaze to the table and toys with the stem of her wine glass.

'I think,' she says, 'I'd be massively pissed off.'

Will sighs and chugs back some more wine. 'Hopefully you won't need to have much to do with him anyway.' He smiles but she doesn't feel at all reassured.

'The funeral was a sad business,' he says suddenly. 'It was all arranged in a bit of a hurry and so none of her school friends were there or anything. Richard was like a zombie and it ended up being him, us and a couple of people who used to work for the family.'

'That's so sad,' says Neve in a small voice.

Will places the glass on the table carefully. 'It's a terrible waste,' he says, eyes cast downwards.

20

The large dinner sits stodgily in the base of her stomach now. Will is staring moodily into his glass. She wonders what Sally is doing. She has been a long time with Matty.

Will seems to rally then and asks Neve about her old job; she tells him about some of the specialist magazines at PCC in a scathing way. Will hoots with laughter, especially at her impression of Fraser.

After a while Sally comes back into the room, bringing a welcome air of brisk practicality. Her cheeks look flushed and her eyes are bright. Neve feels a wave of sympathy for her. It's easy to see that she does most of the heavy lifting around here.

'I'm so sorry about that, Neve,' she says. 'I'm sure Will has filled you in a little on our Matthew. He doesn't mean to be rude. He just has no filter.'

'It's fine,' says Neve. 'I don't really have a filter either.'

Sally smiles and pats her sides. 'Right!' she says. 'Let's move on to coffee and dessert.'

Neve has lost her appetite but she forces down a few spoonfuls of apricot tart and accepts a cup of coffee. Will tops up his wine glass instead and Neve sees his wife flash a look of disapproval his way.

They move through to the comfortable sitting room and Sally shows Neve photographs of their daughter and her two cherubic blonde toddlers, who live in Barcelona. The mantelpiece is filled with images of this sunny family and it is obvious to Neve that this clear-eyed girl with her healthy offspring and sporty ponytail is the Gardners' pride and joy and Neve finds herself feeling a flash of sympathy for lumpen, difficult Matty, who has no filter.

'How long has she lived there?' asks Neve now, trying to rouse herself from a cosy sleepiness that is beginning to drag at her.

'Oh about ten years,' says Sally and then a thought seems to strike her and she sits forward.

'You know, Neve,' she says, 'I'm just thinking that if you did want to get Petty Whin Cottage off your hands, there's a chance my daughter and son-in-law might be interested.'

'Really?'

Sally makes a face. 'Well, I think the whole Brexit thing has complicated things a little. And Lydia has been feeling homesick for a while. I'm sure they would offer a fair price.'

'Okay,' says Neve, 'well, I'll bear that in mind. Thanks.'

The conversation moves on and Neve tries to concentrate but the thought of going back to the unwelcoming cottage is a shadow over her. She half wishes Will and Sally would suggest she spends the night. But as she spots a discreet yawn from Sally, she thinks about something Miri often says: 'It's time to put on your big girl pants,' and with a stifled sigh, she rises from her seat.

'Thank you so much for a lovely evening,' she says. 'But I think I should be getting back now.'

Sally and Will both get up too and Will says he will walk her back. He staggers a little and Neve looks anxiously at

Sally, but the other woman's eyes are elsewhere, her lips primped in a thin line now.

Neve considers suggesting that she return to the house alone. But she's too scared of the dark lane and not completely sure she could even find the cottage.

After hugging Sally and thanking her profusely for the hospitality, she and Will head out into the darkness again. But before they go, Will says, 'Oh, password for the wi-fi. Will you grab it from the study, Sal?'

'Of course,' says Sally and disappears for a moment, returning with a scrap of paper.

The cold air seems to sober Will up a little. Neve feeds him questions about Lydia, the daughter, and he talks expansively about her and the grandchildren all the way home.

When they reach the front door, Neve finds the keys and begins the complicated sequence of opening up. But once she has turned the key in the upmost lock she realizes something is wrong.

'That's weird,' she murmurs.

Will, who is looking at his mobile, the pale rectangle illuminating the tired lines of his face now, says, 'What's that now?'

Neve tries the other three locks but they are all the same.

'I locked all four when we left,' she says, 'but now only one of them is locked.'

'Oh,' says Will. 'Are you absolutely sure you did that? Easy enough not to.'

'I'm sure!' says Neve, her worried voice shrill in the quiet chill air. 'Didn't you see me do it?'

Will makes a sympathetic face. 'Sorry, my dear, I really wasn't paying attention. I couldn't tell you either way, I'm afraid. Don't you think it's more likely that you made a mistake? Unfamiliar door and all that?'

Neve swallows. She's so tired. Is she really sure that she locked them all? After all, her instinct at any door is to lock it once. And she was flustered when Will arrived.

'Maybe you're right.'

'Want me to come in and check everything is okay?'

Neve does, very much indeed. But she thinks about the descriptions of Isabelle as flaky and overly nervous and the idea of being written off as another neurotic young woman annoys her.

Maybe this is how it starts.

'No,' she says, 'I'll be fine. I'm sure I just haven't got used to the locks yet. You go, and thanks for walking me back, and for a lovely evening.'

Will regards her for a moment, swaying slightly on his feet. He pats her on the arm in an avuncular way.

'You'll be alright, young Neve,' he says. 'Nightie night.'

Neve swallows, unexpectedly emotional.

'Night. And thanks again, Will.'

Giving her a wave, Will heads off down the lane and is soon swallowed into the darkness.

Neve enters the hallway and closes the door behind her.

The first thing Neve does is to turn on the lights in every room, even though she's conscious that she mustn't let the meter run out again.

She turns on the radio and searches for Radio 1, needing the cheerfulness of a pop station. Thumping R&B seeps into the room and her galloping heart begins to slow a little. Taking off her coat, which is still damp from earlier, she hangs it over a chair and goes into the kitchen to make some tea. She'd noticed a box of camomile on a shelf and she makes herself a cup, hoping it might help her sleep. Yawning widely, she makes the decision that she must be brave and sleep in a proper bed.

Neve carries her steaming mug into the bedroom and switches on the overhead light, then all the lamps.

It's a pretty room, now she looks properly. But old-fashioned. It feels as though Isabelle wanted to preserve the cottage as it was when it was owned by her grandmother. Bit creepy, she thinks, giving her arms a bracing rub.

The bed has a wrought iron frame and she realizes something has slipped down to the sides of the headrest. Reaching for it, she sees it's a string of colourful fairy lights shaped like roses in dusky pink and purple. She carefully re-strings them through the gaps of the headrest and is happy to note that they are run on a battery and not the mains. Switching them on, she smiles at the effect. The room is much more cosy now.

On the wall above the bed there is a picture of a seaside town. It's all pastel blue sea, white sailing boats and a streaky pink sunset. Neve decides that she'll definitely be keeping this. A moment later she feels guilty for the thought.

Looking around the bedroom again she sees an old-fashioned dressing table with a long rectangular moveable mirror. A series of small photos and scraps of paper are stuck into the frame, including a business card for a taxi company in St Piron, and a couple of photographs that seem to show the couple on display in the sitting room.

The ivory duvet is covered in a proper patchwork quilt and there are two cushions with a vintage rose pattern resting against the pillow. Neve opens cupboards and looks for clean bed linen. She finds it on the top level of a double wardrobe that's crammed with clothes and the uneasy feeling of standing in a dead woman's shoes chills her once again.

Not yet ready to look at the clothes, she grabs some clean sheets and a duvet cover and closes the wardrobe firmly. Definitely a job for the daytime hours, she thinks, and begins to change the bedding, rolling the linen stripped from the bed into a ball and putting it into a corner of the room to be dealt with in the morning. But when she pulls the sheet free from under the mattress something falls with a clunk onto the floor beneath the bed.

Neve gets onto her hands and knees and reaches a hand under the bed. Her searching fingers quickly touch something solid. A handle of some sort, cool against her skin. She pulls it out and then emits a high shriek and drops it back onto the carpet.

It's a knife.

Scrabbling quickly to her feet she stands and stares down at it, breathing heavily.

The blade is curved and ends in a viciously sharp point. It's only by luck that she didn't cut her hand; she can see how keen it is just by looking.

Isabelle clearly had this knife under her mattress. But why? What was she so frightened of? *Who* was she frightened of?

Neve feels something else tugging at her insides now. Anger.

It feels as though she is pulled back into a state of surging adrenaline every time she gets remotely close to relaxing.

After spending several moments debating what to do with the knife, she forces herself to take it to the kitchen and put it back into the rack near the sink.

Neve brushes her teeth in the chilly bathroom, then uses the toilet. The cistern makes a horrible gurgling sound and she watches nervously until the flushing is complete. A plumber is the last thing she can afford.

Really, the sooner she sells the place, the better.

She climbs into the cold sheets, shivering, and gazes up at the ceiling.

Pipes burble away in the walls and then there is an

alarming rattle from somewhere that stops as soon as it starts. Old plumbing is notorious for this sort of thing, she thinks bracingly, sliding further down into the duvet all the same.

Only her forehead, eyes and nose are visible now. Her eyes dart about. Every sense is on red alert. There is no prospect of sleeping with the light off, despite the electricity meter situation.

Something is making a *tap-tap-tap* sound now. An actual dripping tap? Or maybe it's a branch bashing against a window. But there are no trees close up against the building, are there? It stops. She clenches her cold fists and says a little internal prayer for morning to come quickly.

21

In the end, Neve sleeps more deeply than she has for several days. When she wakes she needs a few moments to orientate herself; her body feels welded to the comfortable bed.

Turning onto her other side she looks over at the window. Soft apricot-coloured light spills into the room, spoiled only by the stripes of shadow caused by the bars.

She decides that she must use some of what is left of her inheritance to get those bars removed. After all, there is no way anyone is going to want to buy somewhere with such a ghoulish exterior. She will ask Will and Sally for a recommendation today. There is also the matter of the broken window in the kitchen. Such bad luck that the bird managed to get at the only window without bars.

After showering, she picks through her clothes and finds a long jumper dress, which she wears over her jeans. Her policy of wearing several layers of clothes means she will have to put a load of washing on later. She adds washing powder to her mental shopping list.

Neve makes a cup of coffee and two slices of toast, which she coats thickly with peanut butter. Sunshine floods in through the kitchen window, buoying up her spirits. Looking around, she tries to picture the kitchen redecorated in a cheerful yellow. She will get Lou to help; her sister has always had the best eye for what looks good in terms of décor.

This prompts her to go and get her iPad, which has been charging in the bedroom. She quickly finds the Gardner wi-fi connection and, with a flush of warm gratitude, types in the password.

Settling at the kitchen table, she takes another bite of her toast and opens her emails.

The only one of any interest is from her employer.

Neve knows what it is going to say but she braces herself to read it anyway.

It's from the head of human resources and, sure enough, it informs her that by leaving her post, and failing to inform her manager about her intentions, her employment contract has been severed with immediate effect.

This feels like something abstract. It is difficult to muster any real emotion about it. She hunts again for an email from Miri and there is nothing. Her real life feels far away right now and she can't seem to feel its emotional dimensions. She quickly taps out a WhatsApp message.

I'm online again. Give me news. This place is a total dump. Have you popped?

xxN

This done, Neve sits in the silent kitchen and drums her fingers on the table, thinking.

What can she possibly say to Richard Shawcross? She runs through sentences in her mind and they all seem quite inadequate to the task.

I'm so sorry.

I'm sure she was a wonderful person.

I never asked for anything.

She gets up from the table. It is her duty to at least have

some understanding of who Isabelle was before meeting her brother. So far all she knows is that her house was a tip, she had poor mental health and she didn't mind the smell of potpourri.

Standing in the small study, she looks at the tidy desk and then notices a laptop computer has been slid sideways into a shelf above it. She lifts it down and turns it on.

The screen is black and a message flashes up in white lettering: Missing operating system, insert boot disk and try again.

She remembers Steve selling a computer of Lou's and doing something like this. Formatting it. Something like that. She's not going to be finding any useful information on it, that's for sure.

She gets up and goes to the filing cabinet. The first drawer opens easily and she peers inside.

Cardboard hanging files flutter as she runs her fingers through them. Each one is empty. The same is true of the other drawers, and, when she goes to the desk drawers, she only finds a stapler, some Sellotape, and a couple of pens.

Neve frowns and chews her lip as she looks around the room, thinking hard.

It seems that Isabelle has left no clues about her life whatsoever. There are no stray pieces of paper, no other photographs, no notebooks containing doodles or shopping lists or anything of that ilk at all.

So why keep all the clothes? Why is it only the personal information that has been systematically destroyed or swept away?

It's like she wanted to leave nothing official behind. The clothes, however, feel like another strange gift.

Frustrated by the failure of her search to unearth anything new about Isabelle, Neve decides there is no putting it off. She dresses in her coat and – finally dry – boots. When she

146

leaves the cottage she double checks all the locks on the door. After her confusion the previous evening, she decides from now on she will count 'one, two, three' out loud as she locks them.

Birdsong chirrups all around her. The air is warm and it almost feels spring-like as she gets to the end of the lane and turns into the main road. The walk to Richard's house isn't far but she hopes she has remembered the way correctly after her walk back from the Gardners' the night before. She's certain it was only the next left turning and even she can't get that wrong.

She has no idea what to expect from Richard Shawcross. But for once, she is doing the right thing, the grown-up thing, and this spurs her on.

In daylight she can see that this isn't a lane at all, but a road. She hugs the side of it as she walks, in case any cars come hurtling around the high-walled bends. Within a few moments she passes the Gardners' property and glances up, stopping for a moment, in case anyone is about. She isn't exactly in a hurry to meet Richard and would be glad of the excuse of a cup of coffee.

But there is no sign of anyone and so with a sigh she carries on for a few minutes until she comes to a small churchyard on the same side of the road.

The church itself is a tiny rectangle of grey stone and doesn't look as though it would seat more than fifty people at most. Neve pushes the gate, which is bent and covered with a filigree of silvery lichen and dark moss, and walks into the churchyard.

There are twenty or so graves, some old enough to list sideways like broken teeth in their spongy gum of grass. Towards the back a number are bunched together by a family monument with a cross enclosed in a circle above it.

The name SHAWCROSS appears on the front of the column. This must be the family plot. Neve sees immediately that one of the headstones at the far end is in shiny black granite that looks relatively new. There are some flowers messily scattered in front of it, a small white vase in two cracked pieces.

She peers at the inscription.

ISABELLE ASTER SHAWCROSS

10th August 1982 – 21st December 2016

The winter is past, the rain is over and gone.

A beautiful quote, she thinks, reflecting tactfully that Isabelle was a troubled woman. She hopes she really does have peace now, even though she doesn't believe in anything like that, not really.

Aster . . . middle name, or part of her surname? It's hard to say.

Her attention comes back now to the flowers that have been laid around the grave. An animal must have destroyed them, she supposes. Still, it gives her an uneasy feeling. It almost looks as though someone has stamped on the vase and torn the blooms to pieces by hand. But why would anyone do that?

Maybe she is starting to get paranoid too now, she thinks, pulling a face at no one.

The sharp, bleak caw of ravens above her head make her look up. The sky is now white with cloud; the weather seems to change so quickly here. It's very quiet apart from the sinister rasping calls that seem to be saying she's not welcome here.

Neve hurries back to the gate, almost tripping on the uneven ground, and goes back into the lane.

She only has to walk for another few minutes before she

reaches large, metal gates; the word 'Briarfields' wrought into the framework.

Neve feels a flicker of nerves as she peers through.

Will had hinted that Richard was difficult. Maybe Isabelle really hated him, to leave her house to a total stranger? This thought, once lodged, causes her hands to sweat. She squeezes her palms together as she regards the house before her.

It certainly isn't the grand manor house she'd pictured.

Made from the pale grey stone that seems to be common here, Briarfields is an unusual shape, neither rectangle nor square. It is constructed from two wings that face outwards, angled slightly, connected by a curved middle section. The overall effect is unsettling to the eye, as though the building is neither straight nor round. The two wings are topped by crenelated points. The gravel driveway is lined by trees and a dirty green Land Rover is parked outside the house.

Noticing a buzzer on the gate, Neve presses it firmly, heart fluttering in her chest. Nothing happens. After a few moments she tries again.

Gnawing on her little fingernail, she debates giving up. Richard might not even be in, despite the presence of a vehicle.

That's when she sees someone coming around the side of the house, a dog trotting close by his heels. Head down, the man appears completely unaware of her presence.

With a jolt she realizes she's seen him before. It's the man who burst into the solicitor's office that day, looking for his phone. No wonder Laura Meade had looked so mortified by his presence. She'd presumably spaced out the two appointments, so there wouldn't be any potential awkwardness when Richard met the person who had breezed in and taken possession of his sister's house.

He is currently showing every sign of disappearing around

the other side of the building without seeing her so Neve calls out, 'Hey! Hello?'

Richard Shawcross – because surely this is him – starts and turns. The dog bounds across to the gate, barking hysterically but evidently happy, judging by the manically waggy tail. Neve puts her hand through the bars and rubs the dog's head. Shawcross approaches, his brow pinched with suspicion.

'Help you?' he says curtly.

Neve attempts her sunniest smile.

'I'm sorry to bother you, but are you Richard? Isabelle's brother?'

He frowns so deeply now he is almost wincing.

'That's me.' His voice is low and gruff.

'I'm . . . well, I'm Neve. I'm the person who . . .' she flails then adds lamely '. . . who has the cottage now.'

There is a long silence. All Neve can think to do is rub the dog's velvety head as he lies against the fence, trying to get as close to her as possible. She sees now that he is quite old, with a grey dusting on his chest.

'What do you want?

'Oh,' she says, with a short, nervous laugh. 'Well, I thought I ought to introduce myself. I wanted to say that I'm . . . really sorry.' She swallows and when he fails to respond, she allows the words she really wants to say to tumble out of her mouth.

'Look,' she says, 'I also wanted you to know that I never asked for anything that night. I only met her for five minutes.'

She trails off. Richard is staring at her. With a deep sigh he unlocks the gate from the other side.

'I suppose you had better come in.'

22

Richard marches ahead at speed. Neve struggles to keep up with his long-legged stride. The dog trots along next to her, gazing up with a stupid grin.

'What's *your* name then?' she says to the dog, foolishly.

'It's Jarvis,' says Richard, stopping so suddenly that she almost crashes into his large back.

'Ah!' says Neve. 'You're a Pulp fan?'

Richard looks blank.

'Cocker?' she adds uncertainly. 'Jarvis Cocker?'

'I don't know who that is,' says Richard, blankly. 'It's just a rather very intelligent system.'

Neve can only stare at him in bafflement.

'Just A Rather Very Intelligent System,' says Richard, more forcefully. 'It's an acronym. Comic book thing. From Iron Man. My sister persuaded our grandmother to give it the ridiculous name. Dog was hers.'

'Oh,' says Neve. 'Okay . . .'

They go around the side of the house, from where Richard had originally emerged. This takes them into a large garden with wild, tangled grass.

A few statues emerge from the thick greenery, dotted with

moss. One, of a cherub balancing on one foot, is listing sideways, ivy creeping up and seeming to devour the pale limbs.

'Right, come on in then,' he says as they reach a door. It opens into a kitchen.

This turns out to be yet another country place that doesn't fit Neve's preconception. She'd pictured a range; maybe a huge table with a dead pheasant on it. Copper pots.

But this décor is even older than that of Petty Whin Cottage. There's a free-standing sink, and a couple of sideboards in a faded yellow colour. The floor is covered in greyish lino and there is a pet basket in one corner. A strong doggy smell permeates the air, which is too hot.

At least there is an Aga.

Jarvis walks over to the bed and collapses into it with a loud huff.

The kitchen table is covered in papers, along with a laptop and several smeared plates and mugs with sticky dark rings inside them. A mobile phone lies on the top of some paper files. The top one looks like information from an estate agent called Salter McColl Property.

Neve stands awkwardly while Richard regards the table, rather as if it had appeared like this in his absence.

'Sorry about this,' he says doubtfully. 'Only bloody warm place in the house. I spend a lot of time in here.'

'It's fine,' says Neve with forced cheerfulness. 'You should see how I live!'

Richard scours her with a direct gaze and she wants to cram the words back in. What a stupid thing to say in the circumstances. Now he will think his sister has thrown her house away – the house he should naturally have been left – on some crusty squatter. It's a habit she hates about herself, this need to be the joker; to always have a quip. Abashed, she stands there until Richard rather curtly suggests that she sit down.

She removes a man's jumper and a paperback book with a baffling business title from the nearest chair and places them on the only remaining bit of table, before gingerly sitting down.

'Coffee? Tea?' barks Richard.

'Oh nothing for me,' she says. But he wasn't just being polite and her heart sinks as he goes to fill the kettle. She could kill for a coffee right now.

The only sounds for the next few minutes are the burble of the boiling water and the gentle snores puffing from Jarvis in his basket.

Neve cannot imagine what she could possibly say to continue a conversation with this man.

But Richard, carrying a mug of tea, joins her at the table and speaks first.

'How did she . . . seem?' he says. 'My sister? When you, er . . .'

'Oh,' says Neve, wishing she had a cup of something for distraction. 'It's hard to . . .'

'Right,' says Richard crisply. 'Just tell me what happened.'

Neve takes a steadying breath as she carefully chooses her words.

'Well,' she says, 'I really wish I could tell you more. Or that I had some insight into it. But we literally spoke for a couple of minutes.'

'I understand that.' Richard's face is impassive but his eyes, which Neve sees now are very blue, seem filmy, maybe with tears.

Neve attempts to relay the precise conversation with Isabelle as it happened.

Richard drinks his tea in a series of noisy slurps, his eyes elsewhere.

Neve clears her throat.

'Look, Richard,' she says, 'I don't understand why she

left me the cottage. It doesn't feel right to me to keep it. I'm not sure what I'm going to do, but it's important you know I never asked for any of this.'

Richard blinks a couple of times. Then he covers his face with both hands and rubs his cheeks vigorously, as though running a pair of windscreen wipers over them. His eyes are bright with emotion, but he isn't crying, to her enormous relief.

'Get rid of it then,' he says so bluntly that she jolts. 'Burn it down. I don't care.'

Then he lets out a long sigh.

'I'm sorry,' he says. 'It's all been a bit of a shock.'

Neve clears her throat. 'I bet,' she says with feeling. She hesitates before speaking again. 'Um, I hate to ask this, but what do you want to do with her things? Do you want to come around and look through them?'

'No,' he says forcefully. 'Keep it all. Give it to the charity shop. Whatever you want.'

'Oh.'

Richard gives her a stiff, brief smile. 'Sorry if I'm a little . . .' He takes a swig of his tea. 'I'm not sleeping well and I haven't got time to think about this. I have to go to London for a few days on business and I'm not remotely ready.'

At that moment his phone beeps with a text. He snatches it up and then says, 'Fuck,' loudly. It sounds to Neve like 'fark'.

'Is everything alright?' she asks tentatively.

'Bloody dog sitter,' he says. 'Saying now she can't take Jarvis. *Fuck.*'

Neve glances over to the dog, whose head has reared up at the mention of his name.

She doesn't give herself time to think it through.

'I could look after Jarvis,' she says.

Richard stares at her. 'You?' he says. Finally, she is riled.

'Just a thought,' she says with faux cheer, getting to her feet. 'But I can tell you probably have lots of people to help . . .'

'No,' he says hurriedly, 'I mean, I don't and thank you, but are you quite sure? He's a bit overly enthusiastic sometimes, as you've seen for yourself. I mean, he's quite old, but even so.'

They both regard Jarvis, who stands up and pads over, tail a blur of excited wagging.

'I'm sure,' says Neve. 'You're a good boy, aren't you? Aren't you?' She laughs as Jarvis places his heavy head on her knee and gazes at her adoringly.

'Well, if you're sure, then I am very grateful,' says Richard. 'I'll pay you of course.'

'Oh no need,' says Neve hurriedly.

'No,' says Richard and his voice has gone all tight again. 'I absolutely insist on that. It's twenty-five pounds a day around here and I am going to be away for at least three days so is seventy-five pounds alright?'

Neve opens her mouth and is about to argue. Then she thinks about the work that's needed on the windows, and her current lack of employment.

'That will be fine,' she says.

They make a plan.

Neve will leave with Jarvis now, and Richard will drive over later with the dog's basket and bag of food. Richard hands her a leather lead, soft and cracked with use, and offers a filthy towel, which she regards suspiciously and then asks him to put it in a carrier bag.

They swap mobile phone numbers and, a few minutes later, Neve is walking, or rather being walked by, the dog, who pulls and yanks on her arms and then stops abruptly when he finds an interesting patch of ground to sniff. When they reach the lane and Jarvis stops to munch on a pile of manure, Neve starts to wonder whether she has done the right thing.

Still, she thinks, she might feel a bit less lonely with a dog for company, although she can't imagine Jarvis is much of a guard dog. And let's face it, she needs the money.

As they approach the cottage, Jarvis almost pulls her off her feet in his haste to get to the property.

'Jarvis!' she yells ineffectually. 'Stop it!'

She isn't strong enough to stop the forward momentum of the dog, who is now barking in a frenzied way and almost pulling her arm out of its socket. She has no choice but to run to keep up.

'What is it, you silly animal?' she cries.

It's as she reaches the front of the cottage that she sees what the dog is barking at.

23

'Oh my God.' Her stomach heaves.

The magpie is lying neatly on the doorstep. But this time there is no head, just a ragged hole at the top of the plump black and white chest.

The same one as before? Or another? The gorge rises in her throat.

'*Nature, red in tooth and claw.*' The Tennyson line comes into her head then and she tries to breathe slowly to stop herself from being sick.

Must calm down, she thinks. *Think.* Think how this happened.

It was a cat, or maybe a fox. Yes, that's it. An animal found the badly wrapped bird and played with it, then left it here as a gift. But do foxes do that kind of thing? A cat then. Maybe the cat belonging to the Gardners. The thought that cats generally don't play with dead things churns uneasily in her mind. Isn't the point that they like to play with them before going in for the kill?

It's a different magpie. It must be.

But the more she looks at it, with its twisted wing and rusty bib, she is sure that it is the same one. How can it have moved?

Jarvis keeps taking little steps forward, barking, then jumps back as if scalded. Oh God, she thinks. Will he try and eat it?

Neve looks on, hopelessly. She wishes fervently that someone else could help her.

But there is no one. She's going to have to deal with this. First though, she needs to get past the thing to get inside. But what about the dog?

Looking around, she sees a rusty piece of fencing in the bushes and she pulls a still-resisting Jarvis over there. Slipping the lead off his collar, he almost gets away and she yells at him to stay. He flattens his ears and is submissive for long enough for her to loop the lead through the fence. With a plaintive whine, the dog lies down and regards her, head on his paws.

'Right,' she says a bit breathlessly. 'That's a good dog. Just need to . . .' She looks doubtfully at the magpie and with a shudder leans across the step to begin the laborious process of unlocking the door.

The lowest one is almost within hand-brushing distance of the oily feathers of the decapitated bird.

'Oh shit, shit, fuck,' she whimpers. The smell is unspeakable. Her stomach shudders with nausea and saliva floods her mouth.

Inside the house she gathers bin bags and rubber gloves. There's a plentiful supply, under the sink. Isabelle seems to have been a strange mix of disorganized flake and tidy housefrau. But thank God for it. At least she won't have to touch the disgusting bird.

Jarvis stands and barks in indignation when she emerges from the house, armed with cleaning products.

'Let me do this,' she says, 'and then you can come inside.'

It hasn't taken long, she thinks ruefully, for her to start talking to the dog like an equal. She's dimly aware that this is a slippery slope leading to the animal sleeping in her bed and eating all her food.

Although at the moment, it is hard to imagine eating anything ever again.

Holding her breath at the rotting fish smell, she opens out a bag and then uses another to nudge the bird over into it. It rolls sickeningly and as it flops into the top of the bin bag she sees something that makes her peer closer, despite the smell.

There's a small rusty hole in the bird's chest. It's chaotic with maggots that twist and wriggle and she suppresses a small moan of horror. But she is sure she is looking at a bullet hole.

Why would someone shoot a magpie? Surely they aren't considered vermin like foxes, despite their sinister reputation. Something is yanking insistently at her instincts, telling her the situation is all *wrong*.

The stain on the chest looks identical to the one on the bird from two nights ago, she realizes. She is suddenly sure it is the same bird.

If the bird had been shot dead, then it's hard to imagine how it could have come crashing through the kitchen window so neatly. The one window in the cottage that isn't protected by bars.

This suggests the truly unthinkable thing.

That someone deliberately smashed the window and threw the dead bird into the cottage. Someone who doesn't want her here.

Wasn't that what Isabelle had been convinced of? That someone was trying to intimidate her?

She thinks again of that man in the lane. Of the destruction at the graveside.

Neve's heart ba-booms in her chest and she looks around wildly. The thin, tall trees across the lane sway and whisper. The cottage waits silently behind, door gaping open.

Shivering, she forces herself to continue with her grim task.

Finally, the dead bird is cleared away in the bin at the back of the cottage. She takes Jarvis into the house, where he immediately climbs onto the sofa with a proprietorial sigh.

'Make yourself at home why don't you?' she grumbles gently. Really, Jarvis's presence is a great comfort, even if he is unlikely to be much of a guard dog.

Neve goes into the bathroom, washes her hands then uses the toilet.

Afterwards she flushes absent-mindedly.

There's another deep gurgling sound and then water begins to pour out of the lid of the cistern and onto the floor, soaking her feet.

Neve shrieks and jumps back. The water is gushing now, unstoppably, and it seems like a malign version of that fairy-tale about the magic soup pot that keeps on filling.

'Fuck it, fuck it!'

Throwing the bath towel down on the floor, she rushes to the airing cupboard and grabs another. But the water still gushes. Neve dimly remembers Lou once mending the toilet in the flat by lifting off the lid of the cistern and doing . . . something. Something that magically sorted everything out.

Stricken with this new horror, she forces herself to slosh through the water on the floor and to lift the lid of the cistern. Screwing up her eyes she pushes her hand into the shockingly cold water and roots about, unsure what she is meant to be looking for.

Among the mysterious architecture there she feels something like cloth and pulls at it with the tips of her fingers, muttering obscenities as she does so. There's a strange sucking sound and the cistern dramatically empties of water.

Neve stares at the balled-up piece of material and can't seem to make the necessary mental leap required that will tell her how it got there.

Miserably she throws it into the bin and gives the toilet an experimental flush, but nothing at all is happening now beyond a disappointing sort of clanking thud.

Furiously, she washes and dries her hands and mops up the rest of the water on the floor, using two more bath towels, which she ultimately dumps in the bath in the hope that they will magically wash and dry themselves later. The bottoms of her jeans cling miserably to her ankles and her socks are sodden.

Finding her mobile, she jabs in Sally Gardner's number.

'Hello?' Sally's voice is low and faint.

'Um, Sally, it's Neve,' she says.

'Oh hello,' Sally brightens. 'What can I do for you?'

Neve tells her about the flooded toilet, while the other woman makes a series of sympathetic noises.

'So I wondered if you had a number for a local plumber?'

'A plumber . . .' says Sally, a bit vaguely. 'Let me see . . .'

The line goes quiet for a moment and then Sally is back, speaking in a rush.

'I can't seem to find the number . . . can I call you back in a little while?'

'Oh, okay,' says Neve doubtfully. 'It's just that I can't use the toilet at the moment and it's a bit urgent.'

'Leave it with me,' says Sally and hangs up.

Neve changes into a pair of tracksuit bottoms. They're bagged at the knee and have a tomato sauce stain on the thigh. She pulls on her last remaining pair of socks. Then she drifts into the sitting room, where Jarvis is now sleeping and emitting small snores that sound like popping bubbles.

Scooching in next to him, she strokes his soft ears, making him thump his tail against her thigh.

'I'm going to be straight with you, boy,' she says. 'I don't really know what I'm doing here. I don't like the cottage and I don't think it likes me either!' This causes her to emit a high-pitched laugh that is watery with rising emotion. She wipes her hand across her eyes and glances at her phone, which still hasn't buzzed with the information she needs from Sally.

'Come on,' she murmurs.

Neve thinks about the sodden floor and the broken toilet; the ugly bars on the windows. The loneliness of this spot and the feeling that the cottage is choked by secrets she can't begin to fathom.

The knock at the front door brings her to her feet in one fast movement. Jarvis follows on behind her, barking excitedly.

She opens the front door to see Richard, holding a dog's bed and a bulging carrier bag. Frowning deeply, he's staring down at his mobile. He almost thrusts the contents of his arms at her and she says, 'Oh,' foolishly, then, 'I mean, thanks.'

Neve wants to throw herself at him and beg him to help with the overflowing toilet. But she can just imagine how sneery he would be about this. And he might also think she was ruining his sister's house with her presence.

Richard absent-mindedly pats the fussing dog's head and then turns to leave, evidently feeling no need to say anything. He hasn't really looked her in the eye since he arrived.

'Oh, before you go!' she says.

He turns and looks at her with barely concealed irritation.

'Do you have a plumber's number? It's nothing major. Just a problem with the toilet that needs sorting. Um, fairly urgently.'

Richard regards her as though she speaks some other language entirely, as seems to be his way. Then he reaches into his pocket.

'I know a bloke, Finn, who does everything like that. Hang on a minute . . .'

A few moments pass as he sends the contact by text. She waits for its arrival and thanks him, and then he is gone.

Neve rings the number and lets out a wail of frustration when it immediately goes to voicemail.

'Finn, hi, I got your number from Richard, um . . .' she has a moment's panic in which she can't remember this family's surname before it comes to her '. . . Richard Shawcross. I'm in his . . . his sister's cottage and have a plumbing emergency. Please, please can you call me back straight away. I'm desperate! Thank you!'

Slipping her phone back into her pocket, she moves as though walking through slurry to the bedroom, where she begins to gather up her dirty clothes. She's unsure whether she should use the washing machine while the toilet is blocked; maybe the plumber will want to turn off the water. She feels a thrill of panic run through her at the prospect of being stuck here with no water for any length of time. But she can load the machine, at least.

She shoves the bundle of clothes into the washing machine and looks around the kitchen, wondering what to do and fretting that the plumber won't return her call.

The clothes problem is really pressing now and Neve pictures the wardrobe in the bedroom, which she hasn't been able to bring herself to open. But having dealt with a decapitated magpie and been up to her neck in toilet water, she is now in no mood for superstition. She brings her phone with her and plays music on shuffle through the small speaker. It is tinny and unsatisfying but better than the thick, dusty silence in the bedroom.

Neve opens the dark wooden doors of the wardrobe, which are inlaid with small rose carvings, and a musty smell, tempered with something flowery, enters the room. Running her fingers over the rails she begins to look at the clothes hanging there and sees a small cloth bag with a bow at the top. She twists it around and sees it is some sort of handmade lavender bag, embroidered clumsily with the words 'Best Granny'. Her heart twists as she pictures a young Isabelle, for surely it was her handiwork, painstakingly sewing the scented bag together. She imagines a little girl with skinny arms and maybe blonde plaits, the tip of her pink tongue poking out as she concentrates on her task.

She can't throw this away, it's clear.

Neve forces herself to assess the contents of the wardrobe systematically, pulling out items of interest and throwing them onto the bed. Lots of the clothes on hangers are in slippery dry cleaning shrouds. The implications of this make her shiver. Did Isabelle systematically clean these clothes in anticipation of her own death?

She can't work out whether the idea of this utter certainty makes her feel better or worse about owning the cottage.

When she has done the bed is covered in piles of clothes she plans to explore. There are lots of cotton tea-dresses and floaty chiffon numbers. Some are clearly vintage. Neve guesses these weren't bought from the charity shop, but belonged to the ever-present Granny.

Some of the dresses have full skirts and cinched waists and Neve experiences a little burst of girlish delight. One is stiff pale cotton with green spots and has a green sash around the middle. She fingers the thick material, remembering the joy of playing dress-up with her mother's seventies knee boots and bags, kaftans and miniskirts.

Before she can stop herself, she is tugging off her tracksuit bottoms and pulling off the long-sleeved T-shirt and jumper dress she had worn the night before. Shivering in her bra and pants, her pale skin mottled with goose bumps, she tugs the green dress over her head and pulls it down over her body. It smells only faintly of washing powder and, as she struggles to reach the zip at the back, she begins to hum the song that has come on to her phone: her mum's all-time favourite, 'Dancing Queen' by Abba. She presses the volume button to its maximum capacity and the tiny speaker strains to fill the room with sound.

She can't reach the zip but despite all the drama of the morning, she can't stop herself from humming along to the music.

When it finishes, something slow and moody by Sita comes on. Neve jabs at the phone to pause as a memory washes over her, so powerful she has to sit down to absorb it.

It was a family wedding. Mum was singing the Abba song with slightly drunken abandon, holding Neve by both hands so they danced together. Neve had been eleven and pretending to be mortified. But really she loved the spinning sensation and the wide, happy smile of her dancing mother.

Soon she is a mess of snot and tears, her nostrils red and her eyes piggy. She reaches for a tissue from the box at the side of the bed and finds there are none left.

Neve experiences a bright, hot moment of anger at the unfairness in her life.

She might have had a cottage fall into her lap, but other people her age would have a mum and a dad ready to offer help; to come down laden with decorating equipment and legal advice about what to do with the place. They would bicker good-naturedly and then head off to the pub for an evening meal, where they would complain about tired limbs and gently make plans for the summer.

Neve stands up and goes to the sitting room for her handbag, in search of tissues. Jarvis is standing in the hall, staring at the front door with his tail a blur, and she dimly wonders what's up with him. In the sitting room she blows her nose and then lets out a squeal of pure shock when she sees the dark silhouette of a man peering in the window.

24

She runs to the front door, somehow convinced any delay will mean he has simply dissipated, like smoke, or worse. However often she tells herself she doesn't believe in ghosts, it doesn't seem to penetrate the frightened, superstitious core of her.

As she flings open the front door she is confronted by a man in his mid-thirties, with short dark hair and a small beard. He is carrying a large tool box and his expression is one of complete mortification. Neve swallows, realizing what a sight she must look like and attempts to stand taller.

'Yes?' she says frostily.

'Uh, you called me,' says the man. 'I'm Finn.' He has a soft Irish accent and a low, quiet delivery. 'I've been knocking but you didn't hear me. I'm a plumber.'

'Oh . . .' Neve feels colour creep up her face. 'Right, well, that's good then. Thanks. I mean, come in.'

He nods a little suspiciously and then glances down at Jarvis, who pushes past Neve to nose at his legs, whole body wagging with his tail.

'Um,' says Finn, 'would you mind?'

Neve looks at him blankly for a moment and then says, 'You don't like dogs? Oh, alright, hang on.'

Grabbing Jarvis by the collar, she pulls him with difficulty through to the kitchen and then out the back door.

Then she shows Finn where the bathroom is and hovers by the door as he lifts off the cistern lid. He takes off his heavy jacket to reveal a light blue T-shirt. His arms are covered in fine dark hair that looks soft to the touch. Neve attempts to concentrate on what he is doing.

Finn looks up. 'When I say I'm a plumber, that's not strictly true,' he says. 'I'm more about your general building, odd jobs. But I know my way around most plumbing issues and I know when to call in the experts.'

'Right,' says Neve. 'Well, that's fine. I don't have a working toilet at the moment and I'm a bit desperate. I mean,' she adds, hurriedly, 'desperate to get it sorted it out. I'm not . . . *desperate*.'

Finn nods slowly as though she has spoken words of great wisdom but she sees the side of his mouth crinkle in a hidden smile as he peers inside the cistern.

'Oh well,' he says, 'that's not very helpful, is it?' as if to himself and reaches inside.

'What? What's wrong with it?'

He doesn't reply for a moment, then holds up a round thing she has some dim memory her father referring to once.

'Is that the . . . ballcock?'

The word 'cock' seems to fill the room like a huge inflatable, bouncing off the walls and then gently settling between them. She blushes again and frowns, irritated at herself.

'It is indeed,' he says in his soft brogue. 'And it looks very much like someone has partially disconnected it.'

'Eh?' says Neve. 'Why would they do that?'

He shrugs.

'No idea,' he says. 'There is literally no reason why you would do that if you wanted to have a working toilet.'

She thinks about the wodge of material she had found in there when it was overflowing. When she tells him about this he makes a face.

'Show me where it was,' he says. Neve comes into the room. She is far too aware of the solid heat of his presence in the small bathroom as she leans over and indicates where she found the scrunched-up material.

'Have you had squatters in here or anything, no?' he says.

'I don't know. I suppose there might have been.' She thinks about what Sally said and the state of the house when she arrived. 'You wouldn't think you'd get that sort of thing out here.'

Finn smiles a little. 'I think you get squatters everywhere,' he says. 'But my only explanation for the toilet is that someone has deliberately sabotaged it.'

'Oh,' she says in a small voice, picturing the headless magpie. Then she remembers the business with the locks the other evening.

Suddenly cold, she rubs her arms and shivers.

I hate this place, she thinks.

Finn regards her steadily. 'You must be a bit cold, are you not?' There's that smile again, slow and steady.

It's only now that Neve remembers the back of her dress is still hanging open and with a gulp of embarrassment she reaches behind her back in a vain attempt to hold the two sides together.

'Excuse me,' she says, 'I'll just . . . I'll . . .' and she hurries off to the bedroom, where she pulls off the dress, almost breaking the half-open zipper in the process.

When she comes back to the bathroom, trussed up from neck to ankle in a woollen jumper and the dirty tracksuit bottoms, with a hoodie over the top for good measure, Finn is flushing the toilet. It is making a beautifully normal sound now.

'That's you all done,' he says.

'Oh God, thank you. How much do I owe you?'

'Let's call it twenty,' he says.

Relieved it isn't more, Neve hurries to get her purse.

Despite her embarrassment at the whole open-dress thing, Neve suddenly feels a powerful desire to get him to stay as she hands him one of the twenty-pound notes Richard gave her that morning.

'I would ask whether you could also take the bars off these windows,' she says with a high-pitched laugh, which even to her own ears sounds like a taut wire being twanged. 'But with people sabotaging my bog and bringing me gifts of headless corpses, I'm not so sure!'

Finn's eyes widen.

'Headless whats now?' he says. She makes a rueful face and then tells him about the dead bird.

He listens intently until she has finished and then seems to be chewing over her words.

'Well, you know I'll bet you anything it wasn't the same magpie,' he says. 'Have you actually checked whether the first one was where you left it?'

A rush of sweet hope pulses through her. 'Well, no,' she says. 'I didn't even think of that!'

'Betcha that's what happened,' he says. 'And even if that one has gone, this *is* the countryside.' He says it with a vaguely critical air that surprises Neve.

'You not a country person then?'

He makes a face. 'God, no,' he says, 'I grew up in Dublin. Why, did you think all Irish people lived in farmyards?'

'Oh, no, I mean . . .'

'I'm only messing with you,' he says with a grin. 'Now

then, do you want me to mend that kitchen window? Might not be until tomorrow . . .'

Neve beams in gratitude.

'I won't be able to match what was there in terms of period glass,' he says and Neve assures him this is fine. They walk back to the front door together and as he goes to open it, he hesitates.

'Look, you may have plans,' he says, 'but there's a folk night on at the Hope tonight. I'm going. Want to come along?'

Neve is so surprised she doesn't respond immediately.

'I mean, if you like folk . . .' he says.

'I do like folk,' she lies.

Rain has begun to fall steadily from angry-looking bunches of clouds. Once Finn has gone, she hurries to the back door to let the dog inside. Jarvis is huddled on the doorstep and shoots into the kitchen, patterning the floor with muddy pawprints. Grumbling gently, she goes to the bag Richard provided and finds a smelly dog towel, which she uses to dry the animal, nose slightly crinkled. She orders him into his basket then, and, clearly in fear of being banished into the rain, Jarvis obediently walks over to it, turning in a couple of circles before settling down and curling his nose in towards his tail.

Neve puts on the washing machine, finding soap powder under the sink, and goes back into the bedroom to address the mountain of clothes on the bed.

As she continues to sort through the clothes she is almost giddy at the thought of not having to spend an evening here alone tonight.

She walks to the dressing table and looks at her own reflection.

Then she glances at her phone. Nothing from Lou. Still no message from Sally.

171

It must have slipped her mind, and anyway, it's all sorted out now.

'Okay girl,' she says. 'Go and have a drink with him. You don't have to go crazy.'

25

By the time Neve has tried on, then taken off, several of Isabelle's dresses, she is sweating.

All her clothes, apart from one long-sleeved top and the grotty trousers she has on, are in the wash now. It feels wrong to wear Isabelle's clothes. But what choice does she have?

In the end she settles on a plain white vest top and a soft woollen cardigan in pale turquoise with tiny pearl buttons.

Wearing it, she feels like a slightly different Neve. Someone plucky and resourceful, but feminine too. Maybe this is her new country persona. Lou will get a surprise when she sorts this place out and then sells it at a massive profit, she thinks, making a mental note to find an estate agent to come and do a valuation at some point soon.

Feeling more cheerful now, she slicks on some dark red lipstick and flicks eyeliner along her lids in a feline swoop. Regarding herself in the mirror, she decides she looks just fine.

Neve half-heartedly begins to eat a bowl of cereal, while standing by the sink. She thinks about what Finn had said about the toilet. The first night she hadn't paid much attention to the plumbing. Everything felt old-fashioned and clunky. Will had commented that something seemed wrong when he'd called last night. So it was entirely possible that something had been done to the toilet before she even moved in.

This wasn't a great comfort, but it was something to cling onto. Then there was the whole magpie thing. She stops eating and puts down the bowl. The memory of the rotten smell is still too easy to conjure.

Finn was probably right about the bird, she thinks now. But she decides not to look, just in case.

After feeding Jarvis, who seems to inhale his dried food in one go, she muses on what to do with him tonight.

Do people leave dogs in houses for an evening, or was it like children, where you had to be present? It's the kind of basic knowledge Neve feels ashamed not to possess but she decides that Jarvis is going to have to come with them, whether Finn likes it or not.

She attempts to watch an episode of *Game of Thrones* on her iPad while she waits but the endless bloodshed keeps making her picture the raw wound where the magpie's head should have been.

When her phone rings, she is so surprised that it takes her a moment to place the sound. The signal is so poor it seems she has inadvertently identified the one place it works; on the corner of the kitchen table.

She doesn't recognize the caller's number.

'Hello?'

'Hi, my name is Georgia McColl, I'm with an estate agency in Truro called Salter McColl?'

'Oh,' says Neve, 'hi.' She remembers the file on Richard's table now.

'I believe you might be thinking about putting your cottage on the market?'

'Oh,' says Neve again, and, suddenly aware that she sounds quite thick, hurriedly adds, 'how did you get my number?'

'From your neighbour, Mr Shawcross? I'm sorry, I hope you don't mind my calling?'

Neve feels a flash of annoyance at this. But the woman sounds so friendly and it was on her to-do list anyway.

'No,' she says. 'No, that's alright.'

A couple of minutes later, when she hangs up, she feels a sense of satisfaction.

Georgia McColl is going to come around the day after tomorrow to do the valuation. She had pressed for tomorrow, but Neve felt she needed to get the place in some sort of shape first.

This is the right thing to do. The grown-up thing.

It isn't long after that she hears a knock on the door and gets up, disturbing Jarvis, who had been lying next to her. The dog pants nervously and watches her as she pats her hair and goes to the front door, trying to look as though she was barely aware of the time.

Finn does that little smile, like he is in on a joke no one else understands. She can't decide whether it is really annoying, or whether it makes her want to rip the clothes right off him. It's perhaps a little bit of both.

He's wearing the same woollen jacket from earlier and a pair of black jeans. She can see a deep blue shirt under the collar of the jacket and he smells of something with a subtle citrus zing that sends a little swoop into her stomach.

'How're you?' he says, Irishly, and she grins.

Jarvis tries to poke his head between her legs, which brings her abruptly back to herself. 'Um, yeah, so . . . the dog,' she says expectantly. Finn stares blankly back at her.

'He's coming with us,' she says, raising her chin a little. If he makes a fuss about Jarvis coming to the pub then he's clearly a jerk.

But Finn gives a little nod and gestures towards the opening into the lane where his car awaits. She can't tell whether the corner of his mouth is turned down sourly or not.

26

The pub is in a village about ten minutes' drive away.

Neve thinks her mother would have been proud of her subtle interrogation skills because by the time they are pulling into the car park, she has ascertained the following things about Finn.

1. He moved here from Southampton because his ex-wife grew up in the Forest.
2. She left him a year ago and is now living with a banker in London.
3. He doesn't really like to talk about any of this.

At last Neve has come across something in the countryside here that matches her expectations. The Hope is whitewashed, with beams and horse brasses on the walls. There's even a roaring fire and the whole atmosphere is one of cosy welcome.

Jarvis is glued to Neve's legs and she almost stumbles over him as Finn asks what she'd like to drink.

She considers asking for a Coke. She knows exactly what will happen if she gets drunk tonight. The stresses of the last few days mean her inner bad genie is dying to get out. Does she really want these locals to see her like that?

On the other hand, she isn't going to be living here. She's only staying long enough to get the house sorted and get her head together.

'I'll have a large Sauvignon Blanc please,' she says, pushing down the thought that she didn't end up finishing that bowl of cereal earlier.

It's ten o'clock.

The folk duo, called Hebrides, have moved from their own delicate ballads to crowd pleasers such as 'Whiskey in the Jar' and 'Brown Eyed Girl'.

The main singer is a tiny woman, with pre-Raphaelite curls and pale Celtic skin. She closes her eyes, transported, when she sings in her clear high voice. The singer is accompanied by a bald, chubby man with a beard who plays a variety of instruments, including a fiddle, with astonishing speed and skill.

At some point people get up and start dancing. Neve is sure it wasn't her who started it but by ten thirty she is swinging arms and singing joyously to 'Sally MacLennane' by The Pogues.

Red faces swing in and out, mouths opening and closing as people sing along. Neve feels a sense of belonging to all of them, from the old man clutching his pint at the bar with a grim expression as he tries to ignore the loud music, to the middle-aged woman in the bright pink top whose round freckled breasts are almost popping out as she dances. Then there is Finn. Sexy Finn.

Sexy Finn who has drunk Diet Coke after Diet Coke all evening, while she has had . . . some glasses of wine. She's not sure how many. She's been too busy dancing. But Finn hasn't really moved from the same seat.

178

She dances over to him and gives him a coquettish little beckon with her curled finger. He smiles tightly and shakes his head. Singing along to the music, she grabs hold of his hand and tries to pull him to his feet but he's so heavy and all that happens is she stumbles a bit and ends up next to him on the bench seat.

She can see Jarvis's black nose from his position curled under the bench and she feels a powerful wave of affection for the dog too. He's a lovely, *lovely* dog.

And Finn is a lovely, lovely man. He just needs to loosen up a little bit, that's all. She gazes at him for a moment and then, for no obvious reason at all, the axis of the world shifts a little and there's a sour curdling feeling in her stomach.

'Oh dear,' she says as the room begins to perform an impossible feat of movement and nothing is where it is supposed to be any more. 'Feel a bit . . .'

There is a strong hand under her upper arm now and she is almost levitating outside, where the cold air slaps her around the face. Groaning, she bends over with hands on her knees until the world stops its nonsense and behaves again.

Finn says nothing. She stares down at the domes of his toes in the brown boots as the feeling of nausea passes.

'Oops,' she says, 'I was only going to have one.' She starts to laugh and Finn thinks it's funny too because he's smiling at her, but a bit distantly in a cool way that's suddenly so sexy it makes her groin squeeze. Who wants to stay in the pub anyway? She can do what she wants. She doesn't live here. She never asked Isabelle Shawcross for the responsibility of this cottage in the middle of fucking nowhere.

Might as well enjoy it while she is here.

She moves closer to Finn and sees his eyes narrow a little in a way that is almost unbearable. He's not as tall as her usual type but that's okay because his lips are almost exactly opposite hers and she wonders why she hasn't always gone for men his height when it makes for such excellent kissing engineering. And she's closing her eyes and her lips are touching his softly.

But it's all wrong. Instead of the sweet mashing of mouths she is expecting, there is only air.

Opening her eyes, she sees Finn is standing back and gazing down at car keys that have emerged from his pocket. And she smiles because she gets it now. He's thinking that they can't do it *here*, not in a car park! They'll go back to the cottage and it will make the miserable place feel a bit more welcoming. Like christening it.

But Finn is saying something now and it sounded very much like, 'I think I'm going to take you home, Neve.'

It's clear he doesn't mean 'take you home and shag the life out of you' and she says, simply, 'Oh,' then, 'Why?'

He blows air out through his cheeks and shakes his head.

'You're maybe more of a party animal than me,' he says. Then, 'Maybe I'm just not ready to be dating.'

Neve stares back at him. Who uses the word 'dating'?

But somehow the words in her head have freed themselves from the architecture of teeth and tongue and palate and she says them out loud, accompanied by a snort of derision.

Finn scowls at her. A lurch of discomfort at the awkwardness of this exchange cuts through the fuzz of drunkenness.

It has all gone wrong.

'Right,' she says in what she hopes is a dignified voice. 'Can you take me home?' The word, 'home' feels like a mockery as she follows his disapproving back to the van.

27

Neve wakes at six a.m., bathed in sweat and stumbles to the bathroom to throw up.

Her throat feels lined with broken glass. This alerts her foggily that she isn't just hungover, but properly sick. Neve groans and walks as though through knee-high sand to the kitchen, shivering violently.

Jarvis gets up and pads to the back door where he gives her an expectant look and she sighs, before unlocking the door and letting him outside. She waits, hunched in a miserable curve at the back door for him to pee. She closes her eyes, miserably. Then she realizes she can hear something coming from the living room. A staticky, unpleasant sound she recognizes but can't place.

She goes to the room and realizes that the radio is on again. It is between stations and presumably has been going all night. But when did she turn it on yesterday? She tries to search her memory but her brain is too fuzzy.

It's too much to deal with now.

Neve has been told she is a terrible patient by her sister, by Daniel and by friends at university, when they all succumbed to the same evil stomach virus over one weekend.

But right now she wants her mother so badly that she begins to cry as she hunts for paracetamol and swallows two down with a glass of icy water that somehow scalds her raw throat.

Getting back into bed, she closes her eyes and huddles into the duvet until the shivering stops. Sleep comes like a cosh to the head.

It is the cold draught that wakes her, some hours later.

She has managed to wrap the duvet around herself tightly in an apparent quest to be warm but the parts of her that are exposed – face, one arm and a foot – are freezing.

At first she is too fuddled by sleep to make sense of this and for a few moments her brain works on recreating the disastrous evening before, complete with vivid memories of her trying to kiss Finn and being rebuffed. She winces and then thinks about the early hours when she felt so ill. There was that weird radio thing too.

She experimentally swallows and finds that her throat still hurts, but slightly less than it did earlier.

But why is it so cold in here?

Neve reluctantly untangles herself from the padding of the duvet and hurriedly grabs her hoodie. Thrusting already-worn socks onto her feet, she walks down the hallway to the kitchen. The cool wind on her face seems to get stronger with every step, as does the sensation that something is very wrong.

In the kitchen she realizes two things simultaneously: the back door is slightly open, and the dog is not lying in his basket.

Hurrying to the door, she pulls it open and peers outside.

'Jarvis?' she calls. 'Come here, boy!'

She waits, trying to piece together exactly what she did in the early hours of the morning. She was feeling so ill,

182

but she knows she let the dog out for a wee. She can remember how cold and miserable she felt. She's almost certain she let the dog come back inside. But what if she didn't?

'Jarvis!' She's shouting now as panic begins to pulse inside her. Neve runs to the front of the house and grabs Isabelle's jacket. Pulling it on, she shoves her feet into boots and runs back to the kitchen. Nausea and fear churn in her stomach and a wave of fresh sweat slicks her skin as she runs outside and pulls the back door closed behind her.

Neve starts by checking all around the garden, looking for holes in the fence. It quickly becomes apparent the fence is broken in so many places that it serves no real purpose. The dog could have escaped in any number of places.

She tries behind the property first, climbing the gate into a field where a few bored cows regard her, and shouting Jarvis's name over and over again.

Then she runs back down the lane to the main road, still shouting. All she can see in her mind's eye is the dog mangled and bloody at the side of the road and she begins to cry gently as she sees one car – then a van – barrel past at great speed.

The cold air bites through the thin cotton of her pyjama bottoms and waves of sickly exhaustion wash over her as she calls feebly into the wind. It begins to rain, slow patters that soon become an icy deluge and before long the landscape seems to be hidden beneath skeins of white gossamer.

Neve tries to picture herself telling Richard Shawcross that she has lost his dog and whimpers with fear and hope-lessness.

A small red car turns onto the road and comes towards her. As it slows down she realizes she recognizes the driver. It is Matty Gardner.

Neve looks cautiously into the window as it lowers. At that moment she spots what is on the back seat. It is Jarvis, who stands up and grins happily at her, looking huge in the small space.

'Jarvis!' she cries. 'Hello boy! You're alright!'

Matty mumbles something and she leans in closer.

'How,' she stumbles, 'how come you've got the dog?'

When Matty speaks again, he still doesn't meet her eye but his voice is surprisingly clear.

'I almost ran over him just now. I was going to take him back to Richard.'

Neve takes a deep breath and attempts to pull herself together.

'I'm meant to be looking after him,' she says miserably. 'But he somehow got out and I couldn't find him.'

'Got out,' Matty parrots, deadpan. Neve feels a hot blast of shame. Then he says quickly, 'Could have been killed.'

'Yes.' She swallows. 'Yes, I know. I don't really understand how it happened.'

There's a weighty silence.

'Do you want to get in or not?' he says after it has passed the point of awkward and gone into unbearable.

'Oh.' Flustered, Neve opens the door and climbs in. Jarvis tries to lick her face and she feels a wave of affection for the dog that brings guilty tears springing to her eyes.

She sniffs and asks Matty if he has a tissue as they drive along the road.

'Might be one in there,' he says, gesturing at the glove compartment. She mumbles thanks and opens it. Inside there are a packet of tissues, some gum and a lipstick. With a rush she remembers that the car was Isabelle's.

Looking at Matty he finally meets her eye and blushes. 'I haven't got around to clearing it out yet,' he says and she nods, reaching for a tissue. As she pulls at the packet it falls into the foot well of the car and a piece of paper falls at the same time.

Glancing sideways at Matty she sees he is not looking at her as she picks it up. It is a small paper wristband, of the sort you wear at a music festival; orange, with the word 'Visitor' printed on it.

She's not sure why she does it but she slips it into her pocket with the tissue.

The rest of the short journey passes in heavy silence and at last they are pulling up into the lane next to the cottage. Despite the difference in their ages, Neve still feels as though she has been caught smoking by the headmaster.

As he pulls up in the lane Neve smiles at Matty, who seems to physically shrink in response. She clears her throat.

'Thanks so much for this,' she says. 'But I would be really grateful if you wouldn't mention this to Richard.'

Matty's eyebrows close in together. 'Why would I?' he says and sounds almost offended by the suggestion.

'Oh,' she says, 'well, that's good then. Thank you again. I'll just get Jarvis out the back.'

Neve climbs out of the car and, after fiddling with the mechanism for a moment while Matty waits silently, works out how to move the seat forward.

As she reaches for Jarvis's collar the dog begins to jump out of the car. But something catches her eye just before she closes the door.

There's an air rifle lying on the floor below the back seats. The kind used to shoot wildlife . . . like magpies? She glances sharply at Matty, who stares moodily out of the windscreen and ignores her.

Neve hurries into the house with the dog and doesn't look back.

28

Dearest Granny,

Rich is terribly upset with me. I can live with that, but not if you are too.

I know it seems callous, me not coming to Dad's funeral, but you know what a difficult relationship we had. And the truth is that I simply can't afford to come back right now. Australia is such a long way and it's hideously expensive to fly back.

I expect you will offer to send me the money but I don't believe you can afford it either.

Also, being really honest, coming back to the UK doesn't feel like the best thing for me right now. I've had some problems with my health – but DON'T WORRY! – I am currently trying to get back to full fitness. I'm in intensive therapy with someone new (Rich helpfully said this is one of my 'witch doctors'. Thanks, Rich.)

This chap is brilliant and has specialized in adult and child PTSD. I am still finding it difficult to come to terms with the past and I think this is helping. In fact, I am feeling more positive than I have in some time, despite being sad about Dad.

I hope the funeral goes well and I will send a donation to that charity Dad supported.

Please tell Rich that I love him, whatever he may think.

And so very much love goes to you.

Izzyxxxxxxxxxx

29

After double checking that the entire property is locked up, Neve takes a quick shower. The entire time she is in the water she imagines a gloved hand whipping back the curtain and the precise feeling of a knife blade touching her skin. She's shivering as she comes out and dries herself hurriedly.

Sitting at the table sipping coffee and attempting to force toast down her sore throat, she glances at her phone and sees from the absence of blue ticks that Miri hasn't read her WhatsApp message.

She lets out a long sigh that seems to reverberate around the kitchen and glances down at Jarvis, who is sleeping heavily. Sharp needles of guilt stab at her but her eyes move to the back door. She checks again that it is locked and then stands in the empty kitchen wondering what to do next.

How on earth did she end up here? Freaked out and alone in a dead woman's house.

Isabelle Shawcross feels like an impossible puzzle.

If only Neve can start to understand her a little. To get a glimpse into what was happening in her life at the end. Sleeping with a knife under the pillow is not exactly normal, even in this place, and Neve is sure that something strange is going on here.

That's when she remembers the wristband she found in the car and she hurriedly pulls it from her pocket.

She now sees that the word 'Visitor' isn't the only writing on the thin paper. In small letters there is a stamp that says 'HMP Low Linney'. Her heart jumps and she hurries to the hallway to the waxed jacket of Isabelle's that she has been wearing.

The letters are chiming with something in her mind and she finds that the piece of paper is still there.

HMP LL 14107116. PBH date TBC

HMP LL . . .

Could HMP be Her Majesty's Prison?

Her Majesty's Prison Low Linney.

It rings a bell. Neve goes to her iPad and, giving another silent prayer of thanks to the Gardners' wi-fi, goes straight to Wikipedia.

HM Prison Low Linney

From Wikipedia, the free encyclopedia

Jump to Navigation, Search

HMP Low Linney

Location: South Walling, Worcestershire
Security Class: Adult male/Category A
Population: 670 (as of October 2013)
Opened 1972

HM Prison Low Linney is a Category A men's prison located in the village of South Walling, Worcestershire. It is operated by Her Majesty's Prison Service . . .

Neve sits back with a loud out-breath, which causes Jarvis to look up at her and thump his tail before lowering his head again, eyes beadily focused on her movements.

She doesn't know much about the criminal justice system but she knows that Category A is for serious criminals. A quick search confirms what she thought.

Category A: Prisoners whose escape would be highly dangerous to the public, the police or the security of the state, no matter how unlikely that escape might be.

So who was Isabelle Shawcross visiting in a Category A prison?

An attempt to Google prisoners at Low Linney gets her nowhere. There are only a few stories relating to riots, the murder of an inmate, and a story from the *Daily Mail* about lax security relating to drugs on an inspection in 2010.

Neve gets up and stretches now because her back is aching from her hunched position over the iPad. Her sore throat has crept back and her limbs feel weak and shivery. She makes herself a cup of coffee and goes to the bedroom to get a blanket, which she wraps around her shoulders as she heads back to the kitchen table.

She taps onto her emails and gasps when she sees a reply from Lou waiting to be opened.

Hi, she reads, Soz for slow reply. Whole house been puking. I'm typing with one hand as Maisie finally asleep on one shoulder. Have to be quick. Tx for msg and sorry about going postal at you. I was v worried and didn't know where you were. Glad to hear about the cottage and jam intentions and hope to visit. Keep me in the picture about plans.

Love L

PS Do remember unfortunate trike/wall union! But we had wooden floorboards in that house, not tiles. I still remember the gore!!

Neve sighs and closes her eyes with relief.

But she can't go and stay there again. Not only is the peace with Lou a tentative one, she can't bear to think about the look on Steve's face if she came crawling back. He would be all, 'That's Neve the fuck-up for you. Couldn't even deal with being given a free house.'

She sees now there is a message from an email address she doesn't recognize with a picture attachment. Opening it she quickly realizes it is from Arjan, Miri's husband.

Miri and I are proud to announce the arrival of Farah Savati Johal, 3.64kg, after a caesarean section.

Miri is doing fine but would like me to pass on that she is 'bloody knackered' and 'can't wait to get out of this hellhole'. We would both like to pass on that our daughter is not, as the picture might suggest, wearing a toupee.

We're hoping that mum and daughter will be discharged by the end of the week.

Emotion rises like a hard ball in Neve's throat as she opens the picture attachment and sees the tiny, scrunch-faced baby with a comedy mop of thick black hair. She gives a hiccupy giggle and wipes her eyes. Must get on top of all this crying. She doesn't know what's wrong with her lately. She's like a leaky tap.

But oh, clever Miri. There she is doing heroic things like giving birth and what is she, Neve, up to? Floating around in this strange place where she doesn't belong and trying to untangle a knotted ball of secrets that have nothing whatsoever to do with her. Desperate to tell her friend everything that has been going on, she instead taps out a message of congratulation and thinks about how and when she can get back to London to visit.

The fact remains, she realizes with a sinking heart, that

191

this cottage is the only place she has to stay right now. She looks up and almost feels as though it glares back at her. She gets up, restless, and walks over to the window where she sees that it is snowing. Large, soft flakes are falling at an alarming rate and Neve experiences a squeeze of claustrophobic dread in her chest.

She's ill, alone, and she might run out of food in the next day or so.

Neve thinks about what Will said before. 'She got a bit obsessed about being safe.'

She thinks about the knife.

About the flowers that seemed to have been trampled and destroyed at Isabelle's grave.

For just a moment, the thought that the cottage is haunted drifts into her head.

'No,' she says out loud. 'Not going there.' She's never been one to believe in that stuff and she has no intention of starting now. It feels like paranoia is seeping into her and infecting her blood like a virus.

Jarvis comes over to her and leans, trembling, against her legs. Maybe he's cold, she thinks and decides to make his bed a bit more cosy. It feels like the sort of thing a responsible pet owner would do.

She goes to the hall cupboard, remembering the stack of blankets in there and switches on the small torch to get a better look inside.

The space goes back further than she thought. She sees now there aren't just blankets, but what looks like a sleeping bag too. She gets down on her hands and knees and crawls into the space, feeling the slithery tug of the sleeping bag under her knees.

A bottle of water and a much larger torch lie to the side. The torch flashes bright over the white ceramic eye of an old teddy bear lying near the pillow.

Neve backs out of the cupboard so fast that she bangs her head painfully, heart ramming against her chest.

Who the hell has been sleeping in there?

Neve rushes to the kitchen and grabs her telephone.

Seconds later she hears Sally's voice.

'Hello?'

Almost in one breath, she tells Sally about what she found under the stairs. There is a silence and she hears a long exhalation from the other woman.

'Oh the poor thing,' she says at last.

'What? What?' Neve tries to lower her voice, aware she is almost shouting into the phone.

'Isabelle,' Sally says, then hesitates. 'This was something she did when she was little. Margaret told me about it once. They used to find her all over Briarfields in odd places; airing cupboards . . . an old tea chest. Used to drive them mad.'

'Why did she do it?' says Neve.

'To feel safe,' says Sally sadly. 'It helped her with nightmares she used to have. That's what Margaret said, anyway.'

When Neve comes off the phone she stands immobile for a few moments, picturing the sad, delicate woman she met on Waterloo Bridge crawling into that miserable space, trying to make a nest, huddled against the scary things in her head.

If the scary things *were* only in her head . . .

Neve swallows.

It's either a terrifying thought, or the saddest thing she has ever heard in her life.

And it is this that suddenly galvanizes her. She won't allow herself to be like that frightened woman hiding in a cupboard.

She's going to bloody well find out what has been going on in this house. And then, only then, can she think about what to do next.

She eyes the pile of post that she picked up on the first day, still sitting on the kitchen table. It's as good a place to start as any.

It's mainly junk mail.

There is a letter in a brown envelope, addressed to 'Isabelle Aster Shawcross' about an overdue smear test from a surgery in Truro. Neve moves on to look at the small number of Christmas cards. She is about to throw these away – it's too morbid to see cheery greetings to a dead woman. But then she decides she ought to open each one, in case they contain any useful information at all.

None of the cards seem to have messages beyond the most basic greetings and she quickly tosses them to one side. The final one is thicker, and when she opens it a news cutting falls out.

The card reads:

Dear Isabelle,

I hope this card finds you in good health. You know what Bob is like about things like this but I think you have become friends in this last year and I thought you might like to see this. He's far too shy to show you himself! We are all rather proud of our hero. Hope to see you after the holidays.

Love from us both.

There is one of those address stickers neatly attached on the card that says 'Bob and Linda Dyer' and an address in Sherborne, Dorset. There is a telephone number.

Neve opens out the newspaper cutting and flattens it so she can read. It is from a local newspaper called *The Western Gazette*.

LOCAL TEEN ESCAPES DEATH PLUNGE

A fifteen-year-old from Yeovil was saved by a Sherborne man after the cliff at West Bay subsided onto the beach.

Jade Murphy from the Summerlands area of Yeovil was walking along the clifftop when the cliff face began to crumble.

Retired policeman Robert Dyer of Westbury, Sherborne, was passing at the time and thankfully was able to pull the young woman to safety after she was carried over the side of the cliff. The ex Detective Inspector said, 'I could hear someone crying and realized what had happened. I was able to lie down and slowly help Jade back up.'

Jade said, 'It was so scary. I thought I was going to die.'

West Bay is a popular tourist spot and was used as the setting in the television drama *Broadchurch*, which caused a spike in visitor numbers according to the local Chambers of Commerce. A spokesman said, 'We have been aware of the serious erosion affecting the cliff for some time and the whole area will have to be made safe. It may be some time before the walkway is open again and we apologize for any inconvenience.'

Neve looks at the picture and something pings in her brain. She holds it closer to her face and stares at the middle-aged man who is smiling shyly at the camera.

It's *him*, she's sure of it.

It's the man who was lurking around the house on that first morning here – the one who dashed away in such a panic.

She sits back and picks up the card again.

I think you have become friends in this last year.

Why would a woman of Isabelle's age and background

make friends with some old policeman? And why was he hanging around so furtively?

She lets out a long, slow breath.

It has to be connected with the prison visits. It fits, but she has no idea how.

Neve is aware she is breathing faster now. She reaches for her phone and taps it against her thigh, thoughtfully.

Then, before she can talk herself out of it, she picks up the card again and presses in the telephone number printed on the sticker.

It rings three or four times before being answered.

'Hello?' The middle-aged voice is clear and friendly.

'Uh,' says Neve, realizing she has no idea where to begin. 'I'm, uh, I'd like to speak to Robert Dyer please.'

There is a long pause.

'And who is it speaking?' The woman's voice has tightened now.

'It's . . .' Neve hesitates and then finishes in a rush. 'I'm a friend of Isabelle Shawcross.'

She can hear the woman's breathing on the other end before she says, 'Please wait a moment.'

Neve waits. The woman calls, 'Bob!' in an urgent tone and then there are threads of a whispered conversation she can't quite hear in the background. This seems to go on for some time and she is about to call out to remind them she is still there when a deep male voice finally answers.

'This is Bob Dyer.'

Neve takes a breath. Where to start? She doesn't want to screw this up.

But the words are coming out before her brain has given them the proper clearance.

'Hi,' she says, 'My name's Neve Carey. You don't know me, but I'm the person living in Petty Whin Cottage now.

You were here. You drove off before I could speak to you. Look, I need to talk to you.'

There is another long pause.

'Hello?' she says. 'Are you still there?'

'Look, Miss . . . Carey was it?' says Dyer. 'We are all very upset about what happened to Isabelle. But I don't think there is anything to discuss now.'

'No, but I just want to—'

But he interrupts her.

'I'll say goodbye.'

The phone goes dead.

'What the *hell*?' Neve lets out a long breath of exasperation.

She sits there for a few moments, simmering with irritation, and then she punches in the number again.

'Hello?' The woman answers this time, wary and cold.

'Look, I'm sorry to be pushy,' says Neve in a rush. 'But I only wanted to ask your husband a few things. I don't want to intrude or upset him. It's just that she left me this cottage and I don't know why and there are some odd things going on and . . . well, I just want to know, that's all.' Her words ebb away.

'Look.' The woman's voice is quiet now, intimate in her ear. 'Bob's devastated about what happened to Isabelle. He thought he was helping. Doing the right thing. And now all he thinks is that it's his fault. So please.' The woman's voice trembles. 'Just leave him alone.'

She hangs up before Neve can say another word.

30

Neve sits, simmering and perplexed, for a few minutes before getting up and pacing around the kitchen. Glancing at the window there she tries to ignore the feeling that the fast-falling snow outside is a shroud that will seal her inside the cottage.

It feels like she is back to square one. The dog makes a small sound then and she guiltily remembers she didn't even get round to sorting out his bed with the blanket.

Squatting down to his level, she murmurs soft words and strokes his velvety head. A long shudder passes through him and he begins to pant, his long pink tongue lolling to the side.

Worriedly, Neve quickly starts to touch him all over and quickly finds that he is hurt on the left side of his ribcage.

'Oh you poor doggy,' she murmurs. Jarvis thumps his tail a few times in a game attempt to look lively. Neve leans down and kisses him on the top of the head. 'What am I going to do, Jarvis?'

She gets up and begins to pace up and down the kitchen. Living in the middle of nowhere like this without a car is almost impossible.

But if it is her fault that the dog is injured, then it's her responsibility to do something, isn't it? This has to be her immediate priority.

'Shit,' she says out loud and reaches for her iPad again.

A quick search reveals that the nearest vet is in Truro. Neve makes an appointment then looks for a taxi number, wondering if she'll get the same bloke who brought her here.

She carefully checks all the windows are closed and the back door bolted, while she waits.

Half an hour later she receives a text message to say the taxi is in the lane and she helps Jarvis to his feet. The dog whimpers again and resists but with gentle coaxing she is able to get his lead on and get him to the door.

It's a different driver this time, a thin, Asian man with a small moustache. He gives a friendly smile as she climbs into the back. But then he notices the dog and his expression changes.

'It's an emergency,' says Neve forcefully. 'I have to take him to the vet.'

The taxi driver sighs with exaggerated forbearance and gets out to find a blanket, which he lays on the back seat.

Neve thanks him and is about to close the front door when she has a thought.

She hurries back to the study and picks up the laptop.

'Is there a computer shop in Truro?' she says.

'Yeah, not far from where you're going.'

'Great.'

Neve climbs into the taxi and coaxes a reluctant Jarvis onto the back seat. As they drive down the lane, with flakes of snow fluttering against the windscreen like white butterflies, she feels a powerful urge never to come back.

*   *   *

199

Neve sits now in the noisy reception of the vet's office, chewing anxiously on a nail and worrying about what this is going to cost. She's never owned a pet but aren't vets notoriously expensive?

There are several dogs, some of which are barking with eardrum-piercing intensity. Other people sit with cat cages at their feet, or huddled protectively on their laps. A small, pinched-face woman darts nervous glances around at the other waiting people as if she thinks someone might steal her cat/guinea pig/rabbit.

Neve sighs and tries to distract herself by looking at her phone. She has used up almost all her storage according to a persistent message she has been ignoring for weeks. She spends some time now deleting photos and apps she no longer uses. She notices several she doesn't remember adding: a time-saving app, a kids' game and one she's never noticed before that seems to have something to do with navigation. She is about to delete them when her name is called out.

The vet is a young woman with a high, dark brown ponytail. After a friendly enough start, the temperature in the room seems to change. She glances sharply at Neve, then continues to probe expertly around Jarvis's body, the dog panting with nerves but otherwise meekly accepting her ministrations.

Neve shifts from foot to foot and waits for the verdict.

Finally, the vet looks up, her eyes somewhere to the left of Neve's face.

'I think the dog has injured ribs,' she says. 'I could x-ray but if you don't have pet insurance that's going to be very expensive.'

'Oh,' says Neve. 'If it's not essential then I'd rather you didn't. He's not even my dog,' she says, blushing a bit. 'What do you think happened? How did he do it?' She has given the vet a half-baked version of the story, too ashamed to admit she allowed the dog to be lost.

For the first time the woman looks at Neve directly. Her expression flat.

'I think the bruising is indicative of a kick, if you want my honest opinion.'

Neve gasps and covers her mouth with both hands. Tears spring to her eyes.

'Oh God, poor Jarvis,' she says, stroking the dog's head.

'Do you have any idea how this happened?' The vet's voice is slightly less icy now and Neve quickly mumbles out the story of Jarvis being lost, her shoulders rounded by the shame.

'Okay,' says the vet. 'I'm going to give him an oral dose of Tramadol for the pain and you need to rest him for a few days. But when his owner comes back he should bring him in to see us. We can sort out whether he has insurance and see if he needs more meds or an x-ray.'

'Thank you,' says Neve in a small voice and strokes Jarvis some more. 'Poor, poor dog.'

Who kicked him? Could it have been Matty? But why? He was helping by bringing the dog back to her, wasn't he?

When she is given the printed bill at reception Neve has to stop herself from yowling, like a hidden cat in one of the baskets in the waiting room.

The consultation and medicine together have come to £97. Neve hands over her bank card with a sick sensation in her stomach. That's the money she will earn from looking after Jarvis wiped out then, and more. This jobless situation cannot go on much longer.

Next she heads to the computer shop, a sleepy Jarvis dragging along reluctantly.

Inside the shop, a young bearded man in a T-shirt that

says *Normal People Scare Me* taps expertly for a few moments and then tells her that the laptop has been formatted.

'But some data can be recovered if you can leave it with us?' he says.

'How much will it cost?'

He shrugs. 'About forty-five pounds, I reckon.'

Neve hesitates. She can't afford this. But it might help her to understand Isabelle a little more.

'Okay, yes please. Go ahead.'

She gets a different driver on the way back, a middle-aged woman with dyed black hair and a throaty smoker's laugh, who chats to her about dogs (the driver has three) most of the way back to the cottage.

Neve's spirits fluctuate between a satisfaction at having sorted out some important things, which also included sending a card to Miri, and despair about how much money she has had to spend in the last day. The small pot of her inheritance is shrinking so much that soon she will have nothing left.

A quick calculation tells her she has about £180 to her name now. No job. No prospect of a job.

But she does have a house in a touristy county. And Sally's daughter might want to buy it.

She just hopes it can be done quickly when the time comes.

But not yet. She'll never be able to live with taking that money if she doesn't find a way to shed light on this darkness that shrouds the cottage.

The snow has stopped but the world outside the window in the greying light of the afternoon is still otherworldly and beautiful. She strokes the sleeping dog's head as the car gets ever closer to the place she doesn't want to be.

* * *

As she pays the taxi driver and thanks her, she tries to shrug off the sensation she is returning to a tomb.

Jarvis is sleepy from the medication and she has to encourage him to walk with her from the lane to the cottage. When she arrives at the front door she looks down at the ground and freezes. There are large footprints, which seem to go from the lane around the side of the property.

Heart seeming to ricochet in her ribcage, she follows the footprints and sees that they go to the back door and then towards the woodpile.

Something is wrong about what she sees, in the bright, unearthly glow cast by the snow. Something that doesn't add up.

And then, with a bolt of electric shock blasting through her, she realizes.

The axe that was there before.

It's gone.

31

Neve runs back to the front of the house, dragging the sleepy dog, who seems to be twice as heavy as usual. Her shoulders are hunched, as though this will ward off a blow, and her eyes dart around wildly. All she can picture is a large figure looming out of the fringes of the garden, axe held aloft before it crashes down onto her, splitting her in half. Whimpering with terror she manages to unlock the three bolts with shaking, cold hands and she and the dog almost fall into the cottage.

She slams the door behind her and quickly locks it again. Jarvis, awake now, sits neatly in the middle of the hallway, regarding her with a wary expression that unnerves her even more. Even the dog has stopped feeling like a comfort now; he is an added vulnerability.

Neve begins to slap on every light she can reach without walking across the dark room. She hurries into the kitchen and grabs the knife that had been under the bed. She holds it aloft, her back to the sink, and breathes heavily.

She looks around. After a few moments she registers something surprising.

Her uppermost emotion right now is not fear, but total, white-hot fury.

She will not be reduced to a gibbering wreck, hiding in a cupboard.

No.

'Right, you bastard,' she says, voice obscenely loud in the still room. 'Just try it. Just see what happens.'

Jarvis yawns and climbs into his bed. Neve reaches into her pocket for her phone.

Her hands are shaking as she taps in 999. She feels time telescoping and taking her back to that bitter night on Waterloo Bridge, when all this began.

She doesn't care if they patronize her. Bollocks to them.

When the operator puts her through to the police, she's asked what help is required.

'Someone is trying to scare me,' she says. As soon as the words leave her mouth, she realizes how lame they sound; not like a proper emergency at all.

The woman on the other end asks questions without any apparent judgement and gets Neve to talk her through what has happened at the cottage to frighten her. Neve tells her about Jarvis going missing, cringing as she does so, because she knows how it sounds, then in a bolder voice she describes the footprints and the axe now having disappeared.

The controller tells her a patrol car will call in some time this evening.

Neve hangs up and a strange thought from childhood drifts into her mind. When she had been told off for something, or if she felt she was being ignored, she would say, 'You'll wish I was still here if I was dead.'

Combined with her scrunched fists and determined frown, it used to make her parents laugh indulgently. Now though, all she can think about is the police car rolling up hours from now and her mutilated corpse waiting inside the cottage.

She moves tentatively to the kitchen table and sits down, still holding the knife, and tries to think this through.

Could it be a mistake? Could someone have borrowed the axe without telling her? Is that the sort of thing people did in the country? She itches to call Sally but is aware how needy and pathetic this is. Their son has already had to deliver back the dog she failed to look after properly.

But her mind keeps ping-ponging between two places.

What, though, if someone really *had* got into the cottage this morning and let Jarvis out? That might mean that they have a key and all the locks she is currently relying on are useless.

Neve's eyes dart to the back door. There is a stiff, rusty bolt at the top of the door which doesn't look as if it has been used for a while. No one can undo bolts from the other side, can they . . .?

With difficulty she tries to get it to close and, after a moment, it moves suddenly, painfully trapping the skin of her knuckle.

She sucks the blood away and blinks back hot tears, determined not to cry. If she starts now, she won't ever stop.

The knock at the front door, half an hour later, makes her leap up from the table. She had been drinking a cup of coffee and eating some cereal, despite having a stomach that feels like a closed fist.

As she opens the front door there is a reassuring static emission from a police radio. A short, round female officer with chestnut bobbed hair and keen dark eyes peers at her. Next to her is a male officer, who is tall and thin with heavy brows. His face is folded into grumpy wrinkles.

'Thank God you're here,' says Neve and barely manages to resist the urge to hug them.

* * *

Inside they sit at the table. Slowly, and carefully, Neve goes through the whole story, from being left the cottage in the first place (which prompts an exchange of raised eyebrow glances) to the magpie, Jarvis's escape and injury, to getting back tonight and seeing the axe is missing.

She is aware that they haven't made many notes when she finishes. The silence in the kitchen makes the back of her neck prickle with irritation.

'Look, I know what you're thinking,' she blurts at last. The female police officer's expression remains impassive.

'What's that then?' she says.

Neve hesitates. 'Well, I know how it sounds. You probably think I've let my imagination run riot.'

There is another pause and then the policeman speaks. 'Is it something about this property, Miss, er, Carey?'

Neve frowns. 'What do you mean?'

They exchange glances again.

'Well,' says the policewoman, 'it's just that we have been here before you see. When the previous, uh, owner was here. She seemed to be convinced that she was in danger in some way, despite taking, uh, security precautions.'

Neve leans forward and places her hands flat on the table, palms down.

'I *know*,' she says. 'Bars! Doesn't that make you wonder? That maybe there really is someone lurking around?'

She has to swallow back the quavering note in her voice now.

The policewoman regards her and then sighs.

'We never did find anything out of the ordinary here,' she says. 'But we are very happy to do a thorough search now if that will make you feel happier?'

'Yes.' Neve nods her head vigorously. 'Yes it would.'

They get up and the woman begins to wander about the cottage, while the male officer asks her to open the back

207

door so he can look out there. With difficulty, she opens the bolt again and he thanks her and takes out a thin torch, which he switches on as he goes outside.

Neve hovers nervously in the kitchen. She half hopes they will find something odd, and half hopes they won't. It's hard to work out which scenario would be the least terrifying.

Jarvis pays little attention to what is going on from his basket, only occasionally looking up and giving his tail a few desultory thumps.

The female officer comes back into the kitchen and says the property seems to be secure.

The back door opens again then and the male officer stands in the doorway. He is holding the axe.

'Is this the item you were referring to?' he says.

Neve feels heat flooding her face and neck.

'Yes,' she says. 'Where was it?'

The policeman looks at his colleague and then back at Neve.

'It was just to the side of the wood pile,' he says. 'Can you tell me if that's where it usually stays?'

Neve chews her lip, frowning. 'Sort of,' she says. 'But it's usually on the top. That's where it was before.'

'Don't you think it's possible that it simply . . . fell down?' His tone is so reasonable that Neve feels herself get even hotter and redder.

'I don't see how,' she says, raising her chin and meeting his gaze directly.

'You don't see how,' he repeats. A wave of anger shudders through her.

The woman officer sighs again.

'Look,' she says, 'we understand that it's quite remote out here. It's not for everyone. If you're not used to the quiet, to the strange noises that old houses make . . . well, it can be . . .' she seems to hunt for the right word, 'unsettling for some people.' She pauses and her expression is sympathetic for the first time. 'I think the last lady here was . . . quite highly strung, shall we say, and maybe it got to her. Maybe you might want to think about whether this is the right place for you to be living too?'

Neve breathes slowly through her nose and tries to muster the frostiest expression she can manage, despite the fact her nose is reddening and her vision threatening to become a watery blur.

'How do you explain the dog getting out then?' she says, her voice letting her down by wobbling. 'And the footprints? Look, they're just . . .'

She points wildly at the floor, but there is now no evidence they were ever there. The room seems to lurch and tilt for a moment. Neve's head pulses with confusion.

She's going mad. This must be how it starts.

The male officer's voice cuts into her thoughts.

'Miss Carey, didn't you tell us you'd been out drinking the night this happened? And that you were feeling unwell?'

The implication is clear.

'The magpie,' she says, with a defiant lift of her chin. 'What about the fucking dead magpie then?'

'There's no need to raise your voice or use bad language,' says the female officer and the injustice and frustration of this fizz almost painfully. 'But,' she continues, 'I will admit this could be unsettling, especially to someone from London, who isn't used to the actions of wildlife.'

Neve's emotions begin to still again and she stares coldly back at the two police officers.

'Right,' she says. 'It's quite clear how you made Isabelle feel. And now I'm the second hysterical female to be bothering you, aren't I?'

The male officer starts to speak but Neve's high-pitched squawk of sarcastic laughter seems to surprise them all.

'It's okay,' she says. 'Off you go then. I'll be alright. There are no axe murderers around here, that's for sure. Go on, off you go.'

They exchange glances.

'Miss Carey, if there's anything else we can—'

'No,' says Neve. Too loud again. Too shrill. 'You go and get on with more important police business now. Sorry to have inconvenienced you. I'm all good here, that's for sure.'

'And anyway,' she adds. 'I've got this brilliant guard dog, haven't I?'

All three of them look at Jarvis.

Dreaming heavily, he sticks out a shivering back leg and the kitchen fills with a noxious smell.

A few minutes later she is alone again. She puts on Radio 6 in the sitting room loudly and then goes back and unplugs the radio from the wall. She doesn't trust that radio.

Going back into the kitchen she, somewhat guiltily, wakes up the dog and encourages him to come sit by her side.

'I don't like it here, Jarvis,' she says out loud. 'It's a horrible shitty, creepy cottage and I wish I'd never gone anywhere near Waterloo Bridge that night. I don't like it, and I don't want it.'

She hates herself for being so weak, so 'hysterical' as the police clearly thought. She tries to imagine what it felt like for Isabelle, here in this house, becoming increasingly frightened. So frightened she went to the extremes of getting bars put on the windows.

So frightened that she killed herself?

Neve reaches for the prison band on the table and then remembers the note in the pocket of Isabelle's waxed jacket.

When she gets up the dog gratefully slinks back to his basket.

She walks back into the kitchen, studying the limp piece of notepaper.

HMP LL 14107116. PBH date TBC

Neve pours herself a glass of wine and goes to the table, where she stares at the piece of paper.

The HMP LL part is clear now – Her Majesty's Prison Low Linney. What does PBH mean though? She searches her brain for the possible meaning of the initials but finds nothing.

Neve grabs one of the envelopes she opened earlier and hadn't cleared away and picks up an old Biro that she finds on the table.

She starts to doodle the word 'Prison' and then makes a mind map of words associated.

Bars

Screws

Drug

Lock up

Break out

Free

Parole

The words begin to come to her and soon she finds herself writing down the word, 'Parole' and then, faster, 'Parole board'.

She looks at the note again and the meaning seems to float up from the back of her brain, as though it had been waiting there for her all along.

PBH.

Parole Board Hearing.

Her mind is racing now.

This prisoner that Isabelle was visiting, maybe he was coming out? And if so, could he be the person who was frightening her? But why visit him?

She shifts in her seat. This man could be on the loose, trying to freak out Neve for reasons of his own. This thought causes a sudden sick lurch in her stomach. Her brain floods again with images of hulking men with hidden faces; knives, axes held within meaty hands. Watching her from outside.

From inside . . .

'Get a fucking grip!' she says out loud and the dog starts.

Come on, she says, inside her head now. Think this through. Be systematic for once. Be the logical person. Think about it like Lou would.

So, if there was a person like that on the scene, why would Isabelle go to visit him? Neve taps her fingers on the table rhythmically and tries to think this through.

Whatever was going on, she has a feeling that Bob Dyer, the policeman, is connected in some way. Why was he watching the cottage? Why did he rush away?

Neve reaches for the Christmas card and looks at the address inside:

6, The Fairway, Sherborne, Dorset.

She has no idea how far away this is, or how she will get there. But she doesn't think she can sell this cottage without understanding what happened to Isabelle here.

Bob Dyer seems like the only person who can help her right now.

32

I was doing so well.

Despite grieving for Granny, I was really getting back on my feet. Forcing myself to take on her beloved garden helped, as did the presence of old Jarvis.

And now all I can think about is HIM again.

My letter to the parole board was cathartic but ultimately pointless. He's coming out anyway.

The words in their letter are seared onto my brain even though I ripped it into tiny shreds and then burned it in the kitchen sink.

'We can assure you that the Parole Board fully took the matters you raised into account in its decision-making process. However, the Board concluded that in the light of the length of sentence served, positive reports about his behaviour and the prisoner's recent ill-health, he is safe to be released.'

Safe? I'll never feel safe again.

I thought I was being so brave, booking that visit, when I had word the hearing was due. I knew there must be a chance he would be freed. He had been a 'model prisoner' according to Bob's research.

I suppose I thought if I saw him in the flesh, I could lay it all to rest once and for all.

What a bloody fool I am.

He seemed so ORDINARY. He could have been any whey-faced, overweight, elderly man.

He didn't speak at first, just sat there drumming his stubby fingers on the leg of his grey prison trousers. I made myself sit there for several minutes, looking straight at him. I could see he was uncomfortable and I was glad. How can monsters be so . . . normal? That was what felt so strange, after years of seeing him as twenty feet tall in my imagination for all those years.

I forced myself to utter a single word after a few minutes. The only possible word.

'Why?'

He stared at me with his watery green eyes and for a second something shifted in his expression. He muttered, 'It was a long time ago. I was a different man.' His voice was reedy and high.

There seemed to be no reason to stay after that. I felt suddenly exhausted and I got up to leave. As I was about to walk away he said in a quiet voice, 'Isabelle Shawcross . . .' drawing out all the syllables in an almost luxurious way.

I flinched. Then I realized; he would know my name if I was accepted as a visitor. I didn't even think to tell the prison to withhold that information. And then . . . and then a slow smile spread across his face and he said, 'You look just like her, you know. Same eyes. I remember them still. How they looked up at me.'

I just about managed to get out of the room to get to the Ladies to be sick. There was something so malignant in that smile. As if he deliberately wanted to frighten me. Bastard, bastard, BASTARD.

My one small comfort was that surely this would stop him getting parole. I mean, how couldn't it?

But as far as they were concerned, he hadn't done anything threatening.

They just didn't care.

And now, according to Bob, today is the day he gets out. All Bob's reassurances about keeping an eye on him don't help.

I thought this cottage would be a haven and now all I see are shadows.

33

Neve stays up late planning her journey. She can get a bus to St Piron, then another to Truro. From there she will get a train to Exeter, then another to Sherborne.

It's going to take the best part of four hours. Neve thinks about her dwindling finances and the prospect of selling the cottage quickly. But it will have to wait. She has to see this through now or it will nag at her for the rest of her life.

She looks down at the sleeping dog. Richard is back in the morning and she is dreading having to explain what happened. She just hopes she won't be made to feel like a neglectful criminal. Neve is already sure he's not going to believe that anything weird is going on in this cottage. He has that air, the patronizing one a lot of men have, as if she is a bit of a fool. Not a proper person, to be taken seriously. A pretty face with a head full of fluff.

Is this what Isabelle felt? That no one believed her?

Neve gets up and does another round of checks on the doors and windows to distract herself from the fear, which feels like it could envelop her, tsunami-like, if she let it. Next she checks the electricity meter, anxiety worming in her stomach about the lights going off, knowing this really would be the end of her.

Checks all done, she picks up the knife and her iPad and persuades a sleepy, reluctant Jarvis to come through to the sitting room with her. The dog gives her a forbearing look and lies at her feet, groaning as he settles into place.

Online, she types 'Women who visit men in prison' into Google and finds there are multiple hits, with titles such as, 'Why do women love men who kill?' and 'The Death Row Brides'.

Neve is soon engrossed. She learns that serial killers such as Ted Bundy and Charles Manson received hundreds of letters from adoring women on the outside. Soham Murderer Ian Huntley has received thousands, she reads, with a shudder. There are even specialist websites with names such as MeetAPrisoner.com and InmatesForYou. com.

An article from an online newspaper quotes 'psychologist Lindy Preston, author of *Women Who Love Killers*' who says, 'the type of women drawn to this sort of behaviour are often those with a very poor body image or problems with self-esteem. It may be that they feel these type of desperate men are the only ones they deserve. Alternatively, they may have a strong religious incentive to make contact with men who have committed terrible acts. They may feel that they will be the ones who will show them forgiveness and reform them.'

Neve sits back and idly strokes Jarvis's back as she takes this in. Was Isabelle one of the desperate ones? Surely not. By anyone's reckoning she was a beautiful woman.

What, though, if she had contacted him and then he got out and stalked her?

But then why does no one around here – the Gardners, Richard Shawcross – seem to have an awareness of it?

Neve gives a growl of frustration that makes Jarvis twitch in his sleep.

None of this really makes any sense. She can only hope that her long trip to Dorset tomorrow will lead to some light being shed on this whole scenario.

She tries to stay awake as long as possible but after a while her eyes are so gritty and sore that she can't stop them from drooping. Her chin keeps jerking to her chest and she awakes with small cries that send her heart frantically pounding in her chest. The sickening jolt of it becomes too much after a while and she begins to surrender, making sure her fist encloses the handle of the knife.

As her body sinks sideways onto the sofa, Neve thinks about the first night, and how the cat came into the house and frightened her. Funny that it has never come back, she thinks, as the irresistible suck and drag of sleep begins to pull her down.

At first she is conscious that it is a dream. She even thinks she speaks to the dog to say so. Then she is riding a bike, for the first time in years, down a country road. Sunlight sparkles through the canopy of trees overhead and the colours of everything are more vibrant than in real life. The grass is bright emerald green and the flowers dotting the side of the road a yellow so sharp it almost hurts her eyes.

Suddenly Lou is next to her, also on a bike. They begin to race, going faster and faster, and at first Lou is laughing, then Neve realizes that her sister is wracked with heart-breaking sobs and begging her to stop.

She takes her feet off the pedals and free-wheels but she is crying now too for some reason and the sadness is almost unbearable. It's like she will never get over this feeling, nor will she be able to stop.

When she does, there is no impact, or sensation of shock. She is just sitting in the road with the bicycle next to her, wheels spinning with a *tick-tick-tick* sound. She looks at her hands and realizes they are slick with blood, up to the elbows as if she has dipped her whole arms into a bucket of gore. She doesn't cry or scream, but feels a sense of great curiosity as she holds them up to the light and studies them. When she looks down at the road again, she sees that the entire surface is red and sticky.

She begins to call out to Lou, to tell her about all this, and the room around her swims back into focus.

With a start, she comes to on the sofa, heart pounding.

What a horrible dream. She touches her forehead. It's burning hot. Her throat hurts again too. Groaning, she rummages for some paracetamol in her handbag, which she swallows with a glug from a bottle of water in there of indeterminate age.

Jarvis is deeply asleep. There's barely even any movement of his ribcage to indicate that he is breathing. She gives him a worried, sharp tap on the flank and he shivers slightly, reassuring her.

Looking at the time she sees it is only five a.m. and it will be hours until it's light. But it is a relief that she is no longer in the deep of the night. For some reason, it feels as though she is safer now that morning is near, however bad she feels.

Yawning widely, she forces herself to sit up straighter. She'll sleep on the bus if she has to. Better to be awake and have her wits about her, she thinks.

Neve opens Facebook and spends a few minutes looking at Miri's page, which is filled with congratulations on the birth of Farah. There are several pictures of the tiny girl, face lost in the black explosion of hair, and one that shows an exhausted-looking, puffy-eyed Miri, managing to smile weakly at the camera.

She taps out a quick message promising to come and visit soon and sending love, then spends some time having a desultory look around friends' posts. There's so much crap here, she thinks and is suddenly filled with a strong desire to clean up this one small area of her life.

She has 900 friends at present and she feels a sensation of disgust. Who are these people? She's sure she has only met the smallest handful of them. She vaguely remembers a flurry of friending after she and Daniel went to the Spanish music festival but things have clearly got out of hand.

Neve begins decisively clicking on names and then the 'unfriend' button. It is therapeutic and she finds she can do it without fully being awake. She continues in a daze like this for a while and whole swathes of names are despatched.

It's quite soothing. She is becoming more ruthless as she goes along, half thinking she might get rid of everyone, or close the account, when she chances upon a name that makes her stop.

The name is Izzy Aster. Something fizzes in Neve's synapses and she gets up hurriedly and goes to the kitchen, where the envelope about the smear test still lies on the table.

Isabelle Aster Shawcross.

That's a coincidence. 'Aster' is such an unusual name. And Izzy could be a shortening of Isabelle?

Unsettled, Neve goes back to the sofa and picks up the iPad again. She clicks on this Izzy Aster and sees there is only a picture of a cat lying on the back of a sofa. She taps on the picture to try and get a closer look but it doesn't expand. The colouring of the cat and the appearance of the sofa are shrouded in shadow. She looks around the room uncertainly, suddenly overcome with the strange notion that the picture was taken in this room. Maybe it was the Gardners' cat.

But she didn't know Isabelle Shawcross when she met her that night. She had never seen her before. And the woman didn't seem to recognize her.

What were the chances that they were already Facebook friends?

No, it must be a weird coincidence.

Nine hundred 'friends' is not a lot when you consider that more than, what was it, eight million people live in London? But all the while she is telling herself this, her heart is fluttering uncomfortably again.

Stop it, she tells herself. She really is starting to lose the plot now. It's only . . . Facebook, for God's sake.

There are no revealing posts on Izzy Aster's page at all, just re-posts of annoying aphorisms with supposedly uplifting messages. She goes to check on their mutual friends and sees that they have none.

'Oh fuck it,' says Neve out loud and at this Jarvis struggles to his feet and stares at her blearily. She leans over and rubs his head. 'I'm really starting to go mental, Jarvis my old mate,' she says and smiles as the dog wags his tail with more vigour than since his mishap that morning. 'Got to get out of this place, haven't we?'

By the time Richard's sharp knock comes at the front door, Neve has been pacing around the house, fully dressed for the cold outside, for a whole ninety minutes. Her hair was dirty so she pulled it up into a messy bun and she knows she isn't looking her best, but Richard's face when she opens the door suggests it is worse than she thought.

He blinks and then stumbles backwards, almost losing his footing.

'Oh,' says Neve stupidly. 'What is it?'

Richard's face is deathly pale, his dark eyes almost black. He opens and closes his mouth and appears unable to speak.

Before she really thinks about it, Neve has hold of his sleeve and is hauling him over the threshold and into the house.

'God, what's wrong, are you sick?' she says and he seems to come back to himself. She can almost see his spine stiffening as he clears his throat.

'I'm fine,' he says, in that clipped tone. 'Really. There's no need to fuss.'

'I'm not *fussing*,' snaps Neve. 'You're being *weird*.'

She glares at him and his eyes shift away from her and down to the dog, who has come ambling out to say hello.

'I'm not having a stroke,' he says, reaching down and patting Jarvis awkwardly. 'Low blood sugar, I expect. Had breakfast too early.'

His attempt at a smile now, a slight upward curve to one side of his mouth, does little to make him look more friendly.

'Right. If you say so,' says Neve doubtfully.

'So, er, has this one been much trouble?' he says as Jarvis lies down heavily between their respective feet.

'No,' she says, 'but about that . . .'

She tells him about Jarvis's unintended trip out of the house and the fact that someone had possibly kicked him. She is blushing with the shame of it as she speaks but Richard merely nods along, as though she is telling him about a perfectly ordinary itinerary.

He doesn't seem to be listening, in fact, so she repeats that the dog will need an x-ray.

'Right,' says Richard. 'If you could just get his things.' He clearly can't wait to leave.

Stupid, annoying man.

As he moves to the front door though, she forces the words out of her mouth before she can change her mind.

'Richard, do you know why Isabelle was visiting a bloke in prison?'

He has his back to her and she sees him freeze before turning, his face fixed.

'No, I er, no, I mean.' His gaze swooshes past, and almost, but doesn't quite, land anywhere near her face. 'My sister had all sorts of lost causes in her time. Bit of a law unto herself.'

'Right,' says Neve tightly. 'Okay then,' she adds in a breathless rush, 'so do you know why she was so scared of living here? Why did she put bars on all the windows?'

There's a silence that seems to expand and suck all the oxygen out of the hallway.

His face is so stricken now that Neve prickles with the rawness of it.

'She was . . .' he says and his eyes seem to cloud and redden '. . . she always had an over-active imagination. Even when we were small children, she would be the one who thought there was a ghost in the wardrobe, or, I don't know, a bogeyman at the window.'

Neve thinks about the old manor house up the road and the constipated emotions of the man in front of her. She is filled with a painful hope that people listened to young Isabelle once. That she was reassured at least when she was a child that the bad things weren't out to get her. But maybe the bad things were real?

'Right, well I think we're all done,' she says and Richard practically runs out of the door. Jarvis looks back at her and she feels a tug in her chest.

He's not her dog. She doesn't live here. It isn't her problem.

An hour later, Neve is shivering on the second bus. The snow had been short-lived, but it was still, she thought, about a thousand times colder than London.

As the countryside unfolds around her she thinks about what she intends to say to Bob Dyer when she arrives at his house. She doesn't even have any guarantee that he is going to be there. It's entirely possible that he will be off golfing, or going on a cruise, or whatever retired policemen do in their spare time.

When Neve gets to Exeter, she feels an intense pleasure at being in a city again, albeit a small city. She is overwhelmed by a desire to drink all the good coffee she can find; to buy shoes that will be useless in the countryside and impractical tops in thin, floaty fabrics that are only of use in warm offices and bars. Despite her woolly head and sore throat, she wants to cram it all in, to take it with her when she returns to that lonely cottage again.

She looks around, blinking like a country mouse. She would never have countenanced walking around London looking such a state. This thought seems to pull the plug somewhere inside her and all her enthusiasm swirls and drains away. What was she thinking? She has no money to spend here.

She has no job, no boyfriend. She has nothing, apart from that bloody depressing cottage she doesn't even want and perhaps an inherited stalker.

No mum and dad to look after her any more.

Neve's throat constricts and she squeezes her eyes shut. When she was going out every weekend, having a laugh with Daniel and her friends, it was easier not to be sad.

But she has been alone with herself in this past, strange week, and it's like something is waiting. Something huge and painful, with the potential to smother her.

Neve decides she will have that coffee, hang the cost. And she'll have the biggest cake she can find to go with it, despite her churning stomach.

She is hoping to doze on the train, despite the fact that there is a portly man in a suit whose phone pings with messages every five seconds opposite her and a woman with a disgruntled, whiny toddler across the aisle.

But she makes a pillow out of her jacket and leans against the window, anyway, hoping for some peace from all the thoughts that seem to knot and gather there. This might be a pointless journey. But she's doing something proactive, rather than sitting in the cottage and feeling frightened.

It's only when she feels wetness against her face that she realizes she has been deeply asleep and drooling on her makeshift pillow. There had been no dreams, no awareness of anything happening around her. Simply the soft blackness her body had needed.

She blinks and stretches her stiff neck. Her hair is all bunched up on one side and she attempts to pat it back vaguely into place. The businessman is openly staring at her and she gives him one of her looks. The woman with the toddler has got off the train now and Neve suddenly experiences a moment of panic that she has missed her stop. She doesn't want to have to ask the creep opposite and is saved by an announcement saying that Templecombe is next. Quickly looking at the app on her phone she sees this is the stop before Sherborne.

Neve spends the last few minutes of her journey practising what she is going to say to Bob Dyer.

You HAVE TO tell me what was going on. Who did she visit in prison? Was she in danger? Am I in danger too?

As the train pulls away from Templecombe station, there's an announcement that Sherborne is the next stop.

34

Pale winter sun bathes the small market town as she makes her way out of the station.

Following the instructions on Google maps on her phone, she walks down a long road and finds herself in front of a breathtaking abbey of pale gold brick, which stands majestic in neatly tended grounds. The bells ring out then, rich and strong, and the sound soothes her nerves a little, albeit momentarily.

She walks up a narrow high street busy with shoppers that is crammed with delis and upmarket clothes shops, or small gift shops selling trinkets and expensive kitchenware. The town has a holiday, touristy air. She thinks about how much her mum would have loved poking about in those shops looking for souvenirs.

At the top of the high street she takes a left and it is a matter of minutes before she finds herself outside a row of narrow two-storey houses with a sign saying 'The Fairway'. The houses look relatively new, but have been built in the local light stone and match the surrounding, older cottages.

Neve's mouth is dry and she takes a swig from the water bottle in her handbag. Her hands are shaking a little. She feels like a fake reporter, without any of the nerve or skills to carry it off.

She makes herself lift her hand to ring the doorbell, practising what she might say.

Nothing happens. She rings again and tries to peer in through the net curtains covering the bay window at the front of the house. A dog barks inside, a high-pitched yapping indicative of no one else being there.

'Bugger,' she says with feeling. 'Bugger, *bugger*.'

Neve is suddenly so tired and dispirited that she feels as though her legs won't hold her weight any longer. She sinks down onto the step, feeling the cold bite through her clothes. She puts her head in her hands and lets out a frustrated squeal, thinking about the money she has wasted getting here.

She sits like this for several moments, until, sensing movement nearby, she looks up.

'What on earth are you doing on our doorstep?'

The couple are in their sixties. It's definitely *him*. The man who came to the cottage that first day and ran away. Bulky in a black rain jacket, he is carrying several Sainsbury's bags. The woman looks a little younger, with short hair that's shot through with multiple highlights in colours ranging from russet to yellow blonde. She is dressed in a smart quilted jacket with the collar up and holds a basket looped over her elbow, her hand extended. A pair of sunglasses are perched neatly on her head.

Neve jumps to her feet, blushing furiously. She attempts a friendly smile to show she is a normal, harmless person, and not a mad woman intending damage to their doorstep.

'I'm Neve,' says Neve, the smile on her face becoming a rictus now. 'We've met before, haven't we?'

'I'm sorry,' says Bob Dyer, face set. 'But I really don't see any need to talk to you. Come on Linda.'

Bob Dyer glares at his wife, who stares at him for a moment, and then back at Neve. She lets out a sigh and then reaches into her pocket, bringing out keys.

'Excuse me,' she says, her voice soft and apologetic and Neve hesitates before moving away from the doorstep.

'Look, why won't you just talk to me?' she says, unable to keep the whiny desperation out of her voice as the door opens and the couple bustle past her and go inside.

'There's simply no good that can come of it,' he says. 'I'm sorry.'

The woman, Linda, also mouths 'Sorry' at Neve as she keeps on speaking, her voice getting louder and her words faster. 'I just want to know what was going on! Why was she going to Low Linney prison! Who was she scared of!'

She murmurs 'Please' pathetically as the door is closed firmly.

'Shit!' Neve kicks a small clod of mud that is next to her boot on the pavement. 'Shit!'

She pulls up her collar with hands that shake with frustration and anger and begins to walk down the road fast. A complete waste of time, all of it. What was she even thinking, coming here? This isn't her business. What an idiot she is.

Her phone rings suddenly and she takes it from her bag, filled with an illogical surge of hope that it's Bob Dyer, with a change of heart. She doesn't recognize the caller's number and she quickly answers, a little breathlessly.

'Hello?'

'Yes, hello,' says a cultured voice. 'This is Georgia McColl. I'm outside your cottage waiting to come in and do the valuation we booked?'

'Shit!' she says again. 'I mean, I'm really sorry. Something came up. I'm not there today. Can we re-arrange?'

There is a tight pause before Georgia McColl speaks. She sounds clipped now.

'I guess we can, if you can guarantee you will be here.'

Neve issues flurries of apologies and agrees that the estate agent can come back tomorrow. She hadn't sounded at all pleased to be stood up, but Neve doesn't have the brain space left to feel guilty about this.

She walks slowly back down the high street, thinking about the long journey back to the cottage. The train back to Exeter isn't for another hour. She stops in front of a coffee shop and, despite being neither hungry, nor thirsty, pushes open the door to the steamy, warm interior.

There are only a few tables, which are all taken, but she is lucky; a couple of elderly ladies in matching Barbour jackets are just getting up. They talk at the same time in loud upper-class voices as they harvest handbags and stout shopping bags. Neve manages a weak smile of gratitude as she slips past them into the waiting seat by the window.

The waitress comes over after a few moments. She's a small, round woman about Neve's age, her hair in a tight ponytail that gives her a startled appearance as she asks Neve what she's having.

For a moment, Neve feels overwhelmed by the mental processes involved in this exchange. She can't remember the last time she had a proper sleep, all night, and in a bed in which she felt safe. Not sober, anyway. It's only when she realizes the waitress is now looking at her a bit oddly that she forces herself to make a decision.

'Can I have a Coke please,' she says. 'I mean a fat one. Not Diet.'

The waitress nods and says, 'Right-oh,' before leaving her alone. She rests her head in her hands, feeling that her hair is greasy, and closes her eyes. Her body feels as heavy as if it were made of a series of sandbags. The prospect of dragging the weight of herself all the way back to Truro, and then on a bus to the cottage, seems like a thing of enormous difficulty.

There is nowhere for her to be. Nowhere she can kick off her shoes, puff out her cheeks and say, 'It's good to be home.'

She's suddenly aware of a movement on the other side of the window and she looks up blearily to see the policeman's wife, Linda Dyer, peering in at her.

She gives a decisive little nod and then opens the door to the café.

'Good,' she says breezily, once inside. 'I'm glad I found you. I've been looking all the way down the high street. You mustn't mind my Bob. He's a very good man but he isn't good with people he doesn't know. Can I sit here? I'll just get a green tea.'

All this is delivered in a rush of words and a cloud of perfume is left as Linda takes off her coat and throws it on the chair before going over to the counter.

Neve studies her as she chats to the woman serving as though they are best friends. She is small, only around five feet tall, wearing neat boots with a heel, and fitted jeans. Her hair, now Neve looks at it properly, is of the style that must require constant blow-drying and attention in order not to collapse around her head. Her face is immaculately made-up.

A few moments later she comes back to the table with a steaming mug and sits down in the chair opposite Neve, where she studies her openly.

'So,' says Neve hesitantly, 'Bob and Isabelle were friends?'

Linda nods, eyes still scanning Neve's face. 'That's right.'

'I saw him,' says Neve. 'Near the cottage.'

There is a long pause. 'Wanted to lay flowers at her grave,' says Linda. 'Couldn't get her out of his mind. Such

230

a waste.' She lifts the cup and blows onto the surface before taking a small, birdlike sip. 'Then he thought he ought to check on her place. Make sure it was all in order. Didn't expect anyone to be there.'

Linda takes another sip before speaking again.

'So,' she says. 'How did you know Isabelle in the first place?'

Neve hesitates. She has told this story several times now and it isn't sounding any better with repetition.

'I didn't know her,' she says wearily. 'She was a random person I met on a bridge. I don't even want the bloody cottage.' She realizes this is a non-sequitur by the puzzled pinch of Linda's brow and continues in haste. 'Isabelle gave it to me. Just handed it over to me and I'm not exactly in a position to say no to a free house so . . .' she shrugs and tails off.

'What do you need from my Bob then?' says Linda, her expression even. Neve momentarily sees a flash of what might be the steely core under this perfumed, coiffed exterior.

'I don't know, is the God's honest answer,' says Neve with an attempt at a smile. 'But I think he knows something. I think someone is trying to freak me out and it's connected to the fact that Isabelle was going to see someone in prison.' She pauses, seeing Linda's expression become more focused now. 'Low Linney prison,' says Neve, studying the other woman's face.

She leans forward and lowers her voice.

'Who was it?' she says forcefully. 'You know, don't you?'

Linda lets out a long sigh and sits back in her seat. She takes a moment to sip the tea. The earthy, mulchy smell drifts up Neve's nose unpleasantly.

'Let me ask you a question,' she says quietly. 'Does the name Sofie Lindstrom ring any bells?'

Neve gives this careful thought.

'Nope, don't think so.'

Linda makes a regretful face. 'Well, I suppose it was almost what, thirty years ago now. Time was when everyone recognized that name. For all the wrong reasons.'

'So,' says Neve, 'who is she?'

'Who *was* she.' Linda lifts her cup thoughtfully to her lips and then lowers it again without drinking anything. Neve feels instinctively that she needs to wait, to not press.

'Sofie Lindstrom,' she says after a moment in a heavy voice, 'was a young mother of two who was murdered, brutally murdered, by a man called John Denville.' Linda's mouth curls in distaste as she says the latter name.

'What happened?' says Neve softly. She's aware that she is suddenly breathing shallowly.

Linda lets out a long sigh, her eyes distant. 'Bob had only been a detective for a year,' she says. 'He'd seen murders before, but usually drugs or whatnot. Never anything like this, you see. Nothing quite so . . .' she pauses and looks at the table, 'well, quite so brutal.'

She meets Neve's eyes now. 'He met her when she was a nurse at a local addiction clinic, did Denville. Developed a bit of a thing about her. No one took it very seriously. He was addicted to all sorts of things of course. The usual story.' Linda sniffs dismissively before continuing. 'His defence team claimed he was out of his mind, when he followed her home that day.' She pauses again. 'Stabbed her something like thirty times. Says he didn't even remember doing it.'

'God,' murmurs Neve. 'That's awful.'

'That's not even the worst part,' says Linda, lowering her voice further. Neve has to slightly lean closer. 'Bob said it was the worst thing he has ever seen in his life. Because you see, the kiddies were there. The eldest one was four and the little one only a baby. They were left alone with their dead mother for a whole day.'

Neve can't think of anything to say and simply stares, her lips slightly parted.

'Oh, it must have been terrible,' Linda continues quickly and the edges of her nostrils turn pink. 'The poor little girl had climbed up to get water from the sink and was trying to get her mother to wake up. When Bob and his constable came into the room – they'd had to break in because a friend had been worried – they saw all the blood, and those innocent little children all smeared in it. It was on their hands, their clothes . . .' She visibly shudders and stops speaking.

Neve says something meaningless like, 'How awful.' She's not even sure what comes out of her mouth beyond it being a totally inadequate response to the horrific pictures now flooding her mind.

'And when they tried to get her to come away, she was so hysterical that she bit the police officer. Not Bob,' she adds, as though this were an important detail. 'It was one of his constables. Needed a tetanus shot, the chap, but he never complained about it.' She pauses and her voice has a tone of wonder about it now. 'Never said a thing about it.'

Neve takes a sip of her drink and barely tastes it. Linda is fiddling with her cup and seems reluctant to go on.

'And so,' Neve nudges, 'Isabelle was visiting him, right?' She makes a face of distaste. 'Why? Was she one of those women who gets off on relationships with men in prison?'

Linda turns her gaze back to Neve and her pale green eyes seem to rest on her face for longer than is comfortable. She seems to be debating something internally and Neve begins to feel awkward.

'What?' she says finally. 'What is that you're not saying?'

Linda lets out a long, sad sigh and gives her head a small shake before she speaks.

'She visited him because he was the man who killed her mother.'

'What?' Neve's heart is suddenly pounding in her own ears. 'She's . . .?'

Linda nods sadly. 'Yes. Isabelle was the little girl. She was Sofie Lindstrom's daughter.'

35

'Oh God.' Neve brings both hands to cover her mouth. There isn't enough air in this café. Her lungs are sponges filled with soggy water. The sounds in here are exaggerated – each clink of a spoon sounds like a crashing cymbal and the conversation level presses in on her eardrums.

'Come on,' says Linda decisively. 'You go and wait outside and I'll pay.'

Neve gratefully grabs her coat and bag and almost knocks over the third chair at their table in her haste to get outside. The café door closes behind her and she sucks in the cold winter air.

The story is so upsetting, so . . . vivid, and she suddenly feels such sympathy for Isabelle Shawcross that her whole chest aches with it. But as she starts to feel calmer, she thinks that there are still so many questions left to ask and looks impatiently to see where Linda has got to.

The other woman has moved away from the counter inside, evidently having paid. Now she is delving into her handbag in a hurried manner. She gets out her mobile, frowns and then answers. She begins to speak and then listens intently for a moment. Her expression seems to change and she looks up, almost fearfully, to where Neve is standing.

Linda then puts the phone back into her handbag and hesitates before coming outside.

Her smile seems forced.

'Everything . . . alright?' says Neve.

Linda's smile becomes tighter. Her eyes are not quite meeting Neve's now.

'Yes, that was Bob. I had forgotten there was somewhere I needed to be. I hope you're feeling better?'

'Yes, I'm fine,' says Neve, 'but I still need to—'

'I'm really going to have to go,' says Linda and her voice trembles so slightly Neve isn't sure if she imagined it or not.

'Please!' she puts her hand on Linda's arm and the other woman flinches. 'Can't you tell me why Isabelle went to visit this man? What happened? I'm really grateful for what you've told me so far, but I still don't understand anything really.'

Linda sucks in her breath.

The pavement is narrow and there isn't room for them to stand here with the steady stream of people passing by. An elderly man wrapped up in a scarf and woollen hat looks at them curiously as he steps past them into the street and a mother with a buggy gives Neve a sour look as she dips the wheels down onto the road.

'I'm sorry,' says Linda and Neve sees that her eyes are shining with tears. 'Bob is very upset with me for coming out and finding you. I think he's right that it's a terrible story that needs to be relegated to the past where it belongs. There isn't any good in raking over old coals, is there?'

'But why?' It comes out angrier and louder than Neve intended and she struggles to control herself. 'Why did

Isabelle go to see him? That's what I don't get,' she says more gently. 'Please, Linda. I need to know.'

Linda's nostrils flare as she seems to struggle to control herself. 'She wanted to understand,' she says quietly. 'To understand, and also to try and forgive him. But the sad thing was, she wasn't able to do either.'

'Oh.' Neve feels like there are so many questions left to ask but has no idea where to start. And Linda is already snapping her coat closed at the throat and switching back into her capable, unruffled mode.

'I'm sorry,' she says firmly. 'But I really do have to go. Do what you think best with the cottage. I'm sure Isabelle would understand.'

Linda then pulls her forward into a quick, fierce hug that takes Neve by surprise so she almost stumbles. 'And now I really have to go.' With that she turns away, her small feet in their smart heeled boots tapping out a quick rhythm, head down, as she hurries back up the high street.

Neve lets out a long breath. Her mind is crowded with too many thoughts as she begins to walk back to the station, barely taking in her surroundings. Looking distractedly at her phone for the time, she is aware that the train she was intending to catch back to Exeter leaves in fifteen minutes.

The picture that Linda painted – the tiny girl covered in blood, trying to coax her dead mother to wake up – is so terrible that she experiences a lurch of nausea every time she thinks of it.

No wonder Isabelle was such a screwed-up person, she thinks. But when did she find out?

She wanted to understand the crime and to forgive John Denville . . . that's what Linda had said. 'And she found she wasn't able to do either.'

Was that what had tipped her over the edge? Was the crime just too large and too evil for her to live with for another day?

Or was it the thought of him getting out and stalking her? The thought of this . . . monster watching the cottage causes a surge of nausea.

The station has just two platforms and as Neve looks up at the information board she sees with a pang that the next train going the other way will terminate at London Waterloo.

A powerful surge of homesickness for the capital passes through her and she quickly debates the logistics of changing her ticket. Her mind races as she assesses her dire financial situation and the practical voice inside her head begins to win over.

Where would she stay? She couldn't turn up at Lou's again, not so soon after their falling out. And Miri and Arjan are not a possibility. Not now.

Neve runs through other friends in her mind but there is no one else who she could assume would either have the room for her, or have the room and be prepared to let her stay for more than a night or two. She has no job and no means of paying for rented accommodation after that. And this problem with the cottage isn't going away. She has to get rid of it.

Climbing onto the train a few minutes later, Neve miserably slumps into the nearest seat. Nothing has changed. She is just as trapped as she was a week ago.

The free wi-fi is patchy so she has a frustrating time trying to research John Denville on her phone. The cracked screen also makes it less than satisfactory too.

But she battles on and finds a story that appeared on the *Mirror* website in 2008.

BRIXHAM BUTCHER PRISON ATTACK

John Denville, whose vicious murder of a young mother shocked the nation in 1985, has been moved to another prison after an attack by another inmate.

The now 61-year-old was found guilty of what the Old Bailey judge called, 'one of the most brutal and distressing crimes I have come across in my twenty-year career,' when he stabbed young mother Sofie Lindstrom (26) thirty times in the kitchen of her Brixham home.

Sofie, who was of Swedish heritage, had two children who were believed to be present at the time. The four-year-old girl and a boy, believed to be almost one, were later cared for by social services and are believed to have been adopted into different families.

Denville became fixated on Lindstrom after meeting her at a local addiction clinic, where she was a nurse. The single parent, a widow, was known locally as something of a Samaritan. According to one neighbour, 'she was always kind to waifs and strays. She could see the good in everyone.'

The jury took just one hour to deliberate, unanimously finding Denville guilty of murder. It later transpired he had a string of previous convictions for crimes including domestic violence and the non-fatal stabbing of a man in a pub brawl.

The judge, his Honour Judge Benedict Browne QC, said when sentencing Denville, 'The sheer depravity of this crime means you must be removed from ordinary society for a very long time.'

He will be eligible for parole in 2016 and the *Mirror* has been told that he is 'recovering well' from the recent attack.

She looks around the busy carriage uneasily.
He could be out.
He could be watching her right now.

36

The bad dreams cling to me like succubae in the morning. I see his face constantly.

I smell him.

He's out there. I know he is.

The police won't listen. They say he has alibis for his whereabouts since he was released. But he has found a way to get to me, I know it.

I know it I know it I know it I know it I KNOW IT I KNOW IT I KNOW IT I KNOW IT

Bars on the windows won't stop him. Bricks and mortar, locks and bolts, none of them are enough to keep him out. He's inside my head. He's been there all my life.

Wasn't it me who let him in? I was always being told not to do this without checking first. But I let him into the house. I let him in and he killed her.

And now he wants to kill me too.

I hide all the knives and then I find them laid

out on the table. I think I must have done it while I slept. I hear things. Footsteps outside.

I can't stop thinking about what he said.

YOU LOOK JUST LIKE HER . . .

37

As the train pulls into Truro, Neve waits in the aisle behind passengers who are gathering belongings from overhead and between the seats. A woman with two boys is directly in front of her, looking harassed.

Her eldest, a bespectacled boy of around five with a mop of thick, sandy-coloured hair, is repeatedly kicking the seat next to him as she struggles to pull out a buggy from where it has been stashed between the seats. There is no room to help so Neve can only stand and wait.

The toddler holds onto his mother's leg unsteadily then turns to peer up at Neve, blinking large, sleepy blue eyes. She smiles cautiously down at him, feeling her usual awkwardness with the very young. The boy regards her for a moment before his face splits into a heart-melting grin, all tiny pearl teeth and shining eyes. She pulls a silly face and he rumbles with a giggle, which makes his brother pause in his kicking game and turn to look at Neve too, curiosity and suspicion fighting for prominence.

As she gazes down at the chubby freckled face before her, she suddenly pictures the scene described by Linda Dyer and looks quickly away again. But a thought has lodged in her mind.

Isabelle's birth brother. What happened to him? He would be around thirty now, by Neve's calculations. What if he was even less adjusted to his past than Isabelle was? Could he have found his sister? And could something, somehow, have gone badly wrong?

So much she doesn't know. So many toxic secrets.

When she walks out of the station, Neve realizes with a cold sinking stomach that she can't remember where to get the bus from.

Making a furious noise under her breath she turns, wanting to kick something. Why can't anything ever go right?

Then, across the road, she realizes someone is watching her.

It's Matty, clad in a parka-style coat that's old-fashioned and strange on someone of his age. He turns to look at the window of a bakery with apparent fascination.

Debating whether to speak to him, she sees Sally Gardner coming out of the chemist shop next door. She has a brief exchange with her son and then she turns and looks across at Neve, before giving her a beckoning wave.

Neve hurries over the road with a light feeling in her chest. Sally is so capable and sensible. Matty is lucky to have her, even if his dad is a bit of a drinker.

'Fancy seeing you here,' says Sally. 'Been shopping?' Her eyes slide down to Neve's hands and their absence of shopping bags. 'Or maybe not!'

'I've had a very strange day,' says Neve. 'I've been in Dorset. But I'll tell you about it another time.' She lets her eyes quickly dart towards Matty and Sally seems to understand immediately because she tightens her lips and dips her chin in agreement.

'Where are you going now?' says Sally. 'We're just off home. Been to the dentist, both of us.'

'Well, I was going to look for a bus,' says Neve, mentally crossing her fingers.

'Gosh,' says Sally. 'Wouldn't dream of having you do that. We'll give you a lift, won't we, Matty?'

Matty's cheeks darken and he mumbles something indecipherable.

They climb into the car; Neve in the front. Matty feels like a malignant presence behind her. She can tell he is looking at her as they pass through the city and out onto the main road and wonders again whether he has been behind any of the odd things that have been happening.

But why would he try to frighten her?

Sally is quiet and appears thoughtful. Neve is too exhausted to make conversation and barely knows where to start anyway. She wants to ask if they borrowed the axe from the cottage but is scared to know the answer. What if Sally doesn't know what she is talking about? At the moment Neve can live in a reality in which it is still possible that it was a misunderstanding between country neighbours, the rules of which she doesn't understand.

She also wonders how much Sally knew about Isabelle's quest with John Denville. Did Isabelle tell anyone other than Bob and Linda Dyer about her prison visit?

But these topics weigh too much right now and she is too wrung out. Neve is grateful when Sally reaches to the radio and puts on Radio 4. They listen to the news in silence and from the back of the car comes the tap-tap of Matty's activity on his phone.

Sally's powerful car ticks off the miles back a little too soon. She offers to park in the lane and for Matty to see Neve to her door. Debating for just a moment which is the lesser of the evils she accepts the offer and the large youth shines a powerful torch from the car to light their way as they walk up the icy lane. The torchlight bobs and weaves before them, casting silvery-white flashes over the branches. The wood next to them seems like a malignant mass of darkness, glowering down on their figures.

An owl hoots mournfully and something scurries quickly into the bushes in front of them, causing Neve to flinch and move closer to Matty.

He flinches in turn, as though she is about to touch him.

As they reach the front door, she fumbles with the locks. It seems to take an age to open the house.

The car in the lane toots impatiently and Matty starts. He says nothing and simply hurries off.

'Fuck!' Neve hisses into the night air. 'You might have waited for me to get inside!'

She shoves against the door and almost falls into the chill hallway.

But straight away she knows something isn't right. Her entire skin seems to fizz with the shock as she holds her breath to listen.

The realization that it's only the radio is a relief that feels almost orgasmic and she laughs as she slaps her hand against the light switch and illuminates the hallway. Stupid radio. Got a bloody mind of its own.

But as she comes into the unwelcoming kitchen and looks balefully around, two unpleasant realizations strike her at once.

She unplugged it yesterday.

And she has no idea how long it has been on for. It could have been playing all day.

The lights could go out at any moment, plunging her into darkness again.

38

Neve runs to the draining board and grasps the knife she left there that morning.

She stands at the sink, clutching it with both hands in front of her body; breath coming in loud rasps of terror.

'You can fuck off, Denville!' she yells, then flinches at the loud violence of her own voice.

The house squats around her, mocking her with its total, enveloping quiet.

Neve forces one foot in front of the other, edging forward with baby steps, knife held out so her arm comes to one long point, until she gets to the hallway.

Weapon still brandished, she smacks the door of the study open and it bangs loudly against the wall. Flicking on the light switch, she scans the room. But no one has been here, she can tell.

Next, she checks the bathroom and when she catches sight of herself in the stippled mirror above the sink, she sees a thin, scared woman with a bone-white face. She looks much older than her years.

Turning away, Neve moves to the bedroom and stops in the doorway. Something is wrong here. She can't work it out. But the scene is very slightly off, as though it has been re-painted in the wrong shades.

The bed . . . it's neatly made. Did she make it that morning? She is sure she didn't. But maybe she did? Letting out a groan of frustration, she mashes a fist against her forehead. She can't remember. Sometimes she does and sometimes she doesn't. It's so neat and tidy though . . . almost like a hospital bed.

With a quivering hand, she gently pulls back the duvet, dreading what she might see beneath. But there is nothing, just the smooth flattened sheet. It's just a bed, she tells herself.

Trying to calm her ragged breathing, Neve walks back into the kitchen. She can't seem to put down the knife.

All she can hear is the wind

'Fuck this,' she says, reaching into her pocket for her phone. She thumbs up Sally's number.

Sally picks up almost immediately and seems so unfazed that Neve feels a pulse of humiliation. Sally clearly thinks she is a totally useless moron.

She invites Neve to come to dinner and to sleep over.

Less than five minutes later she hears a sharp rap at the door. She has thrown her bed things and a toothbrush plus some clean knickers into her bag. She hadn't got as far as taking off her coat and boots when she came in. She almost runs out of the front door, pulling it behind her decisively and locking it with trembling fingers. Even as she does this, she experiences a queasy sensation that it isn't enough to reassure her the cottage is safe.

'Thank you so much,' she says breathlessly. Will is wearing a hunting hat with furry side flaps that makes him look like a lumberjack. He smiles kindly but has a mildly puzzled, amused expression.

'It's absolutely fine,' he says. They walk through the gap in the hedge and into the lane, where the four-by-four is parked.

They climb in and Neve is comforted by the bulk of the car. An alarm chimes until they have clipped on their seat belts.

'So, Sally says something has given you a bit of a turn?' says Will as he starts the engine. The big car glides down the bumpy lane towards the road.

'I don't know,' says Neve, feeling stupid even as she says it. She doesn't know where to start on everything she has learned today. 'But it feels like someone is trying to freak me out.'

'Go on,' says Will and glances at her, his face a combination of shadowed angles and light from the dashboard.

She tells him about the axe, even though she is aware that sounds particularly foolish.

'And there was today!' she says heatedly, as they pull up in front of Will and Sally's cottage. 'I swear I unplugged it.' She contemplates mentioning the neatly made bed but isn't certain about this one. It's probably just her error.

Will has listened without comment the whole way and is now parking.

'And there's something else,' she says. 'I've found something awful out about Isabelle.' She can't bring herself to blurt it out yet. The words feel poisonous in her mouth.

'Okay,' says Will with a big out-breath. 'Let's get you inside and get some dinner in you, then we'll talk it through, okay? And tomorrow I will come over and give the house a thorough check for you, alright? But for tonight, let's get you inside, eh?'

For a moment Neve almost loves this big, cuddly bear of a man.

'That sounds brilliant,' she says, opening the door of the car.

Inside the house, Neve's senses are bathed in pleasant smells, sights and sounds. The lighting is soft and welcoming in the hallway, and she can smell garlic over the scent of the candle that burns just inside the door. Some sort of plinky-soft piano music is seeping from one of the rooms. She looks around for signs of Matty but he isn't here and she feels herself relax.

She takes her boots off and Horace the cat appears to weave around her legs, purring loudly.

Reaching down she rubs the cat's head and it leans hard into her hand, purrs revving up so its whole body shivers with pleasure. 'I haven't seen you for ages,' she says. 'Are you not coming to visit me any more then?'

'He doesn't really wander away from the garden these days,' says Sally with a laugh, appearing at the kitchen door and holding a tea towel. 'He's getting a bit old and set in his ways.'

Neve stands up and gives an uncertain smile. 'Oh,' she says. 'It's just that he came the other evening, didn't he? I thought I might see him again.'

Sally turns away with a sharp, bright laugh. 'Apart from visiting Petty Whin Cottage, I meant. Anyway,' she adds, 'more importantly, let me get you a drink. It sounds as though you could do with one!'

Neve follows her gratefully into the kitchen. The food smells are rich and herby and her stomach clenches with hunger.

'It's just veggie lasagne,' says Sally, 'so I hope you're okay with that?'

'That sounds amazing.' Neve sits down at the table, which has been set for three. She wonders whether Matty isn't around, or whether her place hadn't been set yet. But she's suddenly too sleepy to think about it properly. The safety and hospitality feel like a warm bath and she suppresses a yawn. It must be the relief, she thinks. Then, *imagine what it would be like to live like this, all the time*. It feels as though introducing the topic of Sofie Lindstrom and John Denville into this place would almost be an act of violence. And she is too exhausted to bring it up straight away. She'll gather her resources and tell them in a while.

Will comes into the room again with a burst of hand rubbing and enthusiasm.

'Right,' he says, beaming at Neve, 'who's for a drink? Wine? Beer?'

Neve hesitates. She's so exhausted she thinks alcohol is going to knock her out but she decides to have just one and see how she gets on.

'I'll have a beer if that's okay?' she says and a few minutes later Will hands her a bottle of Beck's that is dotted with condensation and a tall, thin glass.

She thanks him and takes a long sip as Sally comes to the table with a red ceramic dish that bubbles with crusty cheese, sending delicious steam into the air. A wooden bowl of salad is placed on the table by Will, who uses the tongs to toss it until it glistens with oil.

'This is delicious, Sally,' she says after putting a small forkful of searingly hot pasta into her mouth. When she has swallowed, with difficulty, she says, 'Where's Matty tonight?'

Sally and Will exchange looks.

'He had something earlier,' says Sally carefully. 'He's . . .' she takes a mouthful of her own food and chews for a moment before continuing '. . . he has taken Isabelle's death rather harder than we realized, it seems. He got upset today, coming up to the cottage with you.'

Neve lowers her fork. 'I'm so sorry,' she says. 'I should have—' but Sally interrupts her by holding up a hand.

'No, it's nothing to do with you, please don't worry,' she says. 'He's just a sensitive boy, that's all. Sometimes I think that living out here is perhaps not the best place for him. He was like a different boy when we visited his sister last year. It was as if the environment suited him in some way.'

She seems about to say more but Will breaks in.

'More salad, Neve?' he says, noticing that Neve has finished the entire bowl while waiting for the lasagne to cool.

'Oh yes please,' she says and then laughs. 'You must think I'm a right greedy guts.'

Will smiles kindly and tongs a pile of shining leaves into her bowl. 'Not at all,' he says. 'It's nice to see a woman with a proper appetite.'

As they eat in silence, Neve feels as if the topics of Petty Whin Cottage and Isabelle are circling like black crows above their heads. She doesn't know how to broach the subject and wants to stay longer in this pretend, safe place where it isn't happening.

But after a moment Will speaks again.

'Neve, we understand that you've had a bit of a rotten time since you came here. I'm so sorry about this. I wish things could have been easier for you.'

'Thank you,' she says, feeling her eyes prickle with emotion. She takes a swig of her beer to compensate and then has a coughing fit because she swallowed too quickly.

'Are you alright?' Sally pats her on the back and her voice is so gentle, it breaches Neve's final defences. No one has touched her for ages, it seems, and she wants to curl her head into Sally's neck and stay there.

And then that's exactly what is happening because she

has dropped her fork and is unable to control the sobs that rip through her.

'Oh shush, shush now,' says Sally gently, her arms around Neve and one hand smoothing her hair; Neve is suddenly conscious that it's dirty.

'I don't even know what I'm doing here,' she says finally with a snotty hiccup, and pulls away to delve for a tissue in the handbag by her feet that she then fails to locate. But it's okay because Sally is magically holding a man-sized one out to her now. Neve takes it gratefully and then uses it to rub at her reddened, damp nostrils.

'It's just that . . .' she lets out a heavy sigh. 'Well, you see, my dad died. And my mum's dead. And I feel like, I feel like . . .' A wave of sadness batters her again and she closes her eyes for a second. Why is she telling them about this? They don't care. No one cares. She must get on with it, mustn't she?

'Go on,' says Sally softly.

Neve laughs and it's too bright, like the sharp *ting* of metal against glass.

'It sounds so stupid,' she says, staring down at her half-eaten dinner. The colours – red peppers, orange cheese, green leaves – seem too vivid. 'But the whole thing with the cottage seems like something I could deal with if I'd been able to get advice from my mum and dad. My mum, actually. She'd have taken charge and had that creepy old shithole looking like a show home.'

The other two laugh politely.

Neve continues. 'I feel like I've been given this supposed opportunity . . . woo! Lucky me!' She sniffs, 'But instead it's like a big ugly albatross on my head.' She laugh-hiccups. 'Or wherever the fuck albatrosses go.' She looks up to see their amused expressions. 'I'm sorry about all my swearing. I'm always being told about it.'

Sally leans across and pats her hand softly. 'Finish your dinner up and we'll talk this through properly. Will,' she says. 'Get Neve a glass of wine or another beer.'

'I'll just have some water, thanks,' says Neve and wonders for a second whether Will looks a little deflated.

They finish the meal and Sally tells Will about the dentist visit she and Matty had earlier in the day. Neve tunes out and eats her food, which doesn't seem quite so delicious now it has cooled and congealed a little on the plate. She feels too tired to be ashamed of her breakdown, fortunately. And God knows when she will get something this good again, so she finishes every last mouthful before placing her knife and fork on her plate and thanking Sally for the food.

'It's my pleasure,' says Sally and gets up from the table. 'Can I clear up for you?'

'I wouldn't hear of it,' she says and makes a sweeping motion to indicate that she should make her way to the sitting room. 'I'll be in with coffee in a moment. You go through.'

Neve carries her water through to the sitting room and sinks into a brown leather armchair. She looks around the room, at the framed pictures of the family on the piano, and the flickering flames visible through the window of the log burner, and tries to think about nothing. But the image of the tiny Isabelle, arms slick with her mother's blood, as she tries to coax the dead woman to drink some water is too powerful and it feels like her mind has imprinted it in the background, like wallpaper on a computer screen.

After a while Will and Sally come into the room. He is holding a tray that contains a cafetiere, a jug of milk, a bowl of sugar and cups. There is a plate of mini Florentines.

'Coffee?' he says and Neve hesitates then nods. She doesn't want to be kept awake but she needs to focus too, in order not to sound like a lunatic.

When they are all sipping coffee to the soft accompaniment of the traditional jazz playing quietly in the background and the whoosh and roar of wind in the flue of the burner, Neve speaks.

'So,' she says, 'I found out something awful about Isabelle today.'

'Oh yes?' Sally's coffee cup is halfway to her lips.

And she begins to tell them what she learned from Linda Dyer earlier, about how Isabelle was visiting a man in prison, and the horrific crime which had put him there. Both faces register confusion and then, when she reveals Isabelle's connection to Denville, shock.

Sally stares down at her hands and mutters that it's a terribly sad story, and Will shakes his head forcefully. 'The poor girl,' he says. 'We had no idea at all. To think . . .' he sighs heavily, 'that she went all the way to Low Linney prison and told no one about any of it.'

Neve agrees quietly. Something catches awkwardly in her mind, like a woollen sock snagging on a misplaced floor tack.

'But that's not the worst part,' she says and then tells them about John Denville possibly having got out of prison.

'God,' says Sally with heat. 'That's a bit disconcerting.'

'I know, right?' says Neve. 'I keep thinking it's him who is doing all this weird shit.'

Will leans towards her.

'But lovey,' he says gently. 'Really, why would he? What would be the motive?'

Neve shrugs.

'Well, I can't say I could begin to ever understand the mind of someone like that but it all seems a bit far-fetched to me,' he says. 'It's much more likely that Isabelle drove herself half mad thinking about it. Life isn't like the telly, is it?'

Neve tries to let this comfort her but she's finding it oddly hard to concentrate, like her brain is wrapped up in thick cladding.

There is silence for a moment and then Will leans over and places his empty coffee cup on the low wooden table in front of him.

'Look, Neve,' he says. 'The offer still stands about our daughter, you know.'

Neve sighs. 'I know, thank you. I think I'll take you up on it. I promise to stop being flaky about it. It's just . . .' she curls her legs up under her to get more comfortable in the chair. 'I feel some sort of obligation to her. To Isabelle. To find out what was going on before I get rid of it.'

'Well, I can understand that,' says Sally gently. 'But you could say that making you part of her suicide was actually rather cruel. And that you ought to take the money and run.'

Neve's head feels as though there is a slowly tightening band of steel around it.

'It's not going to be easy to sell that grotty old place,' continues Sally, 'whatever guff you might hear from estate agents. Its central heating is like something from the Ark, as you've already discovered, and,' she laughs, 'as you put it so succinctly, it's a creepy old shithole.' The words seem made from different angles, coming from Sally's well-spoken mouth, and Neve can't help but smile. But her voice sounds muffled and far away.

Her sore throat has come back with a vengeance and the lasagne seems to sit in a cheesy, oily mass in her stomach. A wave of pure exhaustion washes over her.

'God,' she says, 'I'm so sorry, but I think I need to go to bed. I've got a virus that's been brewing and I suddenly feel a bit shit.'

'Of course, of course,' says Will hurrying to his feet. Sally says nothing and when Neve steals a glance at her she sees the other woman's face is expressionless before softening with sympathy.

'I'm so sorry,' says Neve again. 'I don't mean to be rude. And I do appreciate being able to talk to you. You're absolutely right about the cottage. I need to get rid of it.'

'Come on then, you poor wounded soldier,' says Will and Neve gratefully follows him up the narrow staircase. She glances at more framed pictures of children on the way, mostly, it seems, the Spanish grandchildren, judging by the bright blue skies that are backdrops in so many.

They pass a bedroom from which a low bass thudding seeps out and Will makes a face and directs Neve down another small corridor that leads off the landing.

'Matty has his music on but it shouldn't disturb you down here,' he says, opening a low wooden door and dipping his head to enter.

The spare bedroom is small and neat and the air smells pleasantly of fresh laundry. The walls are a bright cheerful yellow, the curtains pale and sprigged with embroidered flowers. There is a chest of drawers and slightly wonky bookcase painted pale blue; the latter is stuffed with old children's books, from Enid Blyton to Roald Dahl, plus all the Harry Potters neatly lined up in order.

The duvet is also pale yellow and soft as a cloud; the bed piled with pillows. Next to the bed there is a table containing tissues and a bottle of water in deep blue glass.

Neve wants to sink straight onto it. Will must sense her desire to lie down because he begins to back out of the room, hunching his large frame awkwardly.

'I'll leave you to it. Hope you feel better in the morning. Oh, the bathroom is just down to the left,' he says, then, 'Night, night, Neve.'

'Night, Will, and thank you,' she says and he gives a

dismissive wave of his hand as he disappears through the doorway.

Neve finds her toothbrush and walks to the bathroom, barely noticing her surroundings now, such is the almost magnetic pull of that soft, warm bed. She can vaguely hear voices from downstairs when she comes out and she stops for a moment. There's something quiet and urgent about the tone, which comes from one of the other bedrooms, but, fearful of being caught nosing, she hurries back to the guest room.

Five minutes later, she sinks gratefully into bed. Sally has left a packet of Nurofen on the chest of drawers but she is too sleepy, too muzzy-headed to take them. She just wants to sleep, to sleep, sleep, sleep.

39

She's on a bike again; riding it around Will and Sally's kitchen this time. A woman, who dream logic tells her is Isabelle, sits on the kitchen table, cross-legged, but Neve can't see her face. Isabelle shouts encouraging things to Neve and encourages her to ride faster but Neve doesn't want to. If anything, she wants to stop but finds she can't.

Then finally she is slowing down and for some reason she says, 'That's lucky,' when the bike becomes stuck in something that is sticky and black when she dips her feet down to the ground. Isabelle says, 'Have a drink of water. That's all you need,' and Neve is so thirsty. She wants the water badly but can't reach it . . .

Her eyes snap open and she stares up into thick darkness. Her heart is pounding.

She thinks about the stickiness in the dream, the dark mass of it on the floor. No prizes for why she dreamed about that. Her mouth is coated and her throat still sore.

She's desperately thirsty and feels hungover, even though she barely touched her one beer. The duvet feels too heavy and hot now and she throws it back and struggles to a sitting position. She fumbles for the lamp and manages to switch it on. The warm light is the colour of egg yolk against the pale walls. Her phone tells her it is only two a.m.

Groaning, she climbs out of bed to get to the bottle of water. Taking off the lid, she tips it straight into her mouth and shivers when she realizes it is fizzy. It prickles at her painful throat and she puts it down again. Tap water. She needs plain old tap water.

Pulling a jumper over her bed T-shirt, she opens the heavy door, which makes a deep *shooshing* sound over the carpet. Peering out into the dark corridor, she hesitates. She doesn't want to put a light on in case she wakes someone. And with all the doors closed, she can't exactly remember which one was the bathroom. Was it the second or third on the right? The thought of accidentally stumbling into Will and Sally's, or worse still, Matty's bedroom is too awful to contemplate.

At least she knows where the stairs are. She decides to go down to the kitchen.

Feeling her way down the short corridor from her bedroom to meet the landing, she is relieved to see the small dome of a nightlight plugged into the socket in the hall. It gives her enough light to get to the stairs and from there she makes her way down, toes carefully reaching for the next step, hand clasping the bannister.

When she gets to the bottom she can see a light is on in the sitting room and the door is open. There's the rumble of deep, male snores.

Tentatively, she pokes her head around the door. Will is asleep on the sofa, his large bulk not quite fitting into the space, so that one arm with a meaty fist is flung towards the carpet. Her eyes stray down and she sees there is a cut-glass tumbler there and a bottle of what looks like whisky nearby.

Tiptoeing now, she goes into the kitchen and closes the

door behind her carefully. The under-lights of all the cupboards give her more than enough light to find a glass on the draining board and to fill it with cold water, which she drinks greedily. Her sore throat immediately starts to ease and, moving her head experimentally, she realizes that she is feeling a little bit better than when she first woke.

The small, warm bedroom and the suffocating weight of that duvet don't seem as appealing as they did earlier and so she takes her glass and goes to sit at the kitchen table.

Something is still nagging at her and she can't seem to catch its tail. Maybe it was the weird dream, she thinks, sipping her water carefully. She's aware that it could have been much worse. She had been dreading that she would dream about the scene described in that kitchen by Linda Dyer, thirty years ago, or whatever it was. But then, she thinks with a shudder, maybe there are nightmares still to come.

Neve doesn't want to know what Denville looked like, but maybe putting a face to him might stop him from being the vague but terrifying silhouette of a monster in her mind. He seems to lurk there now, like a shadow.

She forces another sip of water down, to try and distract herself from these thoughts, but pictures Isabelle making her pilgrimage to Low Linney prison. Even the name sounds lonely and grim.

Neve pauses with the glass midway between her lips and the table, and then slowly places it down. This is what it is. This is the thing that has been bothering her, at the very back of her mind. But she felt too poorly earlier to pick up on it.

Will had said it earlier. 'The poor girl,' he'd said, 'going all that way to Low Linney,' or something like that.

But Neve hadn't mentioned the actual name of the prison. She's certain about this.

Is she? Her mind races.

When the door opens with a creak, she starts and almost spills the water. At first, she thinks the large frame emerging into the kitchen is Will, then she sees it is Matty, who visibly starts at the sight of her.

'Sorry,' she says in a low voice and hears how hoarse she sounds. 'I was just getting a drink of water. Didn't mean to give you a fright.'

Matty grunts something indecipherable and goes across to the fridge. His large pale feet poke out of his pyjama bottoms and she studies him as he leans in and then takes out a carton of orange juice. Glancing at her a bit defiantly, as if she cares, he lifts it to his lips and takes a long slow drink.

Neve's mind races. She's aware that Matty needs careful handling and simply won't bother to answer any question he finds difficult.

When he finishes drinking he burps loudly and Neve raises her eyes. He clearly expects her to be shocked by his rebellious behaviour.

He puts the carton back in the fridge and closes the door forcefully. He shows every sign of leaving the kitchen without saying anything at all and Neve panics.

'Matty,' she says hurriedly. 'You know Isabelle's car?'

His entire upper body seems to close in protectively and in the pale light of the kitchen he is all frown and shoulders.

'Well,' she forces herself on in a friendly voice, 'did you see that wristband thing in the glove compartment?'

He frowns.

'What wristband thing?' he mumbles. 'I haven't even looked in there. It's her stuff. I can't throw it away.'

Something about this seems, bizarrely, believable. It could be a sort of weird shrine.

Matty lopes back towards the door.

'I'm sorry about Isabelle,' says Neve hurriedly. She only wants to stop him from leaving, but as she says the words, she realizes they are true. She is desperately sorry that this poor woman, with her terrible burden from the past, couldn't find a way to live with herself.

Matty stops and looks at her and it almost feels like the first time he has given her direct eye contact.

'I wish I'd known her,' she says and immediately feels as though she has said something wrong because his brow scrunches in scorn. Or confusion. She can't tell which.

'But you did,' he says. 'I already said that.'

Neve had forgotten about what he'd said that first night. *I've seen you before.*

She spreads her arms in front of her, palms flat against the cool wood of the table, almost in supplication. It's crucial that he trusts her.

'I honestly didn't,' she says. 'What makes you think that I did?'

Matty frowns. For a moment, all Neve can hear is the humming of the fridge.

'On her laptop,' he says finally. 'There were photos. Photos of you.'

40

Neve does what she always does when presented with something so disturbing and strange that her brain is unable to absorb it. She laughs.

'What? Why on earth would Isabelle have photos of me?'

Straight away she realizes her mistake. She has lost him. She can almost see him drawing back into himself and realizes, too late, that he felt mocked.

'Matty,' she starts to say but he talks over her.

'I didn't say I knew why. I just said I'd seen them.' He reaches for the door. 'I'm tired. I'm going to bed.'

'Matty,' she hisses desperately and jumps up but she can see his large feet are already disappearing up the stairs at speed.

Back in the bedroom, Neve climbs into bed, although the prospect of sleeping seems a distant one.

But she's cold, so she tries to snuggle down into the heavy duvet. Questions swirl and dance inside her mind. Why would Isabelle have had pictures of Neve? It makes no sense. He must have confused her with someone else. But who?

Several people have told Neve she looks a bit like a

well-known actress, but Neve thinks this is more to do with the combination of fair hair and brown eyes they share. Could it have been *her* on the computer? But this is ridiculous too, she thinks with frustration. Why would Isabelle have lots of pictures of an actress on her computer?

And she has the strangest feeling that Will and Sally are not telling her everything they know about Isabelle. It may simply be out of respect for the dead woman. Perhaps Isabelle told them about her past in confidence and it felt wrong to discuss the details of this horrible, intimate event.

But she decides to be more circumspect with them now, all the same.

She must get the laptop back tomorrow, whatever happens.

When Sally comes into the kitchen at seven a.m. and sees Neve sitting at the table, with a cup of coffee in front of her, she starts visibly.

'Goodness, you gave me a fright!' she says, recovering a smile. 'You're up very early. I thought we wouldn't see you until much later today, especially as you seemed a little under the weather last night.' She pauses. 'How *are* you feeling?'

'Much better, thanks,' says Neve and it isn't entirely untrue. She had popped a couple of paracetamol she found in a blister pack in her handbag, and doubled up with the Nurofen Sally left out for her the night before. Although her head feels a little fuzzy and strange, nothing actively hurts.

That morning she had been awake early and washed her hair using borrowed shampoo in the powerful shower, enjoying the restorative pounding jets of water on her head. Even though she had brought no clean clothes or make-up, she found a comb to drag through her hair, and a small pot of tinted lip balm for her lips.

It all made her feel a little more in control than the ragged mess she had been the night before.

She has a strong sensation that she needs to have her wits about her. To be proactive and in control. A grown-up, for once.

Sally pours muesli into a bowl and then sloshes it with oat milk from the fridge.

'Sally, I wanted to ask a favour,' says Neve and Sally turns to her, her mouth full of muesli. She nods as if to say, 'Go on.'

'I need to get into Truro and I wondered if you could give me a lift?'

'Well, yes of course,' says Sally. 'I don't work in the centre but it's not that big and I can tell you where to go.'

'That would be great, thank you.'

Sally gives her a puzzled look and then adds, 'Right, well I'm leaving in about ten minutes.'

In the car, Sally puts on Radio 4 and they listen to the *Today* programme in silence. Neve can't think of any small talk and luckily Sally doesn't seem to be much of a morning person, focusing instead on the thick traffic.

Sally drops Neve off on the edge of town, with full instructions about the buses back. She suggests that, if she is stuck, Neve can wait until Sally is coming home again at five. Neve thanks her and gets out of the car. Sally gives her a lingering look and then turns back out into the traffic.

Most of the shops aren't open yet, apart from the odd newsagent and a flower shop. Neve wanders into a shopping centre in search of a café. Inside the various chain stores she can see staff running vacuum cleaners over carpets and sleepily checking window displays. The sky is leaden and the temperature quite warm; it feels like rain is imminent. Neve begins to sweat inside her woollen coat and undoes the buttons, letting it hang open.

She finds a small café that is filled with builders buying bacon sandwiches and takeaway teas and feels several pairs of male eyes running over her as she makes her way to the back of the queue. Idly staring at her phone, she twitches with the desire to go online, to check emails and look at Facebook. But she is all too aware that she is haemorrhaging money right now and is determined to avoid going over her monthly data limit.

It strikes her with an unpleasant slap that bills must be arriving both at Lou's and, very possibly, still dribbling through at Daniel's flat. She miserably turns her gaze to the display of hot drinks available.

Seeing both 'Expresso' and 'Cupoccino' on offer, she decides to order tea.

When she opens the door to the computer shop half an hour later, a couple of bleary-eyed people around her own age glance up at her with a lack of curiosity.

A chubby red-haired girl with freckles and a smiley face pops up from behind the counter, like someone from an old sitcom. Her nose is pierced and her hair is shaved on one side.

'Oh!' she says with an infectious laugh. 'That must have looked funny, me bobbing up like that!'

Neve feels a loosening in her chest and smiles back at the girl. She is acutely aware that she used to be a fun person too, who laughed easily and looked for the humour in situations. Now though, she spends her life either thinking someone is about to murder her, or crying about her mess of a life.

She suppresses an urge to say, 'I'm not normally like this,' but for a brief moment envy for this girl burns like indigestion.

The girl probably lives with her boyfriend in this small market town. They have a dog – some, small yappy thing, which they love as much as a child. One day they'll marry and their mates will come along dressed in jeans and T-shirts. They'll go to the pub and all get pissed.

Neve realizes the girl's smile has slipped a little and she is regarding her curiously now.

'Yes! No,' says Neve and blushes at her own stupidity. 'You're mending a, er, my laptop?'

'Got your ticket?'

Neve hunts for a while in her purse but she knows it is a fruitless search. She has never been able to hang onto things like this, which make the admin of life run smoother. She's had to recover passwords for virtually every website she's ever been signed up to, and once had to wait until a nightclub cloakroom had handed over every single item to other guests until her coat finally emerged.

'Don't worry,' says the girl. 'Just give me the name.'

A few minutes later the black laptop is placed on the desk.

'Now, we had some problems,' Neve is told, 'and I don't know whether we have recovered everything or only the most recent data on the computer. We've managed to find a fair number of photos, but some drives seem to have been overwritten so many times, we could only get a partial recovery. Everything we managed to salvage is on this.'

She slides a CD across the table towards Neve.

'Okay, that's better than nothing, thanks.' Neve gets out her bank card with an uneasy feeling that it might be declined. Thankfully, the payment goes through.

*   *   *

Now that she has the computer in her hands, she feels a strange reluctance to turn it on and look at what is contained within. Instead she mooches around the shops for a while, trying to work up the will to find the first bus she will need to take her back to the cottage. She buys a small amount of groceries, tops up her electricity key, and finally makes her way to the bus stop, just as a light rain begins to fall.

It takes an hour and a half to get back to Stubbington Lane. Her bottom is stiff from the bus seats and, having been caught by the rain in the wrong sort of coat, smells like a wet dog.

The estate agent had phoned as she settled onto the first bus to say, tersely, that she had missed yet another appointment. Apologizing profusely, Neve says she needs more time before firming up another. Georgia McColl tries to press her to a time but she can't think about this now. The other woman is a little frosty when the call ends.

She will do it; sort out this valuation. She will. But her head is crowded with all this stuff right now and she must understand what is going on first.

The laptop in her handbag seems to have become a kilo heavier since this morning. By the time she is dragging herself up the lane and through the gate to the cottage, her shoulder aches and she wishes she had never bothered paying to have it recovered. She could, she thinks belatedly, have waited until she next went to London. Steve would probably have done it for her. He'd have moaned. But he would have done it. But what Matty said was so strange. She has to know.

When she comes into the quiet hallway, with its dim, jaundiced light and smell of potpourri, she feels an overwhelming desire, once again, to get away from here. She listens for a moment, alert to any sound of an intruder. She should get the locks changed. But she has no money for that.

The first thing she does is top up the meter.

She misses Jarvis, acutely.

After making herself a cup of coffee and a peanut butter sandwich, she sits down at the kitchen table and switches on the laptop.

As she is about to slip the disk into the slot at the side there is a rap at the front door.

'Oh, bloody hell,' she slaps the table with both palms. Now that the moment has arrived, she wants to get this over with, to truly *know* that there are no pictures of her. That Matty was just being weird.

Yet as she gets up and goes to the front door, there is a small part of her that is grateful for this hiatus.

The shape behind the glass looks vaguely familiar and when she opens the door, she is unable to hide her feelings.

'Oh,' she says flatly. 'Hi.'

Finn smiles tentatively. 'I've come to sort out the window, as promised,' he says. His nose is red around the nostrils and his eyes look puffy. He does an explosive sneeze into his bent elbow and apologizes, sniffing.

'As you can see,' he says, 'I've been a bit under the weather. It's why I didn't come sooner. And also . . .' He shuffles, awkwardly. 'I think I may have been a bit of an arse the other evening.'

'Okay,' says Neve again, wrong-footed. But she isn't quite ready to let him in.

'It was the first night out I'd had since . . . well, you know,' he says. 'And I'd been feeling crap all day. I didn't want you to think I didn't, well, I didn't . . .'

'It's fine,' says Neve crisply, pushing the door to let him

in. 'Don't give it a second thought. But if you can get the window done quickly that would be great. I'm in the middle of something.'

'Sure, sure!' he says. 'You won't even know I'm here.' He grins at her, and she is irritated that her body seems to respond happily, despite what her brain is telling it to do. He tells her he will be working from the outside and goes to his van to get what he needs.

A few minutes later she sees his face at the back window. He is wearing safety goggles and doesn't meet her eye as he begins to scrape and bang at the broken pane.

Neve sits at the table and stares at the laptop.

She should just get it over with. Having Finn here might be a good thing.

But this feels like something she needs to do alone.

She waits.

It doesn't take him long, anyway, and when she hears the polite knock on the back door, she gets up, hoping this won't cost too much.

'The putty will take a while to dry,' he says. 'But it should do the trick.'

'Thanks,' she says.

'Did you want those bars off?' says Finn. 'Think you mentioned that before?'

'No,' says Neve, too quickly. 'I mean, not for now.' He regards her with a puzzled expression.

'Look, are you alright?' he says gently. Neve feels something shiver in her abdomen.

'I don't know,' she says. 'I might have to get back to you on that.'

They smile tentatively at each other.

'I really am sorry about the other night,' says Finn. 'I think maybe it's just too soon.'

'It's fine,' says Neve wearily. And then, 'Anyway, the last thing I need is a reason to stay in this shithole.'

Finn grins widely at this.

'Well,' he says. 'If you do decide to stay, maybe we could have a drink? As friends? We can moan about the smell of cow shit and reminisce about traffic noise.'

'Okay,' she says with a smile. 'If I stay, you're on. Now how much do I owe you?'

He holds up his palms and shakes his head.

'Not a penny,' he says. 'Consider it my apology for turning down a beautiful woman and being a fucking eejit.'

Neve swoops her eyes. 'Cheesy bastard.'

Finn laughs. 'That's me.'

Neve is still smiling as she walks back into the kitchen. It's a relief to have such a normal exchange. She is suddenly overwhelmed with a passionate desire to get away from here.

But not yet.

She sits down in front of the computer.

There is no password. The screen comes to life with a discordant electronic tune.

The desktop is a blank screen. Neve starts with the documents file first.

Nothing very exciting here. Letters to a GP requesting a repeat prescription of a drug Neve has never heard of; some documents relating to tax.

There are several folders of photos. One is called 'Sadie and Matteo' and contains a bunch of images of two beautiful dark-haired children, who beam with gap-toothed smiles at the camera. Some of the pictures are of the children as babies.

Neve moves on and there are more pictures, apparently taken during Isabelle's time in Australia. Most seem to be of an intense-looking man in his forties, who looks at the camera with a slightly arrogant air. Neve decides this is an ex-boyfriend and, sure enough, she finds one where Isabelle is tucked into his shoulder, smiling. He is kissing the top of her head and looking off to the side. She zooms in on the picture to look more closely at Isabelle and her heart contracts. Although tanned and smiling, there is something in her eyes, even here, that seems deadened somehow. As though she isn't really there. And she is thin; much thinner than when Neve saw her that night. Her cheekbones look too sharp and her collarbones jut above the neck of the blue dress she is wearing.

Other folders contain either landscape shots or the occasional group of people holding up beer bottles under bar canopies. A couple make her peer more closely. There is a woman with the same coarse, dirty blonde hair as Neve. But she has huge eyes that look pale in colouring and a much thinner face. Could this be the person Matty saw? Could he just have really crap eyesight, she wonders?

Neve sits back in her seat. This is no good. This is making her feel like a ghoul.

She decides to look at one more folder before giving up.

It's called 'Hannes'. A person's name, or a place, perhaps. Geography has never been her strong suit.

Neve lifts the coffee to sip and clicks open the file.

Seconds later, she slams the cup back onto the table and is on her feet, both hands crossed over her mouth.

Because every single image in this file is of Neve.

273

41

Neve goes to the sink and tries to hold a glass under the tap with a hand that shakes so hard that water slops out the top. Her brain is jangling like a struck bell. She can't think, she can't make sense of it, so she forces cold liquid into her mouth and gasps and wipes her mouth with the back of her hand as it runs down her chin and onto her clothes.

She stands for a few moments then, staring at the window pane.

Why? *Why, why, why . . .?*

Neve walks back to the kitchen table and reaches for the laptop. She makes herself flick through the images. There are so many:

- Neve, sitting next to Miri on the tube, laughing with her mouth open, hands unconsciously mirroring her friend and resting on her own belly.
- Neve, in a queue for coffee, staring down at her phone and frowning deeply at what she sees. Her hair is scraped into a rough ponytail and she looks hungover.

- Neve, dancing, arms above her head in a sensuous curl. Her face shines with heat and alcohol and happiness.
- Neve, walking along the road to Lou's, carrying a bag of shopping.

There are more but she can't bear to look and she slams down the lid of the laptop.

Someone – Isabelle? – had been stalking her for ages. She tries to place some of the pictures but the only one she can mark for sure is the one in the nightclub. That was the night her phone was stolen, wasn't it? She and Daniel had gone to a new nightclub in Hoxton, London, to celebrate the thirtieth birthday of someone in their pub group.

Neve's heart starts to throb almost painfully in her chest now because something is taking shape in her mind. Something dark and strange.

Everyone had said how lucky she was, to have found the stolen phone that very same night . . .

She thinks about the press of bodies on the dancefloor, almost moving as one. A hand slipping into her bag and removing the phone.

And then leaving it handily where staff would find it.

Why?

Why?

Neve runs across the room to her bag to get the phone now. Once, she would never have been more than two feet away from it, but the signal is so poor here she has become less reliant.

She quickly starts flicking through pages of the screen. Searching.

And then she finds what she is looking for.

E-spy. The app she had noticed for the first time in the

vet's waiting room but been too preoccupied to look at properly.

Nothing happens when she taps on the icon.

She can't bear to lift the lid of the laptop again so hurries to the bedroom to get her iPad, where it has been charging.

She taps, 'What does the app E-spy do?' into Google while she is still walking and gets many, many hits.

'E-spy is the perfect way to keep track of your kids, or even your cheating spouse!' reads one.

'Buy the best GPS spying software,' says another.

Neve drops the phone on the table, as though it is burning her fingers.

The phone feels dirty, poisoned. But she makes herself pick it up and quickly dials Sally Gardner's number. It goes straight to voicemail.

She leaves the phone where it is and doesn't even stop to get a coat before she is picking up her keys and running out of the front door.

Someone knows what has been going on. Someone needs to give her answers.

Neve is sweating when she arrives at the Gardners' cottage, even though there is a mean, bitter wind and threatening black rain clouds bunching together in the sky. Her insides sag when she sees that there are no cars at the front of the property. But she rings the bell anyway and then bangs on the front door.

Stepping back dejectedly, she looks up and sees a movement at a window upstairs.

Matty? Lurking there and watching her, no doubt. She goes back to the letterbox and snaps it open.

'Matty!' she hisses. 'Please . . . I need to talk about Isabelle. There's something . . . terrible.'

She's gabbling but can't pull herself together. Nothing

seems to stir inside the house so Matty clearly has no intention of coming down to talk.

Cursing him, she hesitates for just a moment longer then begins to run further up the lane, towards Briarfields.

When she gets to the large, wrought iron gate, she sees the green Land Rover parked in front of the house. Richard said the security buzzer didn't work and she is about to kick the gate in frustration when she sees that it isn't locked.

She pushes it open, and, trying to get her breath back, stomps around the side of the house to the kitchen. Cold rain begins to patter on her head but she barely registers it. She is still blasted by shock, unable to process what is happening.

Not bothering to knock, Neve wrenches open the kitchen door and steps inside. Jarvis gets to his feet and comes over in a blur of hair and tongue and tail. His silly, soft presence makes her want to dissolve into helpless tears so she only murmurs a few words to him before opening the kitchen door and entering a passageway.

It is panelled with dark wood and is poorly lit. Neve walks until she comes to a wide hallway with a cracked parquet floor and a large staircase curling upwards. Dour pictures of hunting scenes line the walls, while a couple of grim-faced Victorians glower down from the staircase.

Neve gathers her courage and yells, 'Richard?' at the top of her voice. 'Richard, are you here? It's Neve. I need to talk to you.'

She hears movement above then, as though the entire house is breathing out. Richard appears at the top of the stairs, looking tousled and startled, dressed in a tatty blue dressing gown.

'What are you doing here?' he says. 'I was having a nap and then I heard—'

'I need to talk to you. It's important,' Neve interrupts.

He stares at her for a moment and then mutters that he will get dressed and meet her in the kitchen.

Neve doesn't move. She feels that if she lets him out of her sight, he will simply melt away.

Sensing this somehow, he says wearily, 'I'll be there in a minute. Just let me throw some clothes on.' He seems oddly unsurprised to see her here.

Neve mutters agreement and turns back to the kitchen. She sits at the table, straight-backed, not touching anything. Warmth against her leg makes her start and she sees that Jarvis is lying by her feet. She can't stop her fingers from seeking his comforting heat and she rubs his soft head and tries to breathe slowly.

If Richard patronizes her, or makes her feel as though she is overreacting, she thinks she might actually kill him. She is winding herself up so much about this that when he comes into the kitchen a few moments later, she almost starts shouting before he has even begun.

He doesn't look at her as he goes to a cupboard and produces a bottle of whisky, then two glasses from the side of the sink.

'Drink?' he says.

'No,' says Neve. 'Yes. I don't know. Yes. Fuck it, yes.'

He smiles weakly then pours two generous measures into the glasses, which are cloudy from over-use.

Neve takes a sip and then immediately coughs. She hates the peaty burn of whisky but it does help a little, so she takes another.

'Tell me what you know,' says Richard.

Neve takes a breath in and out, forcing herself to be calm.

'I thought she was a total stranger,' she says crisply. 'And she was. To me. But she had been following me. *Stalking*

278

me. She'd put an app on my phone. There are all these pictures of me . . .'

Neve takes an angry sip of whisky. *Must not cry.* But pressure is building in her throat and her eyes are prickling. She blinks hard. Picks up the whisky glass. Puts it down again.

'Why was she doing that?' she says, voice skidding. 'You know something. I can tell.'

Richard bends his big head and looks down at his own glass. His face is hidden for several moments until Neve says, 'Richard!' sharply.

He looks up. His eyes are brimming, his mouth twisted. A terrible sound, half-gulp and half-groan, comes from his mouth and then he is covering his face and sobbing. His shoulders shake and he says, 'Oh God,' over and over again.

Neve sits, rigidly. Her lips feel numb, her face frozen. Terror swells inside her.

There is no prospect, not now, that she will learn anything good. Nothing coming now will make her feel better. She is staring into an abyss. In these few moments, she still has a fingertip hold on the edge. But Richard is speaking again and her grip is slipping.

'I didn't know before, I swear I didn't,' he says, stricken red eyes still lowered as he hunts for a handkerchief in his pocket. It is grubby and off-white and he honks loudly into it before continuing. 'I was pissed off about the cottage, of course I was,' he says with a bitter laugh. 'I assumed she really had done one of her mad things and left it to a stranger. But then, that day, that day when I collected Jarvis . . .'

He breaks off and sniffs, shoulders hunched miserably. Meaty hands clasped around the small glass.

'*What?*' says Neve. 'What happened that day?'

'It was . . .' he stutters, 'it was the way *you were standing* in the doorway . . . the light. I don't know. And, you know, looking a bit . . . well, tired. Plus, your hair was up or something. But I worked it out. I could . . . see it. So clearly.'

Neve is on her feet now. She doesn't mean to screech but she can't stop the high timbre of her anguish.

'Worked what out, Richard? What was this thing you worked out?'

Richard gazes up at her, his expression naked with grief.

'I'm so sorry, Neve,' he says. 'You really don't know? It's not my, it's not really my place to . . . to be the one to . . .'

Neve slams both her hands down onto the kitchen table. This time she speaks slowly and quietly.

'If you don't tell me what you are talking about, Richard, I swear to God I am going to do something seriously fucking violent. I am so not kidding.'

Richard avoids her eye and nods, repeatedly.

'Yes, yes, alright,' he says, 'but first, tell me do you know the circumstances of her adoption? *Christ* please, tell me you do.'

'Yes,' she says curtly. 'I know about Denville.' Saying the name aloud again causes a hard shiver between her shoulder blades.

'Well, that's . . . good,' says Richard and tosses back the rest of his drink in one go. He stares at the table and takes a deep breath. 'Did you know she had a sibling?'

'Yes,' says Neve. 'A baby brother. He was there too, at the murder scene.'

Richard finally meets her eye. His expression is filled with so much sorrow that it forces her back into her seat. Ice spreads in crystalline branches through her bloodstream and into all her limbs. Her fingers might snap off at the knuckles. Her legs have no feeling.

'No,' says Richard, so gently that his voice is almost inaudible. 'The press got confused by the Swedish name, you see. One reporter got it wrong and because of restrictions on details about children, the few facts available just got repeated and repeated.' He pauses and continues in a rush. 'It sounded like a boy's name; Hannes. They thought it was like, well, Hans. But it was a little girl.' Richard takes a deep, shuddering breath. 'I'm so very sorry if you knew nothing of this, Neve my dear,' he says.

'No,' says Neve, getting to her feet. 'I don't think I want you to—'

'I'm sorry, but—'

'No!' Neve yells. 'Fuck off! Stop fucking speaking right now!'

'Neve,' says Richard, getting up and reaching for her, his face wretched.

She bats his hands away. 'Don't *touch me.*'

He steps back, his eyes searching her face, breathing noisily.

'I'm so very sorry that you had to find out this way,' he says in a croaky voice. 'Do you understand what I'm saying to you? Do you? Tell me you do.'

'No!' Neve screams and sees flecks of spit fly at Richard. He doesn't flinch. 'Stop talking shit!' Then, 'I'm not even adopted!'

Richard lifts his hands to his face.

'I think you were,' he says through his fingers. 'Don't you see? You have to be. *You* are Hannes. You're Isabelle's sister.'

42

Dearest Hannes,

You'll never see this letter but I want to write it anyway. I will burn it with everything else when the time comes.

I only wanted to see you from a distance, to know that you were safe. I knew that Denville had no way of finding you, but I had to see for myself that you were happy and unaware of it all.

I feel guilty that I forgot about you for so long.

I remember talking about my sister when I was small but was somehow made to feel that I had imagined you into being. That I had never had a sister at all. But when the memories really started to return, then I knew. I knew that I hadn't been alone with Mor that day.

It was hard enough for me to find you, I must admit. And I do feel a little guilty for reeling Bob – dear Bob – into this. He wouldn't do it at first. Refused point blank. But I told him I would never have peace if I didn't know your new name at the very least. Told him that it would help me heal. Help me to stop being obsessed about Denville. Even Bob has stopped believing he means me harm now but he knows I'm not coping well.

I promised him I wouldn't act on it if he could only tell me your name.

I lied.

Easy enough to find you then, especially as I have discovered you are hopeless about things like online security.

I actually held my breath when I sent you the Facebook friend request, but you didn't seem to question it and when 'You and Neve Carey are now friends' pinged on my screen, I felt the first stirring of happiness in such a long time.

I couldn't stop looking at the pictures of you. I wonder if you know how beautiful you are? You're one of those people who seems to exude energy with a little bit of mischief. When you're unhappy, it's like the light gets switched off.

It's fair to say that you weren't the prettiest baby! I even heard Mor say once, 'She looks like a little potato, but I love her all the more for it!' At the time I was cross. Felt that a mother shouldn't say things like that about her baby.

But later I was glad. Because when the reporter for whatever tabloid it was said that there was an 'angelic little girl' at the scene they also reported on the 'stout baby boy'.

It was the name too. It confused them with its foreignness.

But look at you now, darling Hannes.

Neve.

I must call you Neve.

I wish I could talk to you. Tell you about how I used to push you round in that funny old trolley all the time. Mor used to call me Lilla Mamma – Little Mother.

But maybe you don't know anything about where you came from.

About our heritage of blood.

43

Neve ignores Richard's cries as she thrusts open the back door and runs outside. She can only run. Has to keep moving. It's the only way to avoid the impact. If she keeps moving, this new knowledge can't shatter her bones, squash her organs, splatter her blood.

So she runs on, feet slamming into the cold earth of the lane, rain soaking through her clothes and running down her chilled cheeks. The light is leaching away. Dusk drains colour from the hedges and turns the world monochrome.

The woods are stark against the sky now. Branches reach into the growing darkness and merge with it, so it feels as though the world is closing in.

Panting painfully, Neve arrives back at the cottage. She has left the door open but she doesn't care now. Denville can come and find her. She'll kill him herself if she must.

This is all too much, much too big. It has blotted out all the light on everything else.

She wants her sister so badly. When Lou answers Neve can only breathe heavily into the phone for several seconds and a panicked Lou says, 'Neve? Is that you? What's happened? Are you hurt?'

Then, finally, Neve starts to cry.

Now she is busy throwing things into a rucksack. The door is locked. Richard has been banging on it for several minutes but she ignores him.

Finally, he goes away, after shouting through the letterbox that he is there to talk, if she needs him.

Lou was too shocked to speak at first, then she told Neve to 'come home'. To get on a train and come to London where they could be together and talk.

She clearly didn't know about any of it. That Neve was adopted. It is all new information to her too. She cried when Neve told her, in great gulping sentences, about the murder, and about Isabelle and about the real reason she had been left the cottage.

Now, as she stuffs clothes into the open mouth of the rucksack, a thought comes to her. Maybe Isabelle got the wrong person? The relief this brings feels narcotic but it doesn't last. Something terrible occurs to her and she runs to the sitting room to the photograph of a young Isabelle sitting on the tiled floor.

The childhood accident. The cut head.

The blood.

She had been so sure that this was the flooring they'd had as children but Lou had said no, hadn't she? And Lou never got that stuff wrong.

Now Neve sinks onto the sofa, clutching the picture of young Isabelle, with her curly hair and little daisy dress, Lego scattered around her. It is suddenly clear to Neve.

It was this floor, the one in the picture, she remembered.

Blood on the tiles. But it wasn't after having an accident

286

on her tricycle. That happened much later, when she was with her new family.

It was this other woman's blood. Sofie Lindstrom's.

Her real mother's blood.

The shock finally catches up with her now. All her energy seems to drain out of her limbs and she sinks back onto the sofa, numb.

She can't cry any more. This is too huge for tears.

She doesn't know how long she sits with her head resting back on the sofa, staring up at a frilly damp patch on the old ceiling above. But the wind rattling the letterbox brings her back to herself and she gets up. It's time to get away from here.

Ten minutes later she is locking the doors. She doesn't glance back at the cottage as she walks down the lane. She will ask one of the Gardners to drive her to Truro. She will get on the first train out of Cornwall and never come back.

Then she will try to find a way to survive this new knowledge.

It is dark now but the rain has stopped and she's grateful for this small thing as she makes her way up the lane, following the beam of a torch she found in the cottage.

The hedges drip and rustle. An owl hoots. But it no longer feels so sinister. It's simply what happens here. And what more horror could there be now?

44

When Bob told me the news, I felt only numb. He thought I would be relieved, but he doesn't understand. He doesn't understand.

'Don't you see, Isabelle?' he said. 'Denville can't hurt you any more.' But he can.

A stroke, that's what Bob said. A starburst of blood exploding inside the brain. But that doesn't mean HE IS OVER. I still hear him, even when I climb into my safe place, I hear him. He knocks at the windows and he taps on the door. He calls to me in my sleep.

I know now that I will never be free from him because the monster lives inside my head.

It's time to leave it all behind. I know this will hurt Richard and poor Matty, who has become a real friend. But it's time.

First, though, I want to find a way to reach out to you, Hannes. I have been watching you from afar, for months, ever since the night you lost your phone in that club. (I wish you would take better care of yourself!!) It won't be hard to find you during this party season and to pretend we are strangers.

Now that I have decided what to do I feel calm. I will wear Mummy's dress and I will get my hair and make-up done so I look the best I can be. I will watch and wait and then I will find a way to make it all stop.

But first I will give you all I have. I couldn't be a sister to you in my lifetime, but maybe I can help you in my death.

And now I need to get organized. All of this must go in the fire.

45

The lights are on at the Gardners' place.

When she knocks, it takes some time before Will opens the door. His shaggy eyebrows shoot up at the sight of Neve. But his eyes look dull and he smells a bit stale.

'What's the matter? Has something happened?' he says in a low voice. He moves forward a little, his expression now concerned.

Neve swallows deeply. If he hugs her, she will dissolve. She must remain strong. To get away.

'I want to ask you a really big favour. Please, please, can you take me to Truro?'

'Er . . . now?' says Will and leans against the doorjamb.

'Yes, now. I'm going back to London. Please. Can you take me to the station?'

Will stares at Neve for a few moments. His eyes are reddened and puffy, his face more jowly than usual because of a silvery beard dotting his chin. The collar of his rugby shirt is turned inwards and there's some kind of whitish stain on his chest. He looks as though he is carrying a bad hangover from the excesses of the night before.

She squashes the flicker of worry down inside herself. She has no choice about this. Must get away right now.

'Right,' he says finally. 'We'll have to go in my car. Let's go.'

They climb into a battered old Volvo. It is much tattier and smellier inside than the Range Rover. There are clumps of mud all over the foot well. Will sighs irritably as he adjusts the seat to accommodate his long frame. It had been set for someone much smaller; Sally presumably.

Neve is braced for questions but he doesn't say a word as they pull out onto the main road. Something about this feels 'off', but she is too upset and wired to tell whether it is her own judgement that is skewed. Maybe, she thinks, she's looking so crazy that Will is afraid to ask what's going on. But perhaps this is a good thing. It will only take the tiniest kind word to make her cry all over again.

All her senses feel oddly heightened. Maybe this is what shock really feels like, she thinks.

Will seems to be driving quite fast. But everyone does here, in the country. When they know the roads . . .

There's a close, sweaty smell in the car. The headlights wash icily over the landscape and a wooden sign looms out of the dark. The bright wall speeding by on her left seems too close. Neve sees the quick bright flash of animal eyes and then the road is dark again.

She clutches her phone, hoping Lou will send her another message just for the comfort of it. Her thumb toys with the home button as she glances at Will. He is frowning deeply at the road ahead and hunches forward, as though employing all his powers of concentration.

The strange silence in the car feels suffocating. Isn't he at least curious about what has happened? It is only now, as she sees the slow, heavy blink of his eyelids, that she realizes he is not just hungover, but still drunk. A new

291

anxiety squeezes her, just when she felt she had no energy left to be frightened.

Neve taps her phone against her thigh in an attempt to distract herself but her fingers are sweaty and the phone slips out of her hands, landing somewhere in the darkness of the foot well.

'Shit,' she murmurs, reaching down. Feeling around with her fingers she finds it wedged close to where the seat meets the car floor. As she lifts it her fingers brush against something cool and soft. Neve puts the phone in her lap and then reaches down again, pinching whatever it is between her ring and forefinger.

Holding it up, Neve feels as though something has slammed into her chest. She lets out an audible gasp.

Will turns to look at her and says, 'Oh *shit*.'

46

It's a black and white feather, oily to her touch.

The silence is booming pressure on her eardrums until Will breaks it.

'Neve, let me ex—'

'What the *fuck*?' she says in a low voice. She's surprised to find she isn't scared. Instead what she feels is a pure wash of hot outrage. 'Why did you have a *magpie* in your car, Will?'

Will's face looks hollowed out in the dim light of the car. His eyes are like dark holes.

'I'm so sorry,' he says quickly. 'But you must understand it wasn't personal. I like you, Neve.'

Neve lets out a bitter laugh of incredulity.

'Oh that's alright then. Not personal? How could you *do* that? You utter . . .' she's yelling now. She can't find a word big enough to encompass her disgust.

'I never approved of any of it!' Will's voice has taken on a high-pitched, almost whiny timbre. 'It was Sally, really! We just wanted, she just wanted, you to sell quickly, that's all!'

Sally?

'I don't believe you. She wouldn't do that.'

Will barks a humourless laugh. 'Oh, believe me, she would. And she did. She's not what you might think, with all her homemaker stuff. She's a woman who gets what she wants and what she wants is that cottage.'

Neve's fingers curl against the seat. She's sure they've speeded up. 'All those scary things? And what about the gross way I found the house? The *axe*, for Christ's sake?'

Will is breathing heavily. Almost panting. He looks at her, his expression stricken in the dim light of the car.

'I did block the toilet,' he says in a feeble voice. 'And I'm very *very* sorry for that. But everything else . . . well, that was all her. My darling fucking wife. Started before we even met you. She lifted someone else's sack of rubbish on the way home one night and trashed the cottage as her version of a welcome. Ha! We didn't know who was getting the place but she wanted the first impression to be . . . well . . .' he trails off. 'And,' he adds, heated again, 'she destroyed the flowers someone left at Isabelle's grave. As well as, oh I don't know, lots of things she had no place doing.'

'Wait,' says Neve, sitting up straighter in her seat. 'Did you mess with the radio too?'

Will lets out a small moan. 'Sally did, yes!' he says. 'Easy enough with the remote, even from outside. But . . . we do have keys.'

He pauses and then his words come out in a rush, skating into each other in their haste. 'I would *never* have hurt Jarvis! And I told her, I *fucking told her*,' at this he slams one hand against the steering wheel, 'she'd gone too far that time. I let him out – *okay that's all on me!* – but she *kicked him* in the ribs! Actually kicked the poor old mutt! That's the kind of woman we're dealing with! And I told her! I did, I said "This has gone too far now!" But no, Sally

294

knows best. She's all, "Do it for Matty. Think about Matty!" as though that made it all alright!'

Neve realizes belatedly that he is much, much drunker than she thought. The wall on the left of the car flashes past. A ripple of fear penetrates her fury and confusion now.

'Can you slow down for God's sake!' she cries.

The car does slow a little. Neve places a hand against her chest. As she tries to catch her breath, she can feel the panicked thumping of her heart. The magpie feather is still on her lap and she quickly brushes it away with a shudder of horror.

'Jesus, I don't understand any of this,' she says then. Her head aches. She feels sick. 'Please can you calm down a bit and tell me exactly what has been going on?'

Will gives a small moan and rubs his face. In the light from the dashboard he looks ten years older than he did last night. He gazes at her, his eyes pleading.

'We just wanted the cottage, that's all,' he says.

'That's why you frightened me half to death? So your bloody daughter could have *the cottage*?'

'You don't understand!' says Will. 'It's got nothing to do with Lydia really. She isn't coming home any time soon. That's just what Sally said to you! It was a story.'

Neve lets out a long, exhausted breath of air. Today has been filled with horrifying riddle after horrifying riddle.

'Okay,' she says in the most controlled voice she can muster. 'Talk me through this,' she says. 'Tell me every-fucking-thing.'

They are on a brief stretch of dual carriageway now. The headlights of the oncoming cars send flashes of pain into her tired, aching eyes.

'It's all about the land,' says Will tiredly. 'The cottage is worth nothing much on its own. Our place is worth more, but not as much as you'd think. And Briarfields is falling into the ground. But the land is valuable. If we can sell all three of them to Traemar we can fuck off out of this dismal country and go to Spain to retire. Sally had it all planned out. We'd never have to work again. That bit's crucial, as she never fails to remind me.'

This last part makes no sense at all, but it feels as though the day has been filled with distressing riddles.

'Hang on,' she says. 'Who is this . . . Traemar?'

The silvery ribbon of the road stretches ahead. They seem to be speeding up again, a little. Neve glances at the dashboard and a digital display says they are travelling at sixty-five mph. It feels too fast. But she doesn't want to distract Will when she is on the cusp of understanding everything.

'Traemar Investment Capital,' says Will, wearily now. 'Huge fuck-off property company. Want to build a housing estate and let all the plebs in. Fucking welcome to it.'

'Okay,' says Neve slowly. This still doesn't make sense. She tries to untangle her thoughts. 'But how could they guarantee I'd sell to your daughter anyway?'

Will barks a laugh that makes her jump.

'Because my wife is a clever bitch!' he says.

'I still don't get it,' says Neve. 'Start at the beginning. But first, can you *slow down*?'

Will sighs and rubs his eyes. The car wobbles dangerously but slows.

Neve lets out a breath.

'So Sally heard a rumour,' says Will dully. 'That this Traemar lot wanted the land. Knows someone who knows someone. She cooked up a scheme with her old school friend; estate agent called Georgia.'

Neve lets out a breath as she starts to understand at last.

'So what was she going to do?'

Will glances at her quickly, as though this is a stupid question.

'It's very easy for an estate agent to guide a buyer a certain way, don't you think?'

'Is it?' Neve has no experience of the buying and selling of houses.

'Yes of course . . .' says Will. 'You keep it below the radar . . . make a low valuation. All kinds of ways to do it, especially if you have been recommended.'

Sally and that persistent woman were in on it together.

There's a pause. The road flashes by outside.

'But is that even legal?'

'Of course it isn't!' says Will. He turns to look at her, eyes gleaming, for far too long and the car wobbles. 'Especially when you start intimidating people like she did with Isabelle.' He's pressing on the accelerator again.

It is only now that the full weight of what the Gardners have done presses down on Neve.

'Oh my God,' she says, 'you knew all about Denville, didn't you? And you used that to intimidate her? You drove her to her death?'

Will makes an anguished sound and wipes his face with his forearm. He is sobbing openly now.

'I'm so sorry,' he says, 'I'm so very sorry.'

It feels like the car is devouring the road in front of them. Neve grips the sides of the seat, her knuckles whitening.

Seventy-five mph now.

'Slow down, Will! Let's just be calm, okay?'

'I'm sick of it all!' he shouts. 'The whole thing! Isabelle wasn't supposed to die like that. And Matty hates the both of us! I swear he knows something, but Sally says he doesn't. She's always babied and underestimated him! No wonder he's so fucked up!'

Will starts to make a terrible keening sound. The car presses on, faster.

Eighty mph.

Eighty-five mph.

'Sometimes I swear I could kill her, I just wish I had the—'

Neon white chevrons gash the blackness ahead.

And the car is spinning, spinning, spinning into the dark.

47

Sticky.

Sticky hands.

On her face. In her mouth. Warm and sweet.

She needs to wash it away. But her hands are so dirty. She'll never get it off. Never be able to clean the dirty blood, which keeps on coming.

'Miss? Miss, can you hear me?'

Someone is sitting on her. It hurts. They're pressing on her shoulder, trying to squash her, and she's frightened. She gasps and her eyes are open. The world falls around her and settles into ugly shapes. Everything is odd angles. A window. Darkness.

Neve tries to turn her head but the voice shouts sharply that she shouldn't move.

She understands. She is lying sideways, looking through the car window at someone's face, which is upside down. It's a woman with short black hair and olive skin. For a minute she thinks it is Miri and she starts to cry.

'It's okay, love, we'll get you out in no time,' says the

woman in a crisp Eastern European accent. 'I'm Katya. Can you tell me your name?'

Neve believes she has said it clearly but the woman, Katya, says again, 'Can you tell me your name?'

'S'Neve.' Her voice is thick but loud so she knows she hadn't spoken before.

'Good, that's good.' The face disappears, leaving only the blackness of the window. Panicked, she tries to cry out then she hears the reassuring hiss and crackle of a radio. There are voices outside and more lights that blink on and off.

It's raining. The soft sound of it dropping so near to her face is soothing.

I'm hurt, she whispers. *I'm hurt but I'm alive.*

The moments just before the crash come back to her. She tries to look behind her for Will. But all she can see is a curved section of the pale interior roof. Her shoulder hurts too much to move any further.

'Will?' she calls out in a shaky voice.

But there is only the crackly radio and the shushing rain.

48

Lou is crying so hard she can't speak.

Neve has never seen her like this, not even at their father's funeral, where Neve thought she might actually damage her eyes because the tears wouldn't stop.

She is only just emerging from a fathomless, narcotic sleep and everything feels too fuzzy and muffled for her sister's wretchedness to reach her. All she can do is stare and wait for it to pass.

Finally, heaving a heavy sigh, Lou wipes her nose with several hard wipes of a tissue and attempts a watery smile.

'God, I'm so sorry, I just . . .' She is off again. 'I just couldn't bear it if I lost you too!'

Neve reaches across the rough, hospital blanket for her sister's hand, gripping it as hard as her broken collarbone allows.

When they are finally able to draw breath, Neve says weakly, 'I bet Steve wishes he hadn't complained about my swearing now.'

Lou gives her a quick, shocked look and then starts to laugh, deeply, leaning forward, still gripping Neve's hand. Neve tries to join in but the cosy blurring of the drugs is wearing off and the sharp edges of pain are poking through.

'The thing I love about you,' says Lou, wiping her red, chapped nose again, 'is that you'll always say the thing.'

They meet eyes and both smile weakly.

'Seriously,' says Lou, voice wobbling. 'I'm so bloody glad you're okay.' She pauses. 'It could have been a lot worse.'

Neve thinks about Will for a moment and then lets the thought slide away for now.

'Where are the girls and Steve?' she manages. Her own voice seems to weigh a ton. Dredging it up from somewhere deep is so tiring.

'They're in London,' says Lou. 'I thought it might be a bit upsetting for the girls and well, I just wanted to . . . to. Well.'

For some reason this unarticulated thought makes perfect sense to Neve and she squeezes her sister's hand again.

'They think you might be discharged tomorrow. You're coming home with us, obviously.'

Lou's tone is firm and Neve simply nods. She squeezes her eyes tightly shut again.

She tried to make a new start and she has failed.

All she did was lift the lid on something ugly and painful, and she can't close it again. Knowing that she must process all this as soon as her physical infirmities begin to ease makes her want to burrow down into the pain; break her other shoulder, get back into that car and crash all over again.

There is a tidal wave coming that she has to somehow bear. Lou seems to sense what she is thinking about.

'We have an awful lot to talk about, when you're better,' she says softly. 'But just concentrate on resting, for now. All of it can wait. All of it.'

Neve nods. She can feel sleep beginning to drag at her again and she welcomes it.

Her big sister gently strokes her hair until she is deeply asleep.

49

It's the first really warm day of early summer. Londoners are revealing toes, shoulders and knees and the hot, city air presses on the eardrums with its buzzing energy.

She takes a sip of the coffee she'd forgotten by her feet but it's cold now and the milkiness feels slimy in her mouth. She chases it with a swig from her bottle of water and looks out over the sparkling Thames.

She'd got off at Embankment forty-five minutes ago and walked over Waterloo Bridge.

Pausing exactly where all this started, she'd looked down into the water as people thronged past. Someone was playing a guitar and singing a Green Day song, badly, further along the bridge. Traffic rumbled by and the world felt so benign and ordinary today that it was hard to conjure the dreadful scene that had occurred here in December.

Isabelle's wide eyes and her pale, pale skin.

The churning, black water and the lights of the rescue boat as they carried out their fruitless search for her body.

Looking around self-consciously, Neve had thrown the

small bunch of flowers she'd purchased by the tube station over the side, one by one. No one really paid any attention to her.

She had wanted to get hold of something known as Twinflowers, which, the internet told her, was the unofficial national flower of Sweden. Then she'd discovered this wasn't going to be straightforward at all and so opted for a bunch of cornflowers, just because they were pretty. There was no special significance to today. But she was feeling so much better and it was something she had been meaning to do. To come back to where all this started.

Except, that wasn't really when it began, she thinks now. Isabelle had been living with it for much of her life.

Richard had wanted to come to visit her when she first got out of hospital. But she wasn't ready. Still isn't ready.

Her shoulder was broken and for the first couple of weeks she relied heavily on painkillers and sleep to get through each day. She'd refused visits from Richard, even when Lou had suggested gently it might be a good idea.

But some time later she had tentatively started a communication by email, which felt like the right amount of distance.

She discovered many things during the course of their correspondence, which was usually carried out late at night with only the glow of her iPad screen lighting the darkness while the rest of the household slept.

The most important piece of information was that he'd had no idea about what Sally and Will were up to. He'd been close to selling up when everything happened. He would have had no idea of the real value of his property and Georgia McColl had been confident she could ease the transaction in the right direction. The property company, Traemar Investment Capital, would buy Briarfields for a song. If the Gardners had been able to buy Petty Whin

Cottage they would have been in a powerful position to negotiate a high price with Traemar.

The police had investigated all this but, in the end, there had been little in the way of proof so no charges were brought. Neve has learned that the company is now looking at land on the other side of Cornwall to develop.

Thankfully, Sally, newly widowed, has sold her house to some unknown buyer and she and Matty have moved to Spain to be with Lydia and her family.

Poor Matty.

Richard has filled her in a little more on the Gardners. Will lost his headship after having an affair with a sixth former and had been unemployed since then. Richard says now that he always felt there was something 'a little off' about Sally.

This, of course, is information that has come way too late . . .

Over a series of emails, Neve learned more about his sister too.

Her sister.

She'd tried to kill herself twice before. Once in her late teens and once after a breakdown in Australia.

Their father, he told her, had been a difficult man, and when their mother died of breast cancer at only forty-five, he had become something of a bully. His relationship with his adopted daughter in particular had been an unhappy one. Isabelle had always known she was adopted but it was only after having had the first breakdown that she learned about where she had come from.

'She'd always had these awful nightmares,' Richard wrote. 'Woke the whole house up with her screaming. But our parents had been advised not to connect any of this with any memories she may or may not have had. They believed they were doing the right thing at the time.'

She'd spoken to Bob Dyer too, finally. He had guessed Neve's identity 'the very moment' he saw her at the cottage, he'd said. He feared he had caused potential harm by helping Isabelle to locate her. And he was still struggling with guilt; neither he nor anyone else could ultimately save Isabelle from her own demons.

He had been able to fill in some of the gaps. He hadn't known all the details but had made efforts to find out what she needed to know.

Neve's parents had been well-known foster carers in the area before the pregnancy with Lou that came like a late gift. They still looked after a few children now and then, but only in an emergency.

And when Sofie Lindstrom was murdered, they happened to have been the best and most convenient choice. The girls had been separated because it was believed to be the best decision at the time. Isabelle, Richard told Neve, had been a little too rough with her baby sister. There were fears of her holding her too tightly and hurting her, such was her traumatized state. So it was decided that a clean break and a new start would be best for both children. Isabelle had been adopted quickly by the Shawcrosses.

According to Richard, Isabelle had talked often of having a sister when she was tiny but the sibling had never been spoken of and, after a while, she had stopped mentioning her. It wasn't the Shawcross way to rake up the past, it seemed.

Neve's parents had then adopted her and the whole family moved away. Lou had never known the truth and had been too little to understand that the wished-for baby sister who arrived one day wasn't her own.

Now, Neve raises her face up to feel the warmth of the sun. Gold light dances across her closed lids and she lets out a long sigh.

She's glad she came. She'd been seeing Waterloo Bridge in her dreams for months now. If she had left it any longer, she wouldn't ever be able to face coming back.

But she did it.

Go me, she thinks.

Small steps.

Resistant to therapy as she had been at first, Neve has been cajoled by Lou into the company of a quiet, grey-haired woman called Pam, who is gently encouraging her to talk about everything that had happened.

Lou was often right about these things, annoyingly.

She wonders what Lou will say when she tells her she's leaving again.

Neve has taken out a loan against the value of the property to carry out repairs.

She's never painted a wall in her life, or even wired a plug.

But she can learn. She's bought a big book and been looking at YouTube clips for advice.

And anyway, Finn has offered to help.

He came to visit her in hospital, just after the accident. They've been WhatsApping a bit about her coming back to Cornwall.

He's funny. Something might happen with him. Nothing might happen, and that will be fine too.

The priority is tearing down the bars scarring the windows, re-painting the peeling exterior and tidying up that garden.

Neve looks out at the Thames and takes a deep breath.

She still wishes she didn't *know* any of it: could go about her business in blissful ignorance. But there is no way back now.

And she has a cottage to rent out, once it's all sorted.

She and Lou have talked about taking a trip to Sweden together in the autumn. Lou had been all awkward at first, saying it wasn't her place to come, not in the circumstances. But Neve had pointed out that she was always whingeing about never getting a break and didn't she want to spend time with her own sister?

Lou had got all emotional then. So had Neve.

She takes a deep breath of the dirty air now. Beautiful London, with its noise and filth and life.

But she is going back to the cottage. Things are going to be different this time. There's no bogeyman.

She pushes her sunglasses down over her eyes and stands up, feeling a stiffness in her injured shoulder. She's been warned it might cause her problems for a while so she rolls it back and forwards carefully, just as the physio showed her.

Then, taking one last glance at the glittering Thames, she starts to walk down the South Bank and towards Waterloo station.

The End

Acknowledgements:

Writing a book is such a collaborative effort and I have many people I'd like to thank for helping me with this one. First of all, there were several people who gave me their time to talk about practical plot questions.

Tim Ash from the RNLI was very generous with his advice on the procedures involved when someone falls, or jumps, into the Thames. If you'd like to learn more about the work of this life-saving organisation or to make a donation, this is their website: https://rnli.org/.

Rosy Thornton provided expertise with the thorny issue of wills and the Donatio Mortis Causa gift that ends up in Neve's possession. Paul Dengel and the Mac Repair Shop in Oakwood gave me some very useful advice about computer matters. Phil O'Conner gave me invaluable plumbing advice.

I'm so grateful to you all and any errors made are entirely mine.

My husband Pete Lownds has not only provided a constant stream of advice about the criminal justice system but was an early cheerleader for the book. He provides a huge amount of love and emotional support during the roller coaster ride that is publishing. I wanted, this time, to properly say how much it is appreciated.

My sister Helenanne Hansen is always one of the very first people to read my work and I'm so grateful for her input. I will never forget the train journey when she was near the end of reading the manuscript. She more or less told me to shut up because she wanted to read, and then disappeared into it for the remainder of the journey. She actually gasped at one point, which is up there with my favourite moments of being a writer, ever!

Thanks go to Emma Darwin, who let me run away with her for a weekend to a beautiful cottage in the country, where we wrote like demons, talked writing and drank a fair amount of wine.

Emma Haughton has been a huge support along the way yet again and also Samantha Tonge, who keeps trying to help me get better at Twitter. (I'm getting there, Sam!)

My three online writers groups – the one with the comfy chair, the one with the sea creatures and the one with the police tape – pretty much keep me sane and make me laugh all the time. Special mentions go out to Luisa Plaja, Geri Ryan, Susannah Rickards, Ruth Warburton, Essie Fox, Sarah Stovell and Julie-Ann Griffiths, who helped me wrangle the plot of *In a Cottage in a Wood* right at the start.

Thank you to my fantastic agent Mark Stanton (Stan) for having a sharp editorial eye and believing in me from the start. Sarah Hodgson and Finn Cotton at HarperCollins have been wonderful to work with on both *The Woman Next Door* and this book and I'd like to thank them sincerely for everything they've done for me. Thanks also to Rhian Mckay for spotting those slippery little errors that had slipped through the net at the copy editing stage.

Joe and Harry, my fantastic lads. What can I say about you, other than how grateful I am to have you in my life?

Watching you both turn into young men is an amazing privilege.

Finally, a huge thank you to all the people who bought *The Woman Next Door* and took time to post their reviews and recommend the book to friends.

Readers, you're the absolute best!

Caroline Green, London. May 2017
@CassGreenWriter
http://cassgreen.co.uk/